Seamless

Beth Bear Shields

Very, very special thanks to Jodi Joffe for Seamless's cover artwork and to Neil Stern Photography for author's photo.

Print ISBN: 978-1-54394-688-8
eBook ISBN: 978-1-54394-689-5

Thank you to Sandra Haven for her help in keeping my story, my girls, on track. Thank you to Elisa Drake for dotting every I, crossing every T and making sure I didn't run on and on and on (because I do tend to do that). Thank you to my parents, Hy and Eadie Bear, for setting the bar high but always holding the ladder steady for me and making sure I have a soft place to fall. Thank you to my sister, Shana, who, to this day, would do a puppet show at the foot of my bed if I asked. Thank you to my incredible husband Jon and our children, for truly showing me what love looks like.

You were afraid I would get lost in the woods, but please don't worry about me. You will always be my compass and I'm going to Sears to get a really big chainsaw, as well. This book is for you, Pops, because, *Once a task…,* right?

I miss you.

Let's do this…

A Princess Story…

Becca could feel Oliver's soft hair tickling her forearm. There was barely anything there, really, but it was so soft because it was so new. At only a few weeks old, he slept, ate and pooped and was remarkably comforting for Becca to hold.

"Becca, we're here," Jenna called up as she walked into the house, placing her baby carrier down and watching as her 3-year-old, Carly, grabbed Mason's hand to go play.

"I'll be right there," Becca yelled back as she finished changing Oliver's diaper, then rocked him a little before placing him in his crib to sleep. "I'll be home soon," she whispered to him, touching his leg, knee and finally his tiny foot as she slowly made her way out of his room.

"You look like a princess, Mommy," Mason said, as he ran down the hall and lifted up her dress, ducking underneath. She wore makeup every day without fail, but, admittedly, never dressed up. A concert T-shirt, flannel and 501s had become her wardrobe. The pregnancy weight was gone, it wasn't that. In her mind, a concert T-shirt, flannel and 501s were simply always appropriate. No wonder Mason had thought she looked like a princess today. He gathered the hem around his neck, making it into a cape and started making flying sounds, "rrmm… rrmmm," leaning into and out of turns. Maybe he was chasing a bad guy or just practicing in case a superhero was in need.

"Thank you, Buggle," she said and gave him a kiss. As he and Carly walked down the hall, she caught something shiny in his hand. "Don't put Thomas on your head again!" Becca yelled after him. The battery operated

Thomas Train he had received for his 3rd birthday had some silly warning on the bottom like, "Caution: don't allow on child's head," or something like that. At one time, she had thought that was hysterical, but Mason's hair was only just now beginning to grow in where she had recently cut it off, away from the spinning wheels.

"Thank you so much for coming. We won't be long," Becca said. "It's just a quick dinner with college friends. Ollie is already sleeping. If I'm not back when he wakes up, his formula is in the fridge. The bottle warmer isn't working so well, so you could just put his bottle in some warm water? In that bowl by the sink? He should be good till 8:30, though. Mason and Carly's mac and cheese is in the fridge."

"No worries, Becca. The weather has been calling for rain all day, but I think we'll be able to get outside for a bit," Jenna said, settling in. "You got an umbrella?"

"Intercoms are..." Becca started.

"In the sunroom. I know," Jenna said.

"I'm sitting for you next Saturday night, right?" Becca asked, looking once again down the hall towards Oliver's room.

"Right. Be over at 5:30?"

"Deal."

"You OK, Becca?" Jenna asked.

"Yeah, don't I look OK?" she asked, reaching around, checking the seam in her dress.

Jenna smiled then and pointed at the exaggerated grin on her own face. "Be fun... smile..."

"Right," Becca said, as she closed the door behind her.

People were already waiting at the train station when Becca parked her Jeep in the lot. She had yet to read the manual and was fumbling for the right button to lock the doors as she ran over just in time to hear the "ding-ding" of the signal. Some people smiled at her as she stood there in her pretty dress and Manolos. They were beautiful—hard to walk in, as she had told her friends—but still beautiful. *Be fun, smile, be fun, smile,* she told herself as she carefully made her way up the steps and down the aisle. She sat down next to a lady and her oversized bag. They exchanged smiles as Becca held tightly to her own, worn bag on her lap. The train blew right past the first stop.

"Wow! We're going fast," Becca said.

"It's the express. Downtown 10 minutes earlier that way," she responded.

I can meet Josh at his office instead of the restaurant. I'll surprise him. *That's fun,* she thought, attempting a smile. She watched the suburbs blow by—houses becoming apartments, becoming buildings. The trees got smaller and more people were out walking. Her fingers were now fidgeting with the long string hanging from the stitching on her bag. *An umbrella...* she thought as she rolled her eyes towards the ceiling, smacking the scratched flap. Winter had already made an early visit with snow a month ago, but now the weather was warmer. When she was little, November in Chicago had meant 50s; now, people were out in shorts and T-shirts.

Becca had realized just that morning she had nothing to wear and had settled on her black linen dress, the one that had the long thin belt and bigger buttons down the back. Be *careful with those buttons,* she reminded herself, closing her eyes and leaning back, remembering that night in New York when she had last worn that dress. It was just a few years ago with her friend Dana and the two guys they had liked to hang out with. Dana had been in love with Steve, but Becca had always been pretty sure that he was gay.

Steve had found a great little Italian restaurant downtown and they had eaten outside underneath the red and white striped awning drinking bottles of wine. The theater where they were going to see a play that starred Becca's teenage crushes, Shaun and David Cassidy, was just a few blocks away. But not knowing the city well, they had decided to cab it. Two drinks and 20 minutes of waving later, she had found herself climbing into the back seat, with Steve laughing and squealing behind her. Two buttons had found their way out of their slots, and her butt had been exposed to the world. Since then, she always had a safety pin tucked into the seam to save the world from the horror. Remarkably, the dress had fit today.

Four forty-five, very early, and with a cab instead of walking in the crazy shoes, she would be there 15 minutes before Josh expected her. *That's fun, smile...* When she arrived at his building, she momentarily forgot what floor he was on. He had moved offices so often she was even beginning to doubt she was in the right building, but when the doors opened on the 16th floor, she recognized his assistant, who looked very surprised to see her. He busied himself with something on his desk, avoiding eye contact. "Josh stepped out for a minute, Becca. Was he expecting you this early? I don't think he was expecting you this early..."

"I caught the express," she said, practicing a smile as she walked into his office. The family pictures could be updated, she thought, as she looked around the small room facing west. The last bit of sun for the day was coming through his small window. She looked at some knickknacks on his shelves, all new and all expensive, before hearing him stumbling down the hall and appearing somewhat shocked, rather than surprised, at the door.

Be fun, smile...

"Where were you, Josh?" she asked, noticing him tucking his shirt in just a bit in the back.

"I was out. It was just one drink," he answered, avoiding her eyes.

"With who?"

"Some people from work."

"Girls?" she asked, noticing a slight smell of lilac in the air.

"Yeah," he said, gathering his things. "Ready?"

"You were out with a group of girls?"

"No, just one girl..."

"*The* girl?" she asked, steadying herself against his desk. "*The* girl? The one in your car? That night? The one that was laughing? When you butt dialed me? The girl you said wasn't there? The girl you said was Alan?" she asked again, a bit louder, but placing her hand over her mouth. "You said I was crazy. You said, I'm not doing this with you... You were so dismissive. You made me feel like I was crazy. *That* girl?"

He sighed then, clasping his hands behind his neck, looking at the old ceiling fixture in his now airless office. "Becca," he called, now reaching after her arm as she quickly dodged away. She ran down the hall and pressed the button repeatedly for the elevator doors to open. Finally, stepping inside among the much taller men and women in their suits, she was glad G was pressed because her hands were shaking too hard and she knew soon it would be her legs as well. As the doors opened, she quickly darted around the others and made her way through the revolving door. She immediately sat on the curb, finally able to hear something over his voice saying, "Just one drink, just one girl."

She sat there on the chipped curb, somewhat hidden by a rusty mailbox, her feet in the gutter near a sewage grate. The people walking on the sidewalk passed her more quickly than the cars stuck in traffic. It was 5:10. She should be arriving right about now, but instead, there she sat. She wanted to believe she could blend in, but everyone was going to notice the girl in the black linen dress sitting on the curb, so looking down seemed like it would cause only more attention. *Pick up your head,* she thought. No one looking at her would know that her legs simply wouldn't move.

Sometimes she would meet the wondering, fearful eyes of the younger women walking past her, either on their way home or out with friends. It was easy to figure out what they were thinking, mostly, *"What happened to her?"* or *"I'm so glad that's not me,"* but there was one woman walking past that seemed to have it all together. She may have been just a few years older, but her chunky heels, classic orange messenger bag and big sunglasses covering her apple cheeks made her appear very worldly-wise. She had lowered the large frames just a bit on her nose and met Becca's eyes...

"Get those Manolos out of the gutter, Princess," her arched eyebrow and head tilt seemed to say.

As Becca stood up, she could feel the scrape of the sidewalk on her bottom and the breeze blow through the opening of the skirt.

The shiny thing in Mason's hand…

She reached behind, gathering the fabric of the dress together as she made her way down the street. The first few drops of rain began to fall, and she held her worn bag over her head. *Princess*, she thought, as the black linen billowed behind her in the wind, *it's time to save the world.*

Seamless

It's really quite simple...

Becca just made the train, but only because she ripped off her shoes to run down LaSalle. She put them back on to walk up the three steps and made her way down the aisle, sitting down behind a young couple and their baby. She turned to look out the window and began fidgeting with her rings. They had once been worn by Josh's grandmother, he had told her, as he had slipped the diamond in the antique setting on her hand the night he proposed.

His grandparents had been married for 63 years. *A good sign*, she had thought. Becca took the rings off and slid them into her purse, noticing the scratches on the front flap and touching the loose threads that were beginning to fray. She looked out the window as the train barreled through and then out of the city. There were fewer people walking around outside, the trees were larger, and there were more of them. The buildings became apartments, then houses. When the conductor finally called out her stop, she grabbed her bag and walked down the aisle. At the door, she stepped carefully down the three steps, then slipped her shoes off again at the sidewalk. She could feel the blacktop of the parking lot as she walked to her car through the dark. *This feels familiar,* she thought, as she approached her car.

Pulling into the driveway, Becca could see Jenna sitting on the sofa while Mason and Carly played with his dinosaurs on the floor. She once again fiddled with the keys to lock up the Jeep before heading towards the door.

"That was a short night," Jenna said, standing up to gather her things as Becca walked in. "Everything okay?"

"Ya know, they canceled. Josh will be home soon. He's just making a stop first," she said, taking off her shoes once again and setting them on the entryway table.

"OK, then. Not a peep from Ollie. Mason and Carly ate. Carly, we should go home," Jenna said, reaching down for her carrier, where Grace still slept peacefully.

Carly stood up rubbing her eyes. "Bye, Mason," she said, as she took her mommy's hand and started out for the long walk across the lawn to her own house next door.

"Buggles, time for bed," Becca said to Mason, closing and locking the door behind their friends.

"OK, Mommy," he said, taking her hand and heading down the hall. "Tell me the Buggle story, Mommy, K?"

Becca looked down at the blonde-haired, blue-eyed boy and sighed. "Again?"

"Yeah, Mommy. Again."

"Well, Mason, a long, long time ago, people used to listen to music on these funny little boxes called radios. That's it. That's how we listened to music. One day, music started being played on TV. There was a whole channel, just for music, with short little movies to watch as you listened to the songs. When they introduced the first song, they explained that music on TV was going to change the way we saw the world. Then they played the first song."

"It was a Buggle!" he screamed.

"It was *by* the Buggles, yes."

"And I'm a Buggle cuz I changed your world, right?"

"You got it. You are my Buggle," she said, lifting him into bed. "Goodnight, Buggle."

"Goodnight, Mommy," he said. "I love you."

"I love you, too," she said, as she turned off his light.

Two and a half hours later she heard Josh's key in the lock and readied herself. He leaned into the door and wiggled it out. They had never gotten that fixed, had they? She was sitting on the entryway bench, with the baskets stored underneath for the boys' little shoes, as he walked in. He sat down on the hall chair across from her, took a deep breath and explained it quite simply, actually.

He wasn't attracted to her anymore.

"I'll get some things and stay at Brian's for a while. You and the boys stay here. I'll make arrangements for a new place." He began to walk down the hall, then stopped and turned around. "I'll call in the morning."

She could hear him in their room. They were happy sounds, really. Slide... click. Slide...click. She could hear him zipping up his bag and then his feet walking down the hall. He looked at her with a rather large bag in his hand.

He's going to say 'sorry' now, she thought. He reached for the doorknob and looked at her sadly.

Here it comes, she thought.

He let out a big sigh and looked at his feet. "Can you find those Bed Bath and Beyond coupons? They would come in really handy when I'm setting up my new place."

A short while later, Becca sat in the backyard with her feet up on the bricks of the fire pit. The heat penetrated her slippers, and she hoped there would be no flying embers to set the cozy, down footies aflame. She was wearing her pajamas and cuddled in a blanket. The lights in the backyard were set on a motion detector, so every few minutes, she tossed her arms up into the sky to turn them back on. The night was quiet, except for the boys' breathing that she could hear from the monitor sitting next to her on the pavers.

The stones had just been laid out a few weeks ago. She and Mason had watched as the men had carefully lifted each piece of bluestone and walked them over to the backyard, creating the same shape, like a puzzle, on the grass. They had then carried over the huge bags of sand and gravel, poured them out and smoothed them over with rakes before tamping them with a tool that they had decided looked like a huge potato masher. The workers then had carefully carried each stone back to create the puzzle once again where she now sat.

She had pictured hosting parties here, gathering her friends around the fire pit, drinking martinis like they had in the bars not too long ago. The only catch was that most of her friends were still single in the city. They didn't have anyone to bring to said party and wouldn't leave the city for a martini in the suburbs, anyway.

Becca sat with a glass of wine next to her, throwing little pieces of paper into the pit. Sometimes, they would bounce off the highest flames, then softly fall into the fire, the burning starting on the edges till the paper crinkled up with the black and red smoldering lines growing towards each other.

It was too late to call anyone. Or maybe it wasn't. To her, 9:00 was late, but certainly her friends were up. The question was, who to call. She hadn't told anyone about *the girl*. She touched the message button on her phone, scrolled to her last group text, the one about the awful day in the snow—who would drive, what they were wearing… *Why do I keep this,* she thought. *I really should delete this….*

She typed: *Josh is having an affair*

He just left

I think I'm getting a divorce

Dana responded first, *"I'm leaving now. Give me thirty."*

Allie, *"Me, too."*

Elle, *"I knew it."*

DELETE

He is unpacking his suitcase, or maybe already out somewhere, with someone, she thought. She went over every event in her head, from the moment they met freshman year in college in the dorm, to their beautiful June wedding, to the pregnancy stick turning the littlest bit blue in the tiny window, to buying the house, to this evening.

Becca finally got to the last little piece of paper. She felt its smoothness between her fingers, noticing the glossy finish, as the light from the fire bounced off of it. She tossed it into to the flames and watched as one corner started to burn. The red and the black line slowly creeping across the length of it – the "B" slowly melting away, then the "e" and growing towards the "d." It shriveled up with the other words catching fire more quickly. She tried to think of something witty she could say to him when he would come back for all the coupons that now were ashes at her feet. Maybe she would tell him they expired, or there would be no more bargains, but a smile slowly cracked through her lips as she typed a word into her phone, while the black and red embers reached the last little line of the bar code.

and the bar is open...

Soon the four of them were drinking wine, sitting around the fire pit, as Becca had always hoped they would, though certainly not under these circumstances. Dana, in her pajamas, Allie in one of her many flowy Anthropologie ensembles, and Elle in a rather short skirt.

"This is nice, Bex," Dana said, gesturing to the fire pit.

"Yeah, the yard looks great, too," Allie said.

"It's Josh's house," Elle stated.

"It was always Josh's house," Becca agreed. "From the minute we saw it, I knew. I remember pulling into the driveway the first time and going over that little bridge over the ravine. His mouth dropped open, he slapped my knee and shook it. He was like a little boy. His eyes got really big. I can still see him tipping his head back when we pulled up to get a full view. He looked all around, opening up every door, every cabinet. He asked what kind of wood the floor was, where the tile was from, the name of the color of the countertop and brand of paint in the kitchen. I saw how happy it made him, so I said OK. The couple that lived here before us actually restored the house. They wanted to bring it back to 50 years ago. They even brought in some landscaper for the garden. He spent a lot of time trying to get it just right. He would bring different plants and flowers and stones..."

"How do you know?" Dana asked.

"I spoke with the owner that day. After it was all done, the wife, Milly, was really sad. She spent a lot of time in the garden just walking around," Becca said, gesturing to the now dark yard. "Turned out, she had fallen in love with him."

"With who?" Dana asked.

"The landscaper. She moved out and moved in with him. The husband didn't want to stay looking at the garden the two of them had so clearly created together, that he had so clearly created for her. So they put the house on the market. He was happy to go," Becca said, with a gulp of wine, definitely not a sip.

"I didn't know people talked so much to people buying their house," Dana said. "Well, she sure was brave to share all that with you."

"Actually, I was talking with her husband," Becca said.

"How did he know all that?" Dana asked.

"It's not that hard," Becca said, rolling the glass stem in her hands. "You can tell when someone isn't in love with you anymore."

The three girls looked at each other, looking for someone, anyone, to go first...

"Bex, what happened, exactly?" Dana asked. The light of the fire was bouncing off her silk pajamas. She may have been sleeping before, but now, her straight, brown hair was parted perfectly down the middle with, of course, a new coat of lip-gloss on her perfectly bowed lips.

"I got downtown early. Josh wasn't in his office. When he did get there, he was drunk. He had been with *the girl*, I guess..." Becca answered.

"What girl?" Elle asked, angrily, sliding to the edge of her chair, shrugging, with her Vixen-polished fingernails in the sky.

"I don't know. *The girl. The girl* who has an appropriate dress ready for any occasion and a cool, new bag. Skinny, fun..." Becca started.

"That's ridiculous," Dana said. "You're beautiful, Becca. You gave him two beautiful boys. He's confused. He'll be back."

"Stop it, Dana! Just stop it!" Elle screamed. "Why do you say that shit, Dana? This has been coming a long time. He's a total asshole, Bex. You're better off without him."

Allie hadn't moved or said a word. Her long legs were still, casually crossed beneath her long, patchwork skirt. Her white T-shirt looked both like an after-thought and amazing at the same time, underneath her shredded jean jacket. "You're going to be okay, Bex. You're all going to be okay," she finally offered.

Becca looked at her three friends—Dana the dreamer, Elle the cynic and Allie the artist—by the light of the fire. It could have been a joke, really... *So, a dreamer, a cynic and an artist walk into a bar,* she thought to herself.

Thank God they're here.

This is going to leave a mark....

Becca was still awake when the sun started to come in through the curtains. She had watched as the sky had begun to turn from night to day, sitting silently in the middle of the living room floor. The girls had left around midnight, Allie, with a reassuring hug, Dana, with a "don't worry," and Elle with a "he's a fucking asshole, Bex."

Becca had walked into the living room then to find Oliver's bouncy chair still vibrating and had sat down next to it to turn it off. Five hours later, she was still sitting beside it. Josh had been gone for eight hours now. This would be her first morning of not hearing him climb out of bed, walk into the bathroom, turn the shower on and finally leave without a kiss goodbye. She could hear Mason moving slightly in his bed. Sometimes Mason snored, just the tiniest bit, right before he woke up. Mason's routine was simple—sit up, rub eyes, find Mommy. Mommy was to be in bed, and Becca quickly found her way down the hall and through her bedroom door to climb under the blanket, still neatly made from yesterday. She messed up the blanket on Josh's side and rolled a bit on the mattress before crushing up his pillow. Mason arrived in her doorway at 5:17, just seconds after she had rolled on to her side of the bed and closed her eyes.

"Mommy," Mason said, "where's Daddy?"

"Daddy's at work," Becca answered, wondering what she had missed.

"I didn't hear any 'clunk'," he explained.

The garage door, Mason hadn't heard the garage door…

He was scratching his head and looking around, confused.

"Daddy got a ride today," she offered, cheerfully.

"Oh," Mason said, walking further into her room and climbing into the bed. "It's cold, Mommy," he said, feeling the sheets on Josh's side of the bed and cuddling in closer to her.

"It is?" she asked. "Come closer then," she said, and they lay together in the king size bed, the two tiny figures not even taking up half of it. They watched as the street lights abruptly turned off.

"Night time is over, Mommy," Mason said.

"Yes," Becca said, kissing the back of his head, his blonde hair a bit of a mess from his sleep.

"I hear Ollie," he said, as the monitor on her nightstand began to crackle.

"Me too," Becca said, reaching to turn it down.

"I'll check on him," he said, climbing off the side of the bed and running down the hall.

Becca stepped down as well and followed the funny noises now coming from Oliver's room. Mason was poking his little brother from between the slats as Oliver bent his knees and grabbed at his toes, rocking a bit from side to side. Becca carefully lifted him from his crib and placed him on the changing table.

"Mommy! I found it!" Mason screamed, picking up his board book. Each page had a wonderfully colorful person—a cowboy, a pirate, a police officer—with a poem about what they do.

Blowing balloons,
Riding a tiny bike,
To make you laugh
I'll do anything you like

…read the page opposite the clown. She could hear Mason reciting the words from memory. Although he said "blow-up" and "teeny" instead. The last pages were a mommy and daddy. Their poem,

We'll give you hugs

And kisses, too

We'll always take

Good care of you

That was followed by one that Becca had written in the book as well.

I'll spin you to Daisy

Make you the best cookies around

And always eat goldfish crackers with you

On our favorite playground

Mason remembered that one without fail.

Later, after a bagel and cheese, milk and a bottle, they played in the yard for the morning, Mason digging up worms and Oliver lying on a blanket under a makeshift canopy. Becca had thrown her hair in a pony but was still in her pajamas from the night before. "Mason, we need to go in and get dressed," she said, picking up Oliver and grabbing for Mason's hand. The three of them walked inside, and she placed Oliver in his bouncy seat before turning it on. "I'll be right back," she said, as Mason turned on the TV and cuddled up on the green sofa, stretching his legs and feet to reach the otto-man. She walked into the laundry room and found her stash of soon-to-be-donated maternity clothes stacked on the dryer and slowly reached for a pair of pants with a large elastic panel and a shirt that was cut like a tent.

"Mommy, I'm hungry," Mason said, as she walked back into the living room, wearing her oversized clothes. The sun streamed through the windows and caught the blonder hairs on his head. She could smell Oliver's diaper and picked him up for a change, noticing 12:30 on the cable box. She had forgotten lunch. A quick change and a boiling pot of noodles later, the three of them sat at the table, Oliver drinking his bottle, Mason trying to get the macaroni and cheese from the green plastic spoon to his mouth. "Wee Street soon?" he asked.

"No, honey, not today."

"Playground?"

"No, honey, not today," she said again.

Mason jumped off his chair and went to the iPad sitting on the table and pressed the arrow on the screen centered on the ivory-colored album with the three men in the center.

The plucky piano intro was starting in the next room.

"Daisy?" he asked.

Becca put Oliver in his playpen and held Mason under his arms to swing him around as they sang. Mason's hair blew behind him as she spun him around, his blue eyes laughing as they met hers.

Later, the three of them fell asleep watching TV. Chicken nuggets, applesauce, milk and a bath later, Mason was ready for bed. She was tapping Oliver's back to make the burps come when her cell phone rang and Mason ran to get it. She could hear a bit of the conversation: *When will you be home? I already had a bath. Not by storytime? Oh. OK. I love you, too.*

After reading three stories and tucking the boys in, Becca walked into the living room. Oliver's bouncy chair was still vibrating, and she sat down next to the seat and pushed the switch on the chair to turn it off. The streetlights abruptly turned on, and Becca watched as the sky began to turn from day to night.

Down on Weee Street...

Do nothing, ask your body, reverse; do nothing, ask your body, reverse. She had seen these words on cards at an exhibit at the Museum of Modern Art. The little plaque next to these cards explained that David Bowie and Bryan Ferry had made up a card game of different ideas for when they got stuck in their song writing—just to check in with themselves, make them feel more inspired. The entire pile was on display, but only a few cards could be read and so she had pulled out her phone that day and had typed them in. *Do nothing, ask your body, reverse.* As she looked at these words now on her phone, she wondered what that would look like in her life. Instead, she did just the opposite. She sat up and dangled her feet over the side of the bed as she listened to Oliver crying.

The new bed she had purchased was a bit smaller than the one she and Josh had shared. The marks in the carpet left by the legs of their sleigh bed he had taken were very deep and, sadly, just where she happened to put her foot each day. Slipping her foot into that hole each morning was quickly followed by her tipping her head up looking at the sky. Not as if to say *"Why?"* but more of a *"Yes, I know. That is so funny. Haha."* This day, only her baby toe fell into the flattened carpet, a huge improvement from that first week.

It was then that she saw Mason in the door to her room, his blonde hair all tussled and mashed from his night's sleep, Gap pajamas all saggy in the knees.

She couldn't "do nothing." Her body said, "I'm tired." And there was no "reverse," only full throttle forward.

"Good morning, Buggle," she said with a huge smile on her face. It was 5:07.

These early mornings were kind of nice, really. She had moved the Tiny Tikes table into the living room, and Mason would eat his breakfast there as he watched shows on Noggin, often about being nice, honest and responsible. *Maybe grownups should watch these,* she thought as she placed Oliver on her lap, tapping his back until the burps came. He had been an easy baby to sleep, to feed, to carry. She figured it was her due since Mason had been challenging in all those departments. She placed Oliver on the blanket on the floor, the toys hanging over his head from the crossbars above.

She went to get a cup of coffee and when she returned, the show was just ending. The blue boy puppet was saying "sorry" to the orange girl puppet. He said he would do better next time. The orange puppet had then smoothed her purple yarn hair back before she clasped her hands together in front of her, smiled and rocked forward onto her toes.

Stupid puppet.

An hour and a half later, they were playing in the yard. Becca was using Mason's shovel to empty out the fire pit, the scoops of burnt paper and ash accumulating on the sides of his plastic bucket. Mason was playing in the yard pretending to pick up pieces of stone, carrying them someplace else and flattening the ground. Children copy what they see. She needed to remember that.

Josh was coming to take the boys to dinner tonight. Some of his clothes had turned up in the laundry and they were now washed and neatly folded in a suitcase in the hall. She called Mason to come inside and he stopped his yard work, pretending to wipe sweat off his forehead just as he had watched the workmen do a few weeks ago. She picked up Oliver's carrier in one hand and the little bucket in the other and walked towards the house, carefully setting the bucket next to the garage and helping Mason inside. She fed Mason an early lunch and gave Oliver a bottle.

"Who wants to go on Weee Street?" she called out, faking enthusiasm. Mason could barely contain his excitement as she gathered them both, then buckled them in their seats.

Becca knew this street like the back of her hand. The yellow triangle signs with arrows indicating the many turns weren't necessary. She had been driving the winding street, over the stone bridges and down through the ravines since she was 16 years old. The trees had grown in the last 15 years and they now reached up into the sky creating a canopy from the sun. In the fall, the empty branches would allow a peek at the homes. It had always brought her peace, driving down the winding street, to most people known as Asbury, but to her boys as Weee Street. She could drive it 30 minutes south and turn towards home, and it would be just the right distance to get the boys a nice nap, that is, only after about 15 minutes into the ride. Once they passed the curvy, winding blocks through the ravines, the boys would fall asleep, but, until then, Mason would ask in a sing-song voice, "Are we there yet?" until they reached the top of the hill leading down the rollercoaster-like road. Then she would sing along with the radio, listening to her '70s music and watching the beautiful houses as she passed each one by.

The large white stucco house with the red, shingled roof was rather famous around there, its entry marked by large metal gates that opened up to a circular drive.

Just a few blocks south, three smaller, but equally impressive, homes shared property on the bluff, supposedly built by a father who had wanted to keep his daughters close to home. His charming French Regency mini-castle sat in the middle of the two other castles of different architectural eras.

There was another home down the street that Becca could only see the slightest peak of between the two coach houses that flanked the driveway. Its long cobblestone entry, lined with trees, ended at the front door, framed in the same blue-gray shutters as each of the many windows.

When Becca was little, there had been another house tucked away in the trees. It had numerous windows, their shutters painted blue with white trim. The beautiful whitewashed bricks and the mansard roof peeked through the foliage. It had looked like something out of a French fairy tale. She used to imagine the children running around in berets, the little girls in their swinging coats and the boys in their knickers. Sadly, that house disappeared years ago.

There was one house she had always tried to steal a peek of, but sadly, it was placed behind a stone fence. Three windows cut into the stone would have allowed for a quick look, if they hadn't had tiles stacked inside of them, blocking her view. After all these years, she had never caught even the slightest glimpse, so it remained a mystery. In her mind, it was a sprawling stone home with a patio in the back, overlooking Lake Michigan where the family would finish their days drinking wine watching the sunset. Someday, she would steal a look.

A short while later, Becca slowly turned down her quiet street and into the driveway. The boys slept silently in their car seats, each of them with their heads tipped just a bit to the left. Idling the car in the driveway could usually buy her another 10 minutes or so before they woke up. She would often steal a few minutes then to close her eyes too. On this day, Oliver woke first, crying and waking up Mason.

"You're up!" she sang and climbed out of the car. She opened the back door and found Oliver kicking his feet and Mason slowly rubbing his eyes as he looked quietly around. At 3, he was the big brother and already appropriately annoyed with his younger one. She unbuckled them and carried them to the front door, one at a time, leaving Oliver in his carrier so she could carry in a still somewhat sleeping Mason. "We're home," she said in a sing-song voice, again, carefully wiggling the key in the lock as it always got a little stuck. "Daddy will be here soon."

A short while later, she had the boys changed and fed. They sat so sweetly as they watched TV, and she leaned against the wall and took it in. *Don't ever forget this moment,* she told herself. She grabbed the suitcase, brought it to the front stoop and opened it up. She took out her phone and copied the word she had typed in that night at the fire pit onto a small piece of paper before placing it inside the bag. She then picked up the plastic bucket and proceeded to pour in the ash and soot over the neatly folded clothes. She chuckled just a bit as she zipped the case closed, the word "IRREDEEMABLE" slowly disappearing from her view.

So this is embarrassing...

Becca's knees quivered a bit as she stepped into the attorney's office building. She completely blanked on who she had spoken to on the phone. She looked at the many last names on the screen in the entryway, running her finger down the list before she recognized it. Audrey Light. She wasn't a partner, just an associate. Instead of $500 an hour, she would only garner $250. *Talk fast*, Becca thought, walking up the stairs. There were plastic sheets hanging from the ceiling and bannisters, the smell of fresh paint filled the air. At the top of the steps, cardboard had been taped down to the landing with bright yellow tape to keep the floor from paint dribbles.

"Hello?" called out a voice from behind a desk. "Becca, is that you?" A tall, thin, very young woman stepped out from behind a plastic sheet hanging from an exposed metal beam way up above her head. "I'm so sorry about the mess. Construction started weeks ago. It will look beautiful when we're done. Here's hoping you'll never see the final renovation, though. I'm sure you'd like to get this done before summer, right? Come with me," she said, gesturing her to follow through the opening in the floating panels she had made with her arm. "Did you bring any paperwork with you at all?"

"No," Becca replied. "Was I supposed to bring…"

"That's OK, we're just getting started anyway. Some people bring tax forms, bills, bank statements. Maybe they have ideas already about visitation for the kids. Let's just talk first. How are you doing?" she asked.

"I'm OK. The boys are OK. Josh moved out last week and we're getting a bit of a routine, the three of us," Becca said.

"That's good. I know this is tough, Becca. How old are the boys again?" she asked.

"Mason is 3. Oliver is 2 months," Becca said. "They're with Josh for the weekend."

Audrey started writing then—two boys, 3 yrs. and 2 months. "They're young. Let's just get you out and get some money for you and the kids. There's nothing personal here anymore. It doesn't matter what has happened—drugs, money, he's having an affair... What does Josh do for a living?"

"He's a pharmaceutical rep? For urological devices?" Becca offered.

Audrey held back a small smile. "OK, and do you work, Becca?"

"I did. I'm a teacher. I have a master's in education..." Becca said, quietly.

"That's good. You can get work teaching when the boys are older, when you're ready to go back. You're staying home now? You two had decided that you would stay home?"

"Well, honestly, childcare would have cost more than any salary I would have brought in, so yes."

"Well, child support is a percentage of his salary. You aren't working and haven't been since the kids were born. That entitles you to maintenance, Becca, maintaining your lifestyle, for a little while at least. You can go back to teaching in a bit."

"I suppose..."

Audrey looked up at her from her desk then. "Is there anything else you might be qualified for?"

"No."

"Let's talk about now, then. You and the boys will be taken care of. Let's just get this done. How much does he make a year?" she asked, still holding her pen, awaiting the number.

"I have no idea," Becca said.

"You don't know his salary?"

Becca shook her head, feeling a bit embarrassed.

"I'll need to see the tax returns, then, Becca. You need to get me those," she said, taking more notes.

"I don't know where they are," Becca said.

"Well, find them. How about your bank accounts. Where are they?" She rapidly jotted words down the edge of her paper. "About how much do you have in each one? I need to know if you have any stocks. What is the mortgage on your house? Do you have a second mortgage? How much are the taxes on your property? I need to know what credit cards you share. Even store ones. You'll need to open up your own, under your own name, if you don't have one already. Do that today so you can still use your joint income to apply. Do you have any credit card debt? Student loans?" Audrey asked, then finally looked up. "Becca?"

Becca was watching the plastic sheets swinging over her head. She hadn't really heard anything after *he's having an affair...*

Boys' Weekend, Yea!

Becca was relieved that the boys were with Josh; this way she could have some time to look around the house for all the paperwork Audrey had just told her she needed. She walked down the basement stairs, holding the low handrail they had only recently installed. The remodel on the basement was a mere three weeks old, and the white Berber carpet was still bright white.

Josh and Mason had built a fort in the center. Josh had probably only needed to buy one case of the construction pieces but had bought two to make it extra big. It consisted of foam poles that stuck together at magnetic joints. You would construct a cube, then hang different colored panels from each with clips. It created a very colorful haven, with the yellow and orange poles and the purple, green and blue nylon squares concealing some of the openings. She saw a small red light glowing on the floor inside and bent down. She lifted a green flap to see one of Mason's trucks with the lights left on, then climbed inside and sat down in the little cube. She turned the truck upside down and switched the switch to the off position.

The quiet inside this fabric cocoon soothed her. *I could stay here all day,* she thought to herself as she grabbed for one of Mason's favorite books from an adjoining cube. *He had said he wanted to bring this to Daddy's house,* she thought, as she turned the heavy pages of cardboard. She pulled her cell phone out of her pocket and started to dial Josh, but stopped.

Is he having an affair?

She remembered that night that he had been late coming home. The boys were asleep, and she was in bed when the phone rang. She had answered it to static.

"Hello?" she had shouted. "Hello? I hear you, Josh! Can't you hear me? Are you OK?" She could hear him talking to someone, then there was laughter, his and a woman's. "Hello!" she hollered for what seemed like forever. Then a door opening and closing, and the noise of the car before it disconnected. The phone rang in her hand then.

"Hey, I'm sorry I'm late. I'm on my way now," Josh said when she had answered.

"I've been listening to you in the car. You called here. Who was that? Who was with you?" she demanded.

"It's just Alan. I'm just dropping him off."

"It was a woman! I heard her! Who is she?" she was screaming now.

"Becca, you're being crazy. There is no woman," he said. "I'm not even discussing this with you. I'll be home soon," and he had hung up.

She curled up in the little cube and noticed Mason's lovey in the adjoining one. She reached for it, pulled it close and fell asleep in the colorful box.

She catches the moments (OK, fine, it's just a bit about Allie...)

The phone startled Becca awake and she reached over to look at who would be calling so early on a Sunday. Allie. Allie at 10:30 was actually late for Allie. Actually, 10:30 was pretty late for Becca as well, but with the boys on Boys' Weekend Yea! Becca was able to sleep in. "Hello?" Becca said tiredly into the phone, looking at the beautiful colors being cast from the sun on the new white carpet through the purple and green panels.

"Good morning!" Allie chimed. "I had a thought. You're picking up the boys from the city tonight, right? Meet me at the museum first! I'll buy you lunch! A glass of wine! Please, Becca! It will be fun!"

It always had been. She had met Allie in their Impressionism 121 class, mostly because they were the top two students and competed fiercely against each other. Where Becca was no competition, however, was in the studio. Allie was an artist. Period. Allie had started very young, of course, no training, it just came naturally to her. She had shared with Becca that she had often been pulled out of her classes by her art teacher. She would smile as she told the story of how, as the second-grade class learned their times tables, Ms.

Miller would appear in the doorway. She would walk over to the math teacher and whisper in her ear. Allie would then be called up and then would walk out of the room as the other kids watched with envy. A few moments later, in the basement art room, she would be drawing—covers for the BuzzBook or SpringSing. Allie loved how it set her apart from the others, but had also shared with Becca that art had given her something to do while she waited for her mother at the doctor's office or at the hospital. Her father had explained to Allie after her mother's long illness that she had finally died in her sleep, thinking it would bring Allie comfort. Instead, the 8-year-old Allie believed that if she fell asleep, she might die, too. After that, Allie rarely slept, but pretended to, covering up at night with the blanket over her head, drawing from the light of her alarm clock. Even in college, she had spent evenings in the studio, catching naps in the chairs. After college, Allie had gotten a job at the Art Institute, her dream job—short of having her own work showcased in a gallery, of course—teaching young artists about art, day and night.

Becca and Allie's favorite plans weren't shopping or going for coffee, but meeting at the museum, walking around and talking about the work. After Becca had gotten married and moved to the suburbs, those days became even more special as they occurred only a couple of times a year. The last time they went, she had been pregnant with Oliver. They had been crossing Michigan Avenue when Oliver had shifted and rested on her sciatic nerve. The pain was unbearable and had stopped her in her tracks, literally. The two had stood in the center of the street holding each other as the cars honked and sped by. A police officer had come over and put his arms around the two of them until she had been able to walk again.

Lots of couples have wedding portraits taken on the boulevards of Michigan Avenue. They capture the moment, usually with the car lights speeding past and the couple looking at only each other as the world goes by. Allie had caught their moment, too. Her painting of the two of them holding each other, screaming in the middle of the street was one of Becca's favorite pieces.

"How about around 12?" Becca asked.

"Perfect! I'll get some work done in my classroom, first." Allie said. "See ya then!"

Just a little peek...

Becca had driven that street so many times that she couldn't believe that she had never noticed it before. The streetlights were different—green, green, green, and then black. The green ones were concrete on the bottom with a geometric designed green lantern at the top. Art Deco, maybe? The black ones were more the Beaux Arts style, she figured. They were heavily ornamented with medallions and flowers, and the sharp points from the lanterns pointed up towards the sky. *This must be where the towns change,* she thought. Each suburb had its own style and as she passed into the next town, she noticed them changing once more, this time a simple round light pointing down from a simple tall pole. There is always a beginning and end, it seems; of course, it depends on which direction you're heading, but since she did the drive round-trip each day, each town had a chance to begin and end, end and begin.

On one of her many drives with the boys, she had noticed several masons carefully cutting away the stained stones in a fence surrounding one of the more beautiful homes on Asbury. It looked very complex, taking out a stone, scraping off the mortar. She had read that the house had been built in the early 1900s. The second owner had added a wing, to put artwork in or something like that. It had offset the balance of the house, but had made more room. The next owner had had the addition razed, returning the home to its original beauty.

When she had driven by the wall at the end of that day, there had been an opening where the men had been working. It was a zigzag from top to bottom, leaving just a little peek. The house looked more vulnerable that way, passersby could see into something that had been hidden so well before. The next day, when she had been driving by with the sleeping boys, the masons had come back, carefully placing the stones into where they had been missing. She had figured that there would always be a seam there, a place you could tell that there had been damage done, but then repaired. Instead, she noticed that in that spot, there was no delineation between old and new, broken and fixed. The repair was seamless. Maybe her repairs would be seamless, too. Maybe someone would look closely and, if they did see that something was different, would realize it all fit together somehow just fine anyway…

Allie had texted to meet her in the Modern Wing. Becca had never gone through these exhibits. Down the hall, through the cafeteria, up the stairs to a long corridor with several entryways to different rooms. She recognized some of the paintings, some of the artists' names. She had studied them in school, but had never seen their work in person. It just didn't make sense to her. A bunch of horizontal stripes of different colors, some vertical lines of different shades of gray. The same celebrity in a four-square with different bright hues leaping off the canvas. Becca's final paper in school had been about Claude Monet. She had studied his haystacks, his bridges, his water lilies, and she understood the beauty of them. But she couldn't decipher what most of these modern artists were trying to convey or why.

In front of her on the wall was a large canvas. Muslin stretched out with only the smallest amount of paint applied in scribbles and doodles and splotches and lines. *There must be a story or an idea woven in there,* she thought, *some kind of plan,* but she had no idea what it was. She stood up from the slatted bench in the center of the room and took a peek at the artist's name: Cy Twombly.

"Hungry?" she heard Allie whisper in her ear. "Hey, Twombly! I like him, too!"

Sunday Afternoon at L'Institute d'Art Avec la Fille, Allie...

"So, this is new," Becca said, gesturing to the cafeteria.

"It's nice, right? I usually bring lunch from home and sit in my office. This is a treat for me, too," Allie said, walking into the room in what felt to be the basement. The windows facing the courtyard let in plenty of sun, and they placed their trays down at a table in front of one overlooking the statues on the lawn. "We can't eat out there, but we can go sit later if you have time. When do you need to pick up the boys?"

"Five," Becca said, watching Allie struggle to open the miniature bottle of Riesling they would share and finally pouring some into Becca's plastic cup.

It was her long curls tumbling down after she removed her hair clip. People were noticing her because of her long curls tumbling down after she removed her hair clip. She had gone from art teacher to artist in just a second, like that. "To Girls' Day!" she said, raising her cup to *tink* Becca's. Instead, the cups made a hollow plastic sound before they each took a sip. "How are things going? What did your lawyer say?"

"Nothing yet. Still waiting to see what she thinks about our finances. She wanted all of this paperwork—tax returns, W2 forms, credit card statements... I mean, the list goes on and on and on."

"What's all that for?" Allie asked, as she poked at her Waldorf salad.

"I guess to see how much money he is going to have to cough up for child support and maintenance," Becca explained.

"Maintenance?" Allie asked, pouring more wine into Becca's still half full cup.

"I'm not working. I guess it's something like if *we* decided that I would stay home, then *he* can't change our plans now, or something like that. I'm not sure exactly what it means money-wise, but I do think I can stay home longer with the boys, anyway," Becca said.

Allie cocked her head. "But as I recall, 'we' didn't want you to stay home, right?"

Becca shrugged.

"So, he had wanted you to go back to work and you didn't and now he's going to give you money to stay home? That is hysterical, Bex," Allie said, once again knocking her cup into Becca's that was now set on the table.

"Parenting time is going to be the tricky part," Becca said, looking out the window at a young artist reclining on the lawn. He was on his back with his arms bent behind him for support, looking across the courtyard. It reminded her of the painting of the man lying on the grass in "Sunday Afternoon on the Island of La Grande Jatte," by Seurat. *It's funny, they both wore tank tops, too. I guess some things don't really change,* she thought. "Josh will get the boys every other weekend and for a couple hours a couple nights a week," Becca explained. "We'll split up holidays."

"Sounds fair. They need to see him, too. Besides, you need some time to recoup," Allie offered.

Becca pondered her life now versus then as they ate silently for a minute. "Ya know, it's not so bad," Becca said. "It really isn't too different. The boys get up early, have breakfast and we play. Mason is in school three days a week now till 12 and Oliver naps then. We have lunch, go for a ride down Asbury, nap, have a snack, go to the park, have dinner, have a bath, read stories…"

"Yeah, that sounds a lot like before," Allie said, matter-of-factly. "You ever think about what it would have been like if you had asked him for a divorce a few months ago, like you were thinking about?"

Becca remembered that night when the five of them had all been out to dinner. Becca had shared just a hint, and the girls had listened. "I wanted to make it work. It was worth a shot," she said. "The boys…I needed to try."

"I get it. I do. You ready? What do you want to see first?" Allie asked, gathering up the remains of their lunches and placing them on their trays.

"Impressionists?"

"Always the Impressionists. Bex, so much to see here and it's always the Impressionists," Allie said, flailing her hands. "I was meaning to ask you, I'm thinking of having my students create a self-portrait by designing a CD cover. Thoughts?"

"Why a CD cover? Why not an album cover?"

"Becca, we're lucky they know what a CD is! An album? Kids have never even seen one of those!"

"My kids know what an album is."

"And only your kids would," Allie said with a smile.

"I think," Becca said, "it would make Mrs. Fink roll over in her grave. Do it."

Another reason to take
Weee Street....

By 5:30 Becca had picked up the boys and was slowly heading back towards home on Weee Street. A guy in a passing Jeep smiled and waved at her. She squinted in the rearview mirror as she caught a glimpse of his taillights just over the two boys' sleeping heads, both tipped to the left. At the next stoplight, she snapped up the cover to the mirror. She tussled her hair a bit and noted the dark roots, flattering anyway.

When the light changed, she saw what the holdup had been. Asbury was blocked off, and traffic was being rerouted to the commercial street five blocks away. She never liked this street, too many cars in a hurry, and the storefronts were nowhere as pretty as the beautiful homes on Asbury, but she had no choice today. Old barbershop, bakery for hipsters, Baseball Academy, Chinese restaurant… then she saw the three women in pet shop aprons walking five dogs. The one in the front was on her phone, not noticing that she was too short on her leash, not noticing the little black dog attached to it was spinning in circles.

"Hey," Becca screamed as they walked past. "Hey!" she screamed louder. She was waving her arms wildly now, screaming at the lady when she finally got another woman's attention. "She's too short on the leash! She's too short on the leash!" *Where was the window button?* She looked and pressed every button and lever, looking for the control, but couldn't find it. Finally, she received the stink eye from the lady watching her, and the other woman, still engrossed in her phone, scooped up the tiny dog as they all went inside the store.

I will never drive this way again, ever, she thought, as the boys began to wake up and they made their slow trip home from the city.

It's true, you never forget
your first time....

The next morning, Mason was in her bedroom doorway. His hair was tussled and mashed. His pajamas all saggy at the knees. It was 5:10. Wake up, dip foot into the missing sleigh bed's old imprint, look at the sky. That's done. "Good morning, Mason."

She changed and fed Oliver before buckling them both into the double jogging stroller, Mason enjoying his Pop Tart in his seat. She was wearing the local outfit of yoga pants, matching jacket, running shoes and ponytail. Running down the block was pretty easy, five houses till the stop sign. She jogged in place, watching the traffic go by until she could cross the street. The difficult part would be the trip up the hill. Only five houses, but straight up. By house three, she felt it. Just getting up the hill was going to be her goal today. When she finally made it, she slowed to a walk to finish the route into town, pushing the boys as they cuddled in their blanket. Only one small coffeehouse served this area of their town. She had seen the other mommies sitting, enjoying their coffee, as their kids rested in their strollers. When she finally reached it, she carefully maneuvered the double stroller through the two doors.

Inside, the line of locals was dressed either for work or like her. She blended, she thought, and then she knew that this would be her new routine. *Here, I am like everyone else.* This place, this time, would be her new favorite thing, but, while maneuvering back out the door, with one hand grasping her skinny latte, Becca got the stroller stuck in the doorway. A woman swooped up from her table, held the door open and grabbed Becca's cup just as the first bit of coffee started coming out of the tiny hole in the lid.

"Thank you," Becca said, as she pushed the stroller over the threshold. "I really don't know what I was even thinking trying to do this today. Everyone else makes is look so easy."

"I'm here almost every day and I see it all the time," the lady said with a smile. She looked to be about Becca's age. Becca hadn't noticed a ring on her finger as she grabbed the coffee. "No worries."

Becca steadied her cup and began pushing the stroller though the chairs and tables outside. She turned back to wave and saw the woman still looking at her and the boys. The woman gave a small wave, and Becca tipped her cup in her direction, but she kept moving, slightly too embarrassed to sit to drink her coffee after needing rescue just to get through the door.

While she strolled through the town, the boys slept. The video store had been replaced by a gluten-free bakery. The stationary store with all the stickers and gel pens had morphed into a Gap. Commercial stores were now popping up as the smaller ones disappeared. She looked at the Pottery Barn window and quickly a salesperson opened the door for her.

"Come in," she said. "Take a look around. We have some new things for the holidays!"

The boys slept the whole time. Through every topiary, lantern and candle. That's when Becca saw the answer to her problems, hanging from a metal track on the ceiling…

The next morning when she jumped out of bed, her foot hit the red flower on the border of a blue rug from Pottery Barn. She looked at the sky, smirked, "Good. Done." Why she hadn't thought of this before, she would never know.

So, about the house...

Two days later, Becca sat in her attorney's office with the plastic panels still swinging overhead. Mason was at school while Oliver slept in the carrier at her feet. Becca had finally given Audrey all the information that she had asked for that day with the swinging plastic sheets. They had no money in any accounts, no stocks, two mortgages and three loans. Credit cards to stores she didn't even know of were at their limits.

"So, it doesn't look like you can keep the house," Audrey said flatly. "It's not even the mortgage, Becca, it's the taxes. But when you sell, you'll be able to take the money, pay off the mortgage and the bills and then start new with the boys. I'll get you more than half, though. I promise."

"Where will we go?" she asked.

"Start looking," Audrey said. "Again, think taxes, Becca. You now have a big lot on a quiet little street. Think smaller lot, that's all. You'd be surprised what's out there."

And she was.

Old, falling apart, smelly houses on busy streets. Her realtor, someone's grandma for sure, named Faye, found every one. Becca didn't mind a renovation, she really didn't. It was finding a place that wasn't too old, too falling apart, too smelly or on too busy of a street that was the problem. It reminded her of that TV show where the families see three houses with their "must have lists." They would put a check next to what they wanted that the house did have and an x next to the items it didn't. Each of the houses so far had only one check, and it was next to price. The rest of the items on the list all had an x.

She and the boys would drive around each day scouting "for sale" signs on lawns before returning to their own for sale sign at home. There had been a few curious buyers. They had been interested in the lot, not the renovated basement, not the perfectly painted blue and green rooms for the boys, not the recently paved patio and fire pit. Everything they'd worked to create or improve in their house meant nothing now. *Same as our marriage,* she thought.

"When the right offer comes in, it's going to be time to leave. Sell," Audrey said to her, her waifish body leaning against her big desk, "fast."

Someone's Grandma Faye...

"So, this one is a 1955 spit level," Faye said as she unlocked the door. "Some would say that it's a Midcentury Modern, I mean, you could say that, of course." They stepped into the house and onto the vinyl tiles in the front hall. "Hardwoods in the living area of this floor and upstairs. They need to be refinished, maybe," she added, stepping onto them. "It's a lot of light. West exposure here, north, there." She was gesturing to the windows.

They reminded Becca of the Brady Bunch. The three columns and three rows did bring in a lot of light. "The kitchen needs some work," Faye said as she peeked in through the sliding door. "These are nice for privacy," she added, sliding it back and forth to close off the kitchen from the dining area. The vinyl tile continued in there, as well. The cabinets were just like the ones she had seen dismantled and stacked in the basement of her house, she thought, as she noticed the tarnished brass hinges on the flat plain doors. "It's a Formica countertop," Faye noted, gesturing to the granite pattern. "Nice window, though. You'll want new appliances," she said, making her way out of the kitchen and taking the two steps out to the stairwell. Seven steps up, seven steps down. "Bedrooms or basement first?"

"Bedrooms?" Becca asked as she looked up at the old brass ceiling fan.

"Yeah, I know it doesn't look so good, but I'm sure it's to help circulate the air. It's difficult in a split level. Ignore that for now," and the two of them walked the seven steps upstairs. "Maybe carpet these, with the kids." She pointed to the unfinished steps. To the right was the bathroom, one-inch square pink tiles with one gray tile every once in a while. The matching pink toilet and pink sink were close enough to each other that you could probably brush your teeth while sitting down. Faye slid over the shower curtain to expose the matching pink tub and tile walls. "That's the 1950s for you." The three bedrooms upstairs were all a decent size and had hardwood floors. "Ya know, it's not so bad. Basement now?"

"Sure," Becca said, and they made their way down the seven steps to the kitchen door entrance and turned to walk down the seven steps to the basement.

"Laundry here, storage here," Faye said, as she poked her head into the open doors. "Parquet floors. Nope, take that back, they're tile," she said as she got a closer view. "Ya know, these are 9-by-9 inches; they could be asbestos," she said walking further into the room that had the same three columns of three windows as upstairs. "That was common in the '50s, but we can have the asbestos remediated. Don't worry about that. You could just have those built-ins ripped down," she said, gesturing to the wall with the broken shelves and cabinets. "I bet the fuse box is in here," and she opened up the closet door exposing a tangle of webs. "Those are probably just cobwebs, Becca. I think the spiders are long gone." *Sure they are,* Becca thought. Faye opened up the small metal door on the wall. "Well, this is original to the house, I bet. Some of these aren't even marked. What do we have here? DW, AC, Micro… You might want to invest in a new box. I don't even know what this one says."

Becca turned to look out the nine windows that brought in the light over the sunken patio. "It has drains there and there," Faye quickly interjected, gesturing to the small, rusted grids in the broken concrete, "for the rain and snow. It doesn't look like they've had any flooding," she said, scuffing her foot on one of the fake Parquet—probably asbestos—tiles.

Becca shook her head. "There's nothing to stop the boys from falling into the patio while they're playing in the yard," Becca said, looking out at the weed-covered lawn.

"Actually, those look like peonies, Becca," Faye said, also looking out the windows, and using her hand as a visor to block out the sunshine. "They grow tall enough that no one will go over them." She gestured to the flower beds that rested at the top of the concrete walls. "You know peonies, Becca? Oh, they're beautiful." Faye opened the folder she'd been carrying. "It says there is a powder room on the main floor. How did we miss that? Let's head back up." They made their way up the seven steps to the kitchen entrance once again.

"Ya know, the fireplace here is kind of nice," Faye said, touching the brick wall that also served as a divider for the hallway and living room. "It gives a bit of privacy from the street. Oops, there it is!" she said excitedly as she approached the front door and closed it to reveal the bathroom door hidden behind it. "Same as upstairs, pedestal is chrome. Very 1950s. Well, that's it." She ran a finger down her paperwork. "That's 1,158 square feet, close to the train and the music park. It says if the wind is blowing just the right way, you may even be able to listen to the music in your yard. I bet you get some traffic here since you're so close to the entrance. You probably get lots of foot traffic, as well. People carrying their chairs, blankets, food and stuff. You ever go there, Becca? To hear any shows?"

"No," Becca said, looking at the old, wooden front door that was now closed with a peep hole too high for her to look out of.

"We could keep looking at other places. The bones aren't bad, though. The price is right. Looks like they had accepted an offer, but no closing. It's just back on the market two days ago," Faye said without looking up.

Becca sat down on the card table chair in the living room and looked out the Brady Bunch windows. Asbestos tiles, old fuse box, sunken patio, busy street… "What's a fair offer?" she asked.

"Well, I'd go kind of low. The furnace should really be looked at," Faye said, still looking at her paperwork.

… and an old furnace…

"Yeah, okay," Becca said, gazing at the tarnished bronze chain hanging from the stairway ceiling fan. "Let's put in an offer."

Two piles…

Faye had called with the good news. The house with the asbestos tiles, busy street and old furnace was hers, all hers. A builder had even offered the right price to buy her old house, with the intention to raze it to the ground. That was all she needed to hear. That would be a great day, watching that house—*his* house—come down, listening to the cracking of beams, seeing the dust rise from the mess created there.

Most of the things were packed away, but she had left all the boys' favorite toys in the living room thrown about on the floor. The buyer had told her she could remove anything and everything she wanted, so she collected everything that wasn't nailed down, and even some things that were—vent covers, doorknobs, light switch covers, things like that. The handymen would be coming to take down the kitchen cabinets. They were only three years old, light maple, shiny. Although she hated them—one more of *his* choices—she knew in a new home they would look different. They would survive this move, too, she had decided.

Nearly everything was packed now, but packing the shoes would take awhile. All of her friends kept their shoes on shelves, accumulating dust. Becca's shoes were still in their boxes, with the tissue paper and those felt bags you were supposed to carefully wrap them in when you traveled. Her bags still had the crease they created when they were placed in the box. Becca had often wondered how one would use those bags. Wouldn't the sole of one dirty shoe get the other shoe all dirty anyway? The thing about her shoes was each pair told a story. She could remember events when she had worn them, what she was wearing, who she was with.

Like the black velvet ones with the twist on top. Becca had rush-ordered them for an extra $35, and they had arrived just hours before a black-tie wedding in the city. She had been so relieved when they arrived and so furious at the end of the night when she could no longer walk in them and tiptoed in her nylons down the street in the dark, holding the beauties by their way too pointy and too-tall heels. She had never worn them again but had kept them because of the way they made her feel—like someone glamorous or sophisticated, she supposed.

She had worn the combat boots on days that she needed to "boot-up" to feel particularly brave and prepared. They had no wedge or heel for height—something she had always relied on for a bit of extra confidence—but they had a lug sole and laced to her mid-calf. They made her feel cool, like a rock star, and even though they were 10 years old, they looked like new.

The only pair not boxed up was in a paper sack on the top shelf. Her waffle-stompers from high school, all covered in cobwebs and dust. They were somewhat discolored, and the black and red laces were frayed where the aglet used to be. The soles were worn more on the outer edge, the treads flatter there. She reached inside one and felt the mostly flattened lift that had helped her to gain maybe an inch. Remarkably, the smallest bit of dried pink paint flakes still clung to the rubber edges.

Sometimes Becca's friends gave her a hard time about her shoes—that she spent too much money on them, and they would never do that. She looked now at the shoes she wore that night on the curb…

"You can't afford those shoes, Bex," Katie had said to her one night, so matter-of-factly.

"They were on sale. I only buy on sale," Becca had justified, while pulling at the strap around her ankle and wiggling her toes inside the pointed sling-back.

"They're not even comfortable. I've been watching you all night. You can barely walk," Katie had argued. "You know, you're not fooling me… It's like that kids song that you changed the lyrics to, about how you buy things when you're sad. It makes you feel better, you know, when you buy stuff," she had said and then started humming the tune from one of Mason's songs on his "feelings" CD.

Stop it, Becca, she thought, as she carefully placed them under the tissue and felt bag, before pushing the box to the side.

Sometimes she had waited for months before the big splurge, like the black pointed-toe, suede sling-backs. Other times, it was more spontaneous like the day she bought those two pairs on the bottom shelf. Looking at them now, she realized that wearing them really didn't bring her as much joy as buying them. That day, like many she supposed, was all about the buy. Always a bad idea she knew, but revenge is served oh so sweetly on not one, but two pairs of Pradas.

The day she bought those had started out as a beautiful day in the city. The three of them had all gone to the zoo. She and Josh had spent the afternoon pushing Mason in the stroller and talking with him about each of the animals. "Look at the tall giraffes, Mason!" "Aren't the elephants' feet big?" The conversation was not stimulating, but infinitely more interesting than anything they could have said to each other. They could have played happy family all day that way, smiling at the other young families, watching Mason running in front of the stroller chasing the ducks by the pond, but the rain started, so they ventured further into the city for a break from the storms.

So many families running around in the rain, laughing, holding jackets over their heads. Not them. When the full downpour began, Josh instantly scooped Mason into the stroller, grabbed the handles and pushed him to the nearest doorway, leaving her behind in the rain to catch up. Like an after-thought, he called over his shoulder, "Hurry up!" The mad dash ended with them inside one of the most magnificent stores in the city, standing in silence. They shook off the rain and stomped their feet on the entryway rugs. He brushed at his jacket, but didn't even notice her rain-soaked wrap. She had deserved to have something held over her head, she deserved to be laughing, she had thought. As they meandered through the store, her anger grew, and by the third floor, it was a storm worse than the one raging outside.

The two pairs were quite similar, she could see that now, but on that day, everything was blurry. When the salesman asked which one she wanted, she couldn't choose.

"Both," she replied. It didn't bother her that this store didn't take major credit cards. She knew the store had a policy for only their own store card, checks or cash. "Both," she repeated, and the anger started to change into something else. Was she happy? Was she, dare she say, a bit giddy?

"Both," she said, and the salesman in the very nice suit smiled, stood up, and took them both to the register. He came back with the charge: $851.

"They don't take credit cards," Josh said.

"Then we'll have to pay cash."

"I don't have that kind of cash on me."

"There's an ATM just outside," Becca offered.

"It's raining," Josh reasoned.

"Then you should go quickly."

And that was that. She sat there as he ran in the rain to get the cash for shoes she didn't really care about, but she remembered him counting out the bills and placing them in the salesman's hand. The sight had made her happy and giddy, and the shoes were OK, too.

She put those two pair in a pile. She would make two piles: one for donate, one for keep. She wasn't sure what pile this was quite yet. She went back to the remaining shoes and saw the white box with the block black letters on top. She remembered these too. These were the ones she was wearing that day in the snow. That horrible, horrible day in the snow.

Clickety, clickety, click...

The next morning, the trucks showed up right on time. She had ripped jeans and a T-shirt on, a cap to cover her dirty hair. Becca listened as the three men in coveralls lifted the door of the truck—*clickety, clickety, click* up the rails. One of them began walking up the sidewalk with a clipboard in his hand as she stood in the empty kitchen gazing out the window. When he approached, she gave a smile and waved. *Ask your body, breathe,* she told herself. And she walked to the door.

For two hours and 45 minutes, she and the boys watched as the men came into the house empty-handed and walked out with something new. Mason narrated each of their exits. "There goes my ball pit!" "There goes my toy box!" "There goes Oliver's SuperSaucer!" As the last boxes were loaded onto the truck, Jenna came out of her house and down her walk. She approached Becca slowly with a sad look on her face.

"That's the last of it," Becca said, gesturing as the truck door slowly came down, closing everything inside. "When the bulldozer comes, call me. I want to see it."

Jenna looked back at her own house to see her two girls in the window, "No, you don't," she said, sadly.

Becca stood for a moment staring at her empty house. She remembered the first time she walked in carrying Mason, introducing him to each room. She recalled painting Oliver's room twice, because the first blue was not the exact same color as the "A" patch on his alphabet quilt.

This is the house we first came home to. We made some great memories here…

"Yes, I do. Call me on my cell," Becca said.

Becca and the not so self-portrait…

The movers were quick and, soon, Becca was in their new home, passing off the boys for *Boys' Weekend, Yea!* with Josh. Faye had been right about the fireplace. It did offer a bit of privacy from the street—the boys hadn't been able to see Becca sitting behind it, crying, as they pulled away.

A folding chair leaned up against the windows with a ribbon tied around it. A card attached to it read, "Enjoy the music festival! Enjoy your new home! Faye." Becca stood in the room, the floor covered in boxes, thinking of what to unpack first. She found the box with her stereo inside and took a knife to cut through the strapping tape that ran across the top. She found another box and did the same. After lifting each flap, she saw the albums she had placed inside. Her collection was from her childhood—soundtracks and heartthrobs. If they were in *Tigerbeat Magazine,* they were in this box. She lifted out the first square and flipped it upside down to see the list of songs, then she sat down on the floor leaning against the wall with the various beige paint chips she had collected earlier and taped to it. She put her knees up with the first album on her lap, tugged the box a bit closer and took out the other albums, one at a time, turning them over or opening them up. She looked at the pictures and liner notes and thought about how she used to dance in her bedroom to some and simply sit on her bed intently listening to others.

She could remember dragging her bright yellow bean bag chair down the hall to her brother's room. His stereo was set up in his closet, and he would lounge in there on his green bean bag chair looking at the liner notes of his favorite albums. Sometimes he would let her shove her chair in there, too, so she would smoosh it through doorways until she could plop down with him. They would sit together listening to his albums and reading along in the safe little room filled with music.

The covers were artwork, he had explained to her. They would look at the bright colors and shapes, like the outlined, angular man and woman dancing near the water, and the cartoonish-like character with the shaky hand reaching for a lopsided wine glass. One night, her brother came home from the record store with an album for her that she had been wanting. On the cover, a woman was putting on lipstick, in only her bra and underwear, as a man in the back of the room was placing a record on the turntable. This didn't seem like art to her, and she envied his own new album with the funny letters and polka-dots.

Growing up, art was always something she loved. She even knew each artist's work in her brother's game of Masterpiece. In one of her many high school art classes, Becca had been assigned a self-portrait. As in college, studying art was easier than creating it, and a self-portrait was tricky. It shouldn't be cartoonish, angular or colorful. It needed to look real, and each time she went to draw the oval with the curved line one third of the way down to place her eyes, she erased it again. It wasn't going to work.

Instead, Becca had finally decided to make her self-portrait an album cover. The songs on the back described her—two columns in fun lettering— with "Scrappy" being the album title and first song. "S's Thuck" was about her small lisp. "Born Later" was an homage to '70s music that she learned about from her brother and loved so much. "You're Almost There" was a quote from the doctor who told her, after X-raying her hand, that she was almost done growing. "No One Needs To Know" quickly followed and was about the multiple heel cushions she hid inside her shoes to gain an extra inch. "A Little Too Much" referenced the amount of bleach her hairstylist had used one spring, making her hair way too blonde, just in time for her first driver's license picture. "Going Round and Round" explained the emotional scars she suffered from the ceiling fan hanging over the stairway in her home— as a little girl, she would frequently come home from school to find her beloved stuffed animals perilously perched on each blade before her brother would turn it on, spinning them around to hit the walls before landing two stories beneath. "I Got Your Number" was a metaphor for how she had memorized the address grid of the city—her brother would block the exit to the family room when she tried to get to the bathroom and he'd shout out a number until she named the right street. For example, he would say 3600, and she would have to respond "Addison," or she'd simply pee her pants.

The cover art had been an imprint of her waffle stomper. She had stepped in pink paint then stomped on the 12-by-12 cardboard sleeve. A self-portrait should expose who you are, she had thought, and it did—a short girl who was hesitant to speak up because of her slight lisp, had a fear of going to the hairdresser and who was tortured, yet educated, by her big brother. This felt pretty exposed, naked even. She got a D. "Not a self-portrait" was the only comment, critique or criticism she received from the infamous Mrs. Fink.

As it turned out, 94.7 FM would continue to play all her favorites; she learned to keep the things she loved hidden and safe; she would never get lost in the city; and she had finally attained the perfect ash blonde mane through highlights. Platforms, as well as built-in, hidden wedges were in style, so she could almost appear to achieve the 5 feet the doctor insisted she would never reach. The S's, however, remained a challenge. That is why, although her friends lovingly called her Bex, she always introduced herself as Becca.

As she placed the last album down, she looked at the floor. Becca could see the scratches and stains from the previous owners. Some of the planks had even begun to separate from the others. Most had nail holes from carpeting that had been laid down to cover them.

She sprayed a bit of furniture polish on a stain, placed a rag on top, and used her foot to move the cloth back and forth over it. When she picked up the soiled rag, there was a shiny spot underneath. She sprayed again, threw down the rag and moved her foot in circles. Little clean patches began to appear.

She paused from the cleaning and took an album out of its jacket, blew the dust off her player and carefully placed the vinyl disc on the carousel. She threw the switch to "on" and watched it spin. It had always been so tough to place the needle down on just the right spot. Then she heard the "pop" and took a step back. *Static, click, click*, then words that she hadn't heard since she was a little girl filled the air. She picked up the jacket one more time and gazed down at the cover. There he was, leaning against a white baby grand, his long blonde hair and shiny white teeth. His hands were resting in his pleated white pants, and his silky white shirt was unbuttoned just enough to make a 10-year-old girl giggle. This had not been one of the albums she had only listened to on her bed.

She grabbed the spray polish again and walked through the room, spraying every stain and smudge, then she wrapped the rags around her feet and slid on one foot, then the other, gliding around the room, singing and swirling in circles.

Picking up particular Dana...

A long shower with no interruptions, a glass of wine while doing her makeup, and now listening to some inspiring music as she finished getting ready. She slid the record out of the ivory-colored jacket. The man and woman were simply dressed in black—he in jodhpurs and boots, his hair in a ponytail, and she with her ballet slippers tied around her ankles, the black tulle of her skirt floating behind her. There was no one, no one, cooler than Stevie.

Becca turned up the volume and got to work. She'd gotten better at the boys being gone for the weekend and now, with setting up a new house and the party she was going to, her mind couldn't dwell on their absence as it had previously. Becca hadn't been to a party without Josh in years. She knew eyes would be on her, and she wasn't sure if she wanted to make a grand entrance or just slide in. She reached into the big, brown paper bag that Allie had left on her doorstep the day before. *This is too long. This is too short. This color is all wrong. This isn't the message I want to send out tonight.* She tried another and looked in the mirror. *This makes me look just a little bit skanky—it's a maybe.* She set it aside and attempted another look. This one was kind of itchy. She never wore pink. She preferred to wear neutrals, to blend in. If she wore this, she understood it would be the "grand entrance" kind, not the "sliding in" kind. *They are all going to be watching anyway,* she thought. *Give them something to look at.*

She poured herself another glass of wine and carried it into the bedroom, actually drinking from a real wine glass this time. In the past, she had used a

43

water glass, but she soon discovered that holding a wine glass made her feel sexier and made the wine taste sweeter. It also brought to her attention that her nails weren't done.

"Shit," she said as she put down the glass to check out her nails. Her friends' nails would look pretty and perfect. She was examining the orange stains on hers from the food coloring in the Play-Doh she and Mason had made yesterday when the phone rang.

"I'll be there in five. You ready?" It was Elle. Her nails always looked good. You either loved or hated Elle. She had been married at 22, divorced at 28 and single since. Elle was a bit egocentric, for sure. When she said, "It's all about me," she may have actually meant it, but Becca loved her anyway. She had a relaxed way about her as if to say, "I don't really care," but a purposeful way about her as well, like, "Notice me. I did this for you." Her outfits were well planned, like her shirt hanging out just the right amount under her cardigan. Her jeans, always the right length for her shoes.

"Um, yeah," Becca replied, buttoning up her last clean top, wondering if she should tuck it in or not.

"We can't be too late," Elle said in a sing-song voice.

"I know," Becca said, sweeping her arm back to grab her coat. That's when she knocked that tall wine glass all over her last clean top. "Shit!"

"What was that?"

"Nothing, nothing," Becca said, as she quickly changed it out for a Springsteen T-shirt under a blazer and grabbed her shoes. She was at the door for Elle's third honk.

The highway traffic wasn't too bad, but the neighborhood streets were full. "Gotta pick up Dana. Make her hurry, OK?" Elle said, rearranging her bangs just a bit. "Ugh, I cut them too short. I couldn't get into Dr. Bender before the party. I thought I could just cover these lines. Ugh!" Her hair, although fine and straight, was pliable to any style to go with any outfit. Up in a messy bun, down in a low pony or even just down to her shoulders, like tonight, her hair fit her attitude.

"You couldn't have just waited?" Becca asked.

"With this forehead? I look old or I look like I worry. Not sure which is even worse, really," Elle said.

Becca flipped down her mirror to see if her lines were visible as she stuck her hair behind her ear—her signature move. "Can't just get away with these, huh?" she asked.

"No," Elle answered, pulling the car to the curb and hitting her hazards. "You'll see once you're out there again. It's Botox or bangs, baby. Make that headhunter hurry!"

"She's a 'talent acquisition manager,' Elle. You know she prefers to be called a 'talent acquisition manager,'" Becca said, shaking her head as she closed the car door behind her. Dana hated being referred to as a headhunter. Cutting off the head of someone you have battled with is rather gruesome. Keeping it to show others to earn respect or simply to further mortify potential victims seemed cruel. *Sure, Dana may have brutalized each of the men she dated, but not quite like that,* Becca thought. She did hunt them, engage and fight, but not to the death. She did, however, write their names in a little floral notebook, detailing each of their offenses:

Jay Parker

-3 ½ weeks

-Always late

-Always sent back his food for not being spicy enough

Becca guessed being a name in her book was a little like having your head shrunk and stuck on a stick. Maybe it was worse. She shared the info of her body count with others as a warning or to further humiliate these men, as well. It must have been particularly hard for…

Dan Malloy

-42 days

-Never cut his toe nails

-Ever

-Rolls himself up in several blankets like a cocoon at night

…to get a girl in bed.

"Dana, you ready? Elle's out front," Becca called as she walked into her apartment, peeking around the door while knocking.

"Yeah, just finishing up. Give me a sec," she answered from her bedroom.

Becca slowly walked in, closing the door behind her. She couldn't help but smile as she spotted the perfectly rolled napkins tucked into their rings on the preset dining table. Dana always had the table set, from the floral placemats to the gold-rimmed chargers to the striped dinner plates, floral salad plates and checkered bread plates on top. Dana had saved for months for the settings, only four, of course, but no one needed to know there weren't many others stacked away in the cabinet against the wall. It was behind the glass that she kept the rest of the pattern—creamer, sugar bowl, butter dish, gravy boat… Dana planned on registering for the other eight settings once she got engaged, but, until then, she had the perfectly plated table in her perfectly addressed apartment. She even had a membership with one of those dinner delivery businesses, the ones where they give you all the ingredients and you prepare it, just in case she had a date to impress Monday through Thursday, when her work schedule precluded making an impressive meal herself.

Dana stepped out of her bedroom dressed in white pants and a black blouse. "I just need help picking the shoes. Come here," gesturing Becca into her bedroom. The room was meticulously neat with the shams and throw pillows marked with a sharp chop in the middle, and her throw folded properly at the foot of her bed. Her armoire was open, though, which would have looked a little sloppy if not for the fact that her T-shirts were perfectly folded into color coordinated piles. "These or these?" she asked, holding up a patent leather black flat in one hand and a black sling-back in the other.

"Those," Becca responded, pointing to a leopard print heel in the closet.

"Really? I bought those because I liked yours so much, but I never should have bought them. I don't know what to wear them with. Really? These?" she asked, stepping into them.

"Yeah, that's great. Elle is waiting in the car. You ready?" Becca asked.

"Almost, just need a bag," she said, walking back into and then back out of her closet. This one?" she asked, holding a black, patent leather clutch.

"How about that suede one?" Becca asked, pointing to the small suede handbag with the concentric Gs sitting on the shelf.

"Really? I thought this one was dressier," Dana said, looking at one and then the other.

"It's just Allie's. We're late. We really should go," Becca said, standing up from the bed and turning to flatten the fluffy duvet she had sunk down in.

"OK, OK," Dana said, looking into her magnifying mirror, carefully pulling the few hairs back in place that had gone to the wrong side of her part. She tilted her head up to make sure the black eyeliner was the same thickness on both of her lids, then grabbed a Q-Tip and barely touched the corner of one eye, making the smallest smudge. "I just needed a minute," she said, pulling at the corner of the throw. "Let's go!"

A new found camera (OK, fine, it's just a bit about Dana...)

Dinner was at their favorite place from their twenties that they still considered their own. A tiny Thai restaurant with no chairs, only benches, the five of them having been there as recently as a few weeks ago. It had gone through some changes in the last 10 years. Most importantly becoming BYOB. *Ridiculous concept,* Becca thought, as she pulled her bottle of plum wine out of a paper bag. No one shared in her love for the candy-tasting wine. The girls were marginally more sophisticated in their tastes, pulling out Pinot Grigio to share. She figured the three glasses she wouldn't need to share might actually be enough to get her through the night.

"Did Elle get her boobs done, again?" Dana asked Becca from behind her menu.

Becca noticed the struggle the buttons were going through to hold her blouse together. "Maybe?"

"I think she did."

Becca could hear Elle's voice in her head, *You'll see once you're out there again…*

"So," Dana said, "What are we going to do with *you*?"

Becca startled. Dana was looking right at her, just as she was about to swallow the best spring roll ever.

"What do you mean?"

"Jay is going to be there tonight…" Dana said, nudging her in the shoulder.

Becca hadn't seen Jay since college. Even then, they weren't really friends. They ran in the same crowd, went to the same parties. The only thing she could think of that they had in common was that he was divorced, for a whole year now, and she would hopefully be soon, too.

"Mmm, that's interesting. Who else?" Becca tried to change the subject. She was not looking for a boyfriend; she had just started to like not sharing her bed.

"Hey, Bex," Dana said, in an excited voice, leaning forward with her hands on her lap like she was ready to pounce, "I found something really fun for us to do Saturday. You said the boys were away next weekend, right?"

"Yeah, they're going to St. Louis with Josh," Becca responded, leaning back to Dana's lean in.

"You love tours of Chicago, and I found the best one. A double decker bus tour for beginner photographers! You bring a camera, or your phone or whatever. They give you some quick hints on taking good pictures, then they drive you around and you shoot all over the city! How cool is that?" Dana almost screamed.

"I had no idea you were even interested in photography. Do you even have a camera?" Becca asked.

"I do! I just got a new one yesterday. It's red. It's really cool," Dana said, with an enormous smile on her face.

"Wow! Well, that's great. That's exciting. I've never known you to be so interested in stuff like this," Becca said, now warming to the idea.

"I heard about it from Luke..." Dana began.

There ya go.

Dana dated, a lot, often trying on the personality and exploring the interests of the guys she dated. Becca didn't mind, though, because each guy Dana "dated" taught Becca something new, like the guy who had lived in Japan for a while. He had explained that everything was just Becca's height there, that at restaurants, her feet would actually touch the floor when she sat down. Or, at the grocery store, she would never need to ask others to reach things placed too high for her, because nothing would be out of her 70-inch reach. Most importantly, she would be able to finally peer out of peep holes in doors, something she had always wanted to do.

The art history guy was interesting as well, but even Becca had known he wouldn't be around for long. Dana had brought him to the Art Institute to meet Becca and Allie one Sunday afternoon. He had stood in front of the gigantic paintings, explaining the artists' stories and techniques, but when he approached Paul Gauguin, it happened...

"Gauguin is one of my favorites. You can tell his true love of women by the way he so beautifully portrays them in his work. He actually discovered Haiti," he said, his arms stretched out to assure her of not only his knowledge, but confidence in it.

Allie shook her head, then whispered in Dana's ear, "Gauguin's wife was a child, a little girl. And it was Tahiti. And he didn't discover it." And that guy was history.

The guys didn't usually last for long anyway, maybe a month. The shortest relationship was probably the guy who could do magic. He had been an Orthodox Jew with five kids living in East Rogers Park. His life was pretty typical, as typical as it could have been, anyway, until his wife told him that she was gay. After the divorce, he had gone astray a bit. Dating a lot. Going on websites. Dana had swiped him to the right, or something like that, and they began talking on a daily basis.

On their first date, they went for sushi and then back to his place. He excused himself to go to the bathroom and when he returned, he stood in front of her in only his underwear. Dana politely said that she wasn't interested, but he made a deal with her—if she picked a card from his deck and he could tell her what it was without looking, she would take her clothes off, too.

When Dana had told Becca the story, she couldn't believe that there were really guys like that out there.

"What did you do?" Becca had asked.

"Well, I picked a card."

"And then what?"

"He guessed it."

"So, what did you do?"

"Well," Dana said, "He guessed my card…."

Later, Becca had Googled the trick. He had peeked at the bottom card of the deck and simply placed her card right underneath it. Becca would never tell, though; no one wants to ruin a magic trick.

True to form, of course, the sudden interest in photography was about a guy. "Who's Luke?" Becca asked, now a little less warmly than before.

"He shops in the grocery store below my place. I see him all the time. He was in line in front of me talking on his phone about a tour and I just happened to be listening…"

Eavesdropping…

"Anyway, he was talking about all the buildings on the tour to some client or something and when he hung up, I told him that my friend was really interested in architecture and tours of the city," Dana said with an even bigger smile.

"Dana, I am not interested in being fixed up."

"No silly, not for you! Anyway, that's when I told him I had just found this camera in my closet that an old boyfriend of mine had left. I told him I was thinking of just throwing it away, but that this might be fun," Dana said, with a little bounce.

"I thought you said you just got the camera yesterday."

"Well, I did."

Becca thought for a second. "So you bought a red camera yesterday that you are telling Luke you found in your closet and it belonged to an old boyfriend."

"Red doesn't work, does it," Dana said thoughtfully, looking more disappointed that she might have to exchange it than at how silly the story was.

"Why an old boyfriend? Why not just being interested in learning how to take pictures? Interested in a tour of Chicago?" Becca suggested.

"I don't want to seem like I'm interested in either of those things. I mean, if we end up hitting it off, I wouldn't want it to seem like I would want to go on these tours all the time. Like I would want to go take pictures all over the city. Like I would be into cameras," Dana explained.

"So, you'll seem to have the same interests in him by default. The camera in the closet and a friend who likes city tours," Becca said, finally figuring it out.

"Exactly," Dana said, the smile back on her face.

"You could have just said that it sounded like fun and maybe you'll try it, right?"

"I wouldn't want to seem so desperate. This seems more like luck. I just happened to overhear his conversation, that's all, and I just happen to have a camera and a friend..." Dana said, cocking her head to the side with the same smile.

"OK, I'll go," Becca said. "But don't you think life would be easier if you tried to *seem less?*"

A signature move...

After leaving the restaurant, walking down the street brought up so many memories. The shoe store they had all gone to every week, the coffee house they'd met in after work, the gym they had all joined for a year but had gone to for all of three weeks. Turning the corner, they saw Allie's townhouse. She had lived there for three years already, and everyone was still jealous.

Allie lived in one of the newer parts of town. Newer parts, meaning that at one point, this part of town wasn't cool or hip at all. It was always *there*, just not discovered by the twenty-somethings until five years ago. Allie's dad's attorney explained that buying in this area would be a good investment, so he bought a warehouse and let it sit and sit and sit... Ten years later, his

abandoned building was worth $12 million to investors who built these con-
dos on its footprint. Her dad then purchased Allie's for a cool $750,000.
The most recent buyer purchased one just last winter, for a much warmer
$1.8 million.

All three floors served as an art gallery. Everything Allie saw was art to
her. Every relationship was colorful. Every one of her many parties that she
threw was creative. She had even thrown a wedding shower for Becca. When
guests arrived, they were given smocks and painter's caps. Upon entering,
everyone found a miniature easel with a 4-by-4 canvas on it, paintbrushes
set up in vases and artist pallets with perfect circles of Becca's favorite colors.
Becca still had the little canvases created by her friends and planned on hanging them on her new bedroom wall. A framed photograph of the group of
them covered in paint was already next to her bed.

The girls all made their way up the stairs to the main floor. The entry wall
was covered in mirrors of different shapes, colors and sizes. Then, one by one,
they each reached into their bags to pull out their wigs. It was Allie's first Wig
Party. She had thrown all different kinds before—costume parties, a fortune
teller, a wine tasting with a piano player. She actually had bought the baby
grand with the free, as yet unused lessons, because nothing else would fit on
the odd landing. Becca took the itchy pink wig out of her bag and pulled it
on, carefully hiding her bangs underneath and, with her signature move, she
tucked the pink, wiry hair behind her ears.

Becca wished she could have gotten lost in that sea of wigs. Maybe she
would go unnoticed for a while, but she knew once she was spotted, other
wigs would gather around. There would be three kinds of wigs there, she figured: the good wigs (her friends who were truly invested and cared), the bad
wigs (the ones who just wanted the dirt) and finally the scared wigs (they were
the ones that asked all the questions). The scared wigs always wanted all the
details. She had been friendly with a scared wig once, now that she thought
about it, from Mason's preschool class. Every day at pickup and drop-off, she
was asking questions and telling Becca how brave she was. One day, Becca

had brought Mason to her house for a play date. Again, at the door, she told Becca how brave she was. Then, as Becca's hand touched the doorknob, she heard it.

"He's cheating on me…"

Becca had taken her hand off the doorknob then. Poor scared wig. They talked a long time. The woman was going to give him another chance. It wasn't love. It was a mistake. He wanted to work things out. Sometimes wigs were like Venn diagrams—they could be scared and dumb at the same time. That's why Becca would be nice to the scared, dumb wigs. She had been one, too.

Becca felt a hand on top of her head. It made the wig itch even more, if that was possible. It was Elle, very drunk. Her wig was fabulous, of course. Long, cascading auburn locks. She looked so glamorous. She always did.

"Lots of guys here," she sang, as if to gather some excitement from Becca. That's when Becca noticed them. No, those were not Elle's boobs at all—Dana had been right. "That guy in the dreadlocks has been looking at me all night," she went on. Looking around the room, there were actually three guys in dreadlocks. One had them pulled back from his face. One had them up in a bun. One was standing just in front of Jay and the girl Jay brought with him.

"I think he has money," Elle went on, but Becca could hear nothing. Jay was cuter than she had remembered. He looked like he had survived his divorce just fine. He also looked very happy with his date.

Elle had made her way towards the piano and was now talking to the guy with the dreadlocks pulled back. Becca saw her friends watching the show and laughing. Now, she couldn't retreat back to them. Elle had been her friend since kindergarten. Maybe she was someone to make fun of sometimes, but she would never do it, and would never be around people when they did. She wandered further into the party when, suddenly, she was picked up off the ground by a green-wigged man who spun her and bounced her around. Gary was one of her closest friends from college. Sadly, he was friendly with one of the meanest wigs at the party. Naturally, Becca landed right at the mean wig's feet when he set her down.

"How are you?" Joy asked, in a rather affected tone. "I heard all about it from Gary. I'm so sorry. How are the boys?"

I hate you, Becca thought.

Lesson one: Always lie to the bad wigs.

"The boys are great."

Lesson two: Always be polite.

"Thanks for asking."

Lesson three: Always make a fast getaway.

"Oh, I think I see Allie!" Becca stomped on Gary's foot as she made her way through the crowd. She could hear his "Ow" as she easily ducked and weaved through the crowd and under their raised glasses, finally bumping into the tall pink Marie Antoinette wig on Allie's head.

"You're here!" she screamed, giving Becca a huge hug. "I was really hoping you'd wear that pink one!"

Stumbling back through the crowd, Becca was abruptly yanked aside to the wall. It was Dana, pulling her right into Jay. "Look," Dana said. "Jay is here. He came with his sister." With that, Dana was gone in a flash, smiling and waving to Becca over her shoulder as she made her way through the room.

Becca turned to look at Jay, who must not have read the invite. No wig. She was glad she had her big girl shoes on, as even with them, he was a solid foot taller than her. His hair was cut shorter than in school, but his brown eyes and quirky smile were the same. You know, the kind of smile where it goes to one side of his face more than the other, and his eyes sparkle? Yeah, like that… She had no idea what to say to him. She didn't remember how to talk about anything but her kids and her divorce, two things no guy wants to hear about. He motioned to a bench and they sat down not far from the bartender making custom martinis. Becca decided to try her signature move, tucking her hair behind her ear. That's when she felt the itchy, pink fibers between her fingers. She carefully took off the wiry wig and placed it on her lap. She crossed her legs and tried to look pretty, knowing that her hair was probably mashed down and a bit sweaty from the pink mess. *Don't talk about the divorce, don't talk about the divorce, don't talk about the divorce…*

"I heard you were getting a divorce," Jay said.

OK, obviously this is what people do, just don't talk too much. Think, think, think. You could talk about kids. You both have kids. You could talk about college. Although that was 15 years ago. That seems boring. You could talk about your interests, only you don't have any interests… Twenty minutes later, they were still talking about the divorce, but she didn't remember any of it as her glass was empty, like the four she had filled at dinner. The room was getting warm now. Jay asked her a question. *What was he saying?* He looked so sincere. *Listen! Ignore your phone vibrating in your bag. What is he saying?*

"Can I ask what happened?" Jay asked.

"He said he wasn't attracted to me anymore." *Shit! Seriously? Get up. Leave. Say you need to get another drink.*

Jay was looking at her. Was that shock or was he embarrassed? She brought the glass to her mouth and sipped the very last drop that had been hiding on the bottom. She met his eyes.

"He's lying," he said, his eyes soft and taking in every feature of her face.

I'll sleep with him, she thought.

A friendly wave...

These rides down Asbury were even more fun now that the boys got a good bump once in a while. Mason's giggles would fill the backseat each time she entered the construction zone—bumps, swerves and, unfortunately, long waiting times. This was throwing off their naps and her days. She would take different streets on the way home, but this was part of their routine, and sitting for the last seven minutes in the ravine watching the Bobcats and cement mixers was great fun for Mason, but was cutting into her time to get them home, ready and off to "Dinner with Daddy."

Another guy waved at her as she sat waiting in the growing line, now actually forming up to the top of the hill. She again pulled down her mirror and took a look at the tired reflection that was definitely in need of full, not partial, highlights.

He had been in a Jeep. The other guy had been in a Jeep, too. She was beginning to wonder—Is there some secret Jeep community that she didn't know about? She moved up just a few feet before the man dressed in orange held up his STOP sign. Becca slid her phone out of the pocket of her diaper bag next to her on the seat and began typing... *is there a Jeep*, and it popped up just underneath... *Is there a Jeep wave?* Apparently, "All Jeepers are responsible for upholding the tradition of the Wave." Upon seeing a fellow "Jeeper," you are encouraged to wave, unless they fall lower than yourself on the hierarchy of the many different Jeeps and then you are encouraged to wave, but those lower should wave first and are to continue waving until they are acknowledged or out of view."

One more responsibility, she thought, and she kept her eyes alert for her first fellow Jeeper to pass her in the longest line ever in the ravine on Weee Street . A few minutes later, the worker turned his sign to SLOW and motioned the many cars up the slowly winding, rubble street. The boys were finally asleep by the time she reached the stone fence with the three windows cut into it, the tiles carefully stacked inside, but today on the fence was a large sign: SOLD. Someone new would be moving into the very curious house. Maybe they would remove those tiles, or maybe not.

Another man dressed in orange was just a block past, waving her west. *No, no detour past the pet shop. OK, do not look out the window,* she told herself. The women in their shop aprons weren't out walking on the busy street today. What a relief, but there in the window, there it was, the dog. He looked sad, gazing out onto the busy street, his little black paws resting on the glass. *You deserve a better view,* she thought, as she slowly inched by with the other cars.

The shelf with the useless things...

"There are still some things at the house," Josh said as he buckled the boys into their car seats for dinner that night. "In that closet down the hall."

That was the one with the shelf 7 feet up where she would put her useless things. That's where she had put the box with the cellophane window on the front. Where, when you looked inside, you could see just the top of her wedding dress.

God, it was so beautiful. The first time she saw it, she knew it was hers. She had been walking downtown and it had been in the window of one of the bridal shops. In its day, the shop was one of the more exclusive stores; now, she knew, like most things, its shine had faded a bit. The neckline was very simple, just straight across the top, then alternate satin ribbons around the bodice. Audrey Hepburn, her style icon, would have bought it right then and there. Becca had needed to wait for a proposal, and when it finally arrived, her first stop was the store with the dress in the window. To her surprise, the dress had been replaced with something too froufrou for her taste—mermaid tail, lots of sequins, you know, Audrey Hepburn's nightmare. When Becca asked where the dress had gone, the sales associate had no recollection of it whatsoever. Even after Becca had painstakingly described it, it was obvious the dress had made no impression on the lady at all. If not for the owner arriving at that moment, the dress would have been gone forever, leaving Becca with only the thought of what could have been. It had been from a trunk show, the owner had said, and was packed in the back. Would she like to see it in cream or white? Would she like to try it on? White and absolutely. And that was it.

Becca hadn't seen it in three years now and there it was on the top shelf of that closet where they used to keep cleaning supplies. In fact, packs of toilet paper and paper towels were still stored on the bottom shelf. *This must be what he was talking about,* she thought. Becca carefully stood atop the paper towel rolls and knocked at the box until just the corner hung over the side of the shelf. She grabbed it and pulled it down. She could still see the white ribbons through the thin layer of dust.

Becca carried the box into the living room as she alternately kicked the paper towels and toilet paper packs down the hall. Left, toilet paper, right, paper towels, until she finally stood in the center of the empty living room. It was always easy to find the middle of that room. There were three beams running across the ceiling and, if she stood just beneath where the second beam hit the highest point of the ceiling, she knew it was the middle. She had stood there many times looking up at the beams debating between staining them dark to match the floor or leaving them as they were to keep with the style of the '50s ranch. But now, there she stood, with the beige walls and weathered beams above her head. One more great plan never put into play.

That room had been her favorite. All windows facing south. The sun in the afternoon was brilliant, and she could remember swinging Mason in circles, singing as the sun bounced off his blonde hair. This time, the sun bounced off the cellophane of the box. She knelt to look at it again. The caterer had actually offered striped linens to match her dress. Now, she couldn't imagine why that had been a selling point to her. She had matched the napkins and tablecloths. But the bottom of the dress… she couldn't remember the bottom. She believed it had just one ribbon along the hem, but wasn't sure. *Was it two? Oh, please don't say that ribbons were all the way down the skirt.*

She couldn't resist and finally gave in to opening the box just a bit, then a bit more, and then finally opening it to see all of its beauty. She lifted it up by its shoulders, the form it hung on left it looking like a little person was still inside it. The sunlight now bounced off the satin and the one ribbon at the hem—just one ribbon. She laid it gently on the floor and looked at the beautiful stripes and remembered the moment she put it on. She had felt like a princess, just like they say you will.

She looked around the room as the sun lit up every little particle of dust floating in the air. Before too long, the demolition would start and the beams above her head would come crashing to the floor. She looked up to the point where the beams met the ceiling. The highest point of the room. She figured when they fell, they would land maybe just a few inches to the left of where her dress now lay. She took a tug at the satin hem and pulled it in that direction.

She grabbed her toilet paper and paper towels and left the big sunny room.

The little blue pill...

"I just shut down your furnace," the man said as he entered the kitchen the next afternoon. Becca and Courtney had just left Mason and Andy playing downstairs. They were standing, drinking coffee next to the only piece of furniture in the room, a stepstool she had been using while trying to reach the light to change the bulb. She had counted on asking this man dressed in the gray polyester shirt and matching pants for help. She hadn't caught his name, or the plumber's, or the asbestos guy's. There had been so many of them.

The house truly was a fixer-upper, she had known that, but she had thought it would be fun to choose paint, tiles and appliances on her own. Watching them curtaining off the basement and putting on hazmat suits was almost comical. Walking past the laundry room to find a big pile of shit by the floor drain, funny. But thousands of dollars later, she had chosen no paint, no tiles and no appliances.

"Won't it get cold in here with the furnace off?" Becca asked. The man in the gray polyester was looking at Becca in a way she couldn't quite figure out. She looked at Courtney and then back at him.

"Your furnace has five tunnels," he explained. "Three of them have cracks."

Still nothing. Becca looked at Courtney, again.

"Lady," he said, taking off the matching gray cap. "It's leaking carbon monoxide. You need a new furnace. I can order you one today, but it will take a couple days to get you some heat." That was all it took: the asbestos, the shit, the furnace, and finally, the tears. She sat down on the stool and laughed as the first one fell. In her view of the ugly tiles beneath her on the floor appeared a little red shoe with Spiderman webs around the edges.

"Why are you crying, Becca?" Andy asked. He looked so worried and so curious.

Becca quickly wiped the tears away and faked a smile. She had been getting pretty good at that. "I'm just tired. You cry when you're tired, right? Grownups do that, too," she said.

"You should take a nap," Andy said sweetly, then he turned and walked out of the room. *He's right.* She thought of those little blue pills in her cabinet. Her brother, a psychiatrist now, of all things, had decided that she had lost too much weight because she was depressed. She thought that was pretty funny since she was actually ecstatic about fitting into her old jeans. *Tonight would be as good a night as any to try one,* she thought. She thanked the man dressed in gray, gave him her credit card and packed up for her parents' house. Since the workmen had made her new place unlivable, the boys had loved these nights at Grandma and Grandpa's, sleeping on the sofas and waking up to company in the morning.

Later that night, Becca tucked them in for a good night's sleep and sat down for a moment in a kitchen chair. She looked at the tiny blue pill engraved with the small letters and grabbed a glass to fill from the water dispenser in the fridge door. She thought about that day she had been in the family room of the old house putting pictures in frames to hang on the wall. It should have been easier, but taping the photos on the mats, fitting them in place and turning the brads had taken awhile. She had been listening to Mason laughing hysterically in the other room. He was busy, which was good, because she was, too. Sometimes, it just worked out that way, that she would get lucky. When she had finally finished, she had gone into the next room, but Mason wasn't there. The laughing had been coming from the kitchen, and that's where she had found him, pressing the water dispenser button on the fridge, dancing in the water that had flooded the floor.

She looked at the pill one last time, put it on her tongue and took a sip. *Now, things will be easier.* She placed the cup down, went into her parents' living room and cozied up near the boys on the sofa. She could hear their breathing and it lulled her to sleep.

Only a couple of hours later, her body awoke with a start. Her heart was banging in her chest, the sweat dripping off her face, and she was so, so thirsty. She army-crawled to the kitchen as sweat dripped onto the floor. *"Boom, boom, boom"* was all she heard as she reached to get her glass, then pushed it up against the dispenser to wait for the water to stream out. Becca gulped it down and lay on her back on the cold, hard tiles. Her heart raced, and the room spun.

This is where they'll find me, she thought, and she drifted off.

She awoke awhile later to water splashing on her face, Mason giggling as he danced about. He had found the water dispenser button on the fridge door.

I'll get a fridge with a water dispenser inside, she thought.

"Good morning, Mason." It was 5:15.

The caffeinated kickboxer enters the scene (OK, fine, it's just a bit about Hillary…)

It was an unlikely dog, a 12-year-old standard poodle. They say you start to look like your dog or your dog starts to look like you, but Hillary and Lucy looked nothing alike. They were truly a mismatched pair, if not for the accessories. Lucy, with her black collar and leash, and Hillary with her more-than-likely, knock-off black shopper bag—and that was about all they had in common. Hillary's long, flat-ironed auburn hair was carefully pulled away from her perfectly round baby blues, while Lucy's curls were out of control, some of the longer ones even covering her somewhat crusted brown eyes. Lucy had trouble just standing, while Hillary could walk on those 3-1/2-inch heels all day.

"She's an Emotional Grabber." Hillary was talking about Dana. They were walking together after Becca's now habitual morning stroller-jog/caffeine stop. She was responding to the story Becca had just told her about her SnapChicago Tour coming up on Saturday. If it were true that Dana was an "Emotional Grabber," then Becca figured it could be said that Hillary was an "Emotional Expulsor." She didn't want too much, too soon, at all. "Look, I'm no expert. I have a boyfriend with no job. But this much I know: This girl wants too much, too soon. Guys are not good at multitasking. If you give them too much to do, they give up. They are not savvy, like we are. When she tells him, 'You don't have enough time for me'—and she will—he doesn't hear, 'I want more time.' He thinks, 'Really? OK!'"

Hillary had lots of doozies like that. "My therapist says you need four seasons to get to know someone. One full year. Don't plan a future with someone until you've seen all the seasons change." Hillary was now in season three, winter, of getting to know Barry. She had explained that she had met Barry last summer, but that summer shouldn't really count, or at least do summer twice because everything always seems better in the summer. It's sunnier longer so there isn't as much time for things to go wrong. Like, in the summer, Barry was working, writing short stories for the local paper. Bad things seem to happen later in the day or when it's dark and in summer, there are fewer hours for that. Like in the fall, when Barry quit his job to write the next great American novel about, of course, a writer, writing the next great American novel. Becca had wondered if Hillary's philosophy came from her therapist, a book or something Hillary had just made up on her own, but it made Becca laugh anyway. *Get to know someone for four seasons to plan a future. Got it.*

Hillary had been in therapy for nearly a year, just one week short of when her divorce started. She had come home from vacation with girlfriends, walked into the apartment, and had found things packed in the front hall. Her husband had been lying on the bed when she had found him. He had simply sat up and announced it—"I'm leaving you"—and was gone. The therapy had been helpful. She had learned better ways to deal with her anger than kickboxing, which she was amazing at, by the way. And she really did sit at the coffee house almost every day between her appointments. The audiologist she had partnered up with was just upstairs in the offices above the shop. Hillary taught sign language and lip reading to his clients after he diagnosed them with any hearing loss. Her clients were mostly children, so she was usually busier after school got out, but once in a while, in the morning, it was an elderly person in the community brought in by his or her own child complaining that their mom or dad couldn't hear anything. Usually, the parent argued that there really just wasn't anything that they had wanted to listen to anyway. Sometimes, Hillary sat in her glass office and watched as they walked in. She could read their lips as they argued, "*You can't hear anything!*" "*There's nothing I want to hear anyway!*" Once the son or daughter was alone in the waiting room on the phone with a friend, she would read their lips as they explained to the person on the other end of the line how incredibly challenging their parent was, as they thanked them for saying what a wonderful, devoted child they were. Hillary always waited until the phone calls were over before walking her clients out, protecting them from getting the littlest bit of the conversation. She had read her husband's lips one day while he had been sitting in his car. Reading lips is difficult, she explained, but it's easy to figure out, "I love you." She just hadn't realized that day that he wasn't saying it to his mom.

Hillary had noticed that Becca wasn't wearing a ring that day she struggled through the doorway of the coffee shop. Their friendship had formed shortly after, when Becca had been on her phone talking to her attorney about "maintenance" and "visitation" for the boys, and Hillary had read her lips.

Hillary had smiled, waved and had introduced herself by saying, "I'm here all the time cuz I just got divorced and can't stand to be in my apartment."

"I'm getting a divorce," Becca had shared and, with that, a friendship was born.

"So, any more crazy nights at your parents'?" Hillary asked.

"No. The asbestos is gone. The pipe is fixed. The furnace is replaced. They even told me to get a sump pump with a backup or something. I mean, we're on the east side of the street, I think the water will just run down the hill, but at this point, why stop?" Becca said, pushing the double stroller as Hillary dragged Lucy along.

"What about your parents? They around?" Becca asked as Lucy squatted the littlest bit to pee but instead just stared out at the mailbox.

"They died when I was 20," Hillary said, as she waited rather impatiently for Lucy to get up.

"I'm so sorry," Becca said. "I had no idea."

"Yeah, they came to visit me at school. They decided to make a road trip through New England afterwards, on their way home. My dad fell asleep. They actually ended up in the woods. The only reason they were found as soon as they were is because their dog wandered up to the street," she said, gesturing to Lucy. "Someone found the dog and then found them."

"You were still in school?" Becca asked as she watched Hillary give Lucy a little treat only to have Lucy growl and gnash her teeth. "Hillary, what did you do?"

"I married my ex-husband," Hillary replied.

"That makes perfect sense," Becca said.

"Yeah. Ya know what my therapist said that was really important? Be with someone who knows the woman you really are, but also understands the woman you want to be. Or something like that… Look, have fun on your tour," Hillary said, as she lifted Lucy rather awkwardly and placed her in the backseat of her car. "Let me know all about it!"

Becca pushed the stroller towards home while the boys quietly slept. *Someone who knows me for the woman I really am but understands the woman I want to be… I know that person,* Becca thought, as she looked through the contacts on her phone. She strolled and scrolled. Finally. It had been so long, it was bound to be uncomfortable. How do you call someone after so long? She quickly pressed the number: one ring, two rings, three rings…

"Becca! Is it really you?" the excited voice shouted into the phone.

Seeing that someone…

The block had changed a lot since she had lived here. Everything was so new and there were people everywhere, young people, old people, people with dogs, people with babies. She looked at the two glass and steel condominiums, the shorter matching townhomes, the dog park and coffee bar. Could this have really been the gravel parking lot she used to walk through to and from work? During the day, the white dust from the rocks had covered her shoes as she had walked through and the only sound had been the gravel underneath them. At night, she would walk through quickly, keeping her eyes on the lights of her building one block away. Her unit on the seventh floor lit up to guide the way.

She crossed the street carefully, noticing how many of the drivers stopped their cars in the middle of the crosswalk. *Well, that hasn't changed,* she thought to herself as she maneuvered around a car and then back up on the curb. Her salad place was gone. It was a breakfast chain that they now even had in the suburbs. She walked up the three concrete steps and pulled open the still very heavy glass and steel door. The building had been a warehouse in the '50s, a wholesale store with everything from T-shirts to toaster ovens. Four stories high then; now the top three were apartments and the bottom one...

"Becca!" he exclaimed, running towards her and giving her a hug and kisses with a matching "mwa" sound. "How *are* you?" he asked, really looking at her, with his voice now a little less enthusiastic and a bit more concerned.

"I've been better, Tony," she managed to get out before her eyes filled with tears.

"Come," he said, grabbing her hand and pulling her through the chairs and mirrors that lined the room. "Sit," he said patiently, waiting as she stepped on the steel footrest and turned into the chair, spinning just the littlest bit. "What's wrong?" he asked, standing behind her, gently putting his hands through her hair.

"Well, I'm getting a divorce," Becca started, not knowing exactly where to start.

"From that awful man with the briefcase, right?" Tony asked, looking at her reflection in the mirror in front of them. She had forgotten all about that day. The day Josh had met her at Tony's after work, when he had left his suitcase for her to take home, knowing she had plans. She had to drag it out after her haircut when she went out with friends, carrying his burden with her. "Ooh, I hated him!"

"I have two children with him," Becca said.

"Well, he's awful, Becca, just awful. I'm glad he's gone. Did he do this to your hair?" he asked, now holding just the tips between his fingers out to the sides of Becca's head.

"I've been busy. I found someone closer to home..." she started.

"Do not tell me who you have been cheating on me with, Becca. I'm not interested. I love you, so I forgive you and we're moving on," he said, finally resting his hands on her shoulders. "What are we doing today?"

"I don't know. Lighter? Layered? Someone told me to get bangs," she offered.

"No, not bangs, you will hate those," he said. He *did* understand the woman she was.

"Well, they told me, 'It's Botox or bangs, baby' to cover my lines," she explained, pointing to the large creases above her eyebrows.

"No, that is only Botox, and I have a great person for you already," Tony said.

"What do *you* think? I just don't know," Becca said, tilting her head back so the tears wouldn't fall. "I'm feeling a little lost these days."

"We'll find you," he said, with a kiss on the top of her head and a smile in the mirror.

Click!

Becca was closer to the woman she really wanted to be, now. Her highlighted, choppy hair blew in the wind just an hour and a half later. The tour sign wasn't far from the others. Many tours began at the intersection of Ohio and Clark. If you got in a different line, you could end up going on a mobster tour, a movie location tour or even a serial killer tour, but SnapChicago made it easy, a big sign in the shape of a camera, the lens cut out to pose in for a photo op. Becca waited patiently with her phone in her hand for Dana to arrive.

"And you are?" the man with a short haircut asked.

"Becca Gold," she answered, watching him go through the list of names on his phone.

"There you are," he said, checking her in. "I'm Luke, your teacher guide today. You shooting alone today, Becca?"

Becca held her tongue. *What was the story again?* "No, I'm meeting a friend here. She found an old camera, she doesn't really take pictures, I love tours..." *Shut up, Becca.*

"Well, that's great, Becca. You let me know when she gets here," he said with a smile and turned to the next person in line.

Becca took a good look at him as he greeted the next person in line. He only sort of looked like Dana's type. His hair was short, conservative, but he was somewhat more casual than the other guys Dana dabbled in. His Levis were ripped in one knee and seemed to be on maybe their second or third day of wear, with sagging and folds in the thighs. His boots were practical for the weather, but not trendy. His sweater was for warmth, not fashion, and his scarf could have been knitted by his grandma, who probably lived up in Minnesota somewhere.

"Sorry I'm late!" Dana said, rushing over to Becca and squishing in line. She stood with a large, camouflage camera case clenched in her hands. "Did you already check in?"

"Was your fictional boyfriend a hunter or something?" Becca asked.

"Overboard, right?" Dana wrinkled her nose, glancing his way.

"Yes," Becca said. "I met Luke. He seems nice," Becca said, sticking her hands in her pockets and bouncing a bit to keep warm.

"Oh good. Did you say anything to him?" Dana asked, fixing her hair that had blown astray in the wind.

Becca thought for a second. "No, not really."

"Oh good," Dana said, smiling his way.

Luke walked over with his phone in his hand. "And you are?" he asked Dana.

Dana looked shattered that he didn't recognize her. "Dana Meyer," she said, disappointedly.

"Yup, there you are," he said, looking at his phone. "Welcome, Dana." And he walked up the line again.

Dana stood silently holding the silly camera in her hands as Becca turned towards her to shield herself from the wind. "Dana, I think you would have to remind him. I mean, he does this every day. He sees so many people…"

"From FoodWorks, right, Dana?" they heard a voice from further up the line asking. It was Luke, with a thumb in the air.

The pink in Dana's cheeks could have been windburn, but Becca knew better.

"So," Luke said, after everyone had boarded the bus. "Welcome to SnapChicago. A little bit about myself. I'm from Superior, Wisconsin. That's about 10 hours from here. Way up north by Minnesota…"

Wow, I was close, Becca thought, still contemplating his scarf.

"…I used to visit my family in Chicago every summer growing up, and I knew that one day, I would live here. I studied architecture in school and fell in love with all your buildings and tried to catch pictures of them on different architecture tours I would go on. It only seemed to make sense to create a tour where everyone was given an opportunity to do that as well. Whether you've been taking pictures for a while or this is your first time, today will be fun. First thing I'll tell you is that big cameras are overrated."

Dana looked at the huge case in her hands, then at Becca. "Just use your phone," Becca said, moving the case to the side.

"Second," he continued, "shoot what you love, but also, don't. Don't just go for a *pretty* picture, go for a *meaningful* one. We will see many buildings today. Some are old, some are new and some are still coming up. Some bridges are rickety, some are contemporary. Each part of our city has a history, and you can see it as we travel through it. You can take a snapshot to remember a place, but it's always just a little better if you take a picture of a feeling as well. You know?"

"I love him," Dana said.

"Dana…" Becca moaned.

"I do. I love him, Becca," she said.

"OK," Becca said, raising her phone to Dana's face and snapping a picture. Becca looked at the picture on the screen. Dana's eyes sparkled, her cheeks were pink, her smile spanned from ear to ear.

"Now, we'll be driving for a few minutes, but when we get off the bus, feel free to go and explore. Get as close as you can to your subject. Fill the screen and try to frame your subject. We'll be seeing lots of shapes today, lots of archways, columns and beams. Shoot through them. Perspective is *everything*. If you shoot from above, that will diminish the subject; instead, crouch down, make your subject more dynamic. Be aware of the background, too. Look out for people that may be a distraction, a garbage can, an ugly sign. Those things will actually distract from what you're trying to convey."

Dana was mesmerized, hanging on every word. Becca looked out the window as the bus went over the bridge, turning right and following the river. She looked again at the picture of Dana. *Is that what love looks like?* she thought to herself, staring at the shot.

"Finally, you probably have already heard of the rule of thirds, but I'll remind you: This is when you cut your frame into thirds using both vertical and horizontal lines. Place your point of interest over the cross sections of the grid, not in the center of the shot. OK, we're here. This is the Civic Opera House, built in 1928. You'll notice its Art Deco details in the exterior."

Luke continued his lecture as they all disembarked from the bus. They stood on the sidewalk, shivering in the cold until Luke was done, then they walked off in different directions, shooting around the columns and through the promenade while crouching down. Dana had taken particular interest in something, walking away from Becca and shooting on her own. Becca stood as the others wandered around shooting. She couldn't find an angle or perspective that spoke to her and began taking pictures of the people in her group: the heavy-set guy who grunted each time he sat down and stood up on the bus, the girl with the blue hair, and Dana standing near one of the columns.

"All right, everyone. That's time," Luke called. "Back on the bus." Everyone filtered back in and sat in their designated seats before the bus took off again, this time, heading further south before turning east. "This is the Chicago Board of Trade Building, built in 1930 by Holabird and Root. Again, another great example of Art Deco…" They disembarked from the bus again, silently, and began to take photos of the incredibly tall and beautiful structure that seemed to close off the street in a rather ominous way. Becca knew all too well where she was and what was just steps behind her so, instead, she focused on the large windows in front of her. She caught the old Beaux Arts street lamp in the upper left part of the grid in her frame, but as she looked in the top, she saw the clock. It was only about 2:30, but all she could see in her mind's eye was 5:15. She turned and saw the curb she sat on not too long ago and approached it slowly.

"The woman on top is Ceres, the goddess of agriculture. She's actually three stories high, though you would never guess from this perspective. She's made of aluminum…." Luke was saying, but his voice sounded distant, a meaningless drone.

Becca's heart raced in her chest and, the canyon, as they called this part of LaSalle, seemed to close in on her. She steadied herself on a streetlamp and looked at the exact spot. "Bex," she heard as Dana approached. "Shit. Come here," she said, grabbing her arm and pulling her away.

"No," Becca said, wrenching her arm from her friend, taking a deep breath and trying to steady her phone in her hand. She could see it now. The rusted legs of the mailbox, the chipped concrete of the curb, the sewage grate with a wrapper of some sort wadded up and stuck partially inside. She stood above and aimed the screen down, positioning the front tire of the car parked near the curb in the upper left part of the grid.

Click.

It's a very unusual setting...

"It's a very unusual setting," the jeweler said. He was an older man in a little shop just 20 minutes from home. Lake Forest was a wealthy community, its streets lined with huge estates. In the late 1800s many of the wealthiest families in Chicago had built here for vacation time. The town square still looked as though they could be walking around there, with their parasols and handbags dangling from their elbows. Commercial retailers hadn't moved in yet, really. Those that had, had taken up shop in these same storefronts. It was almost comical to think of those wealthy Chicagoans spending a weekend or summer here now, walking into and out of these very same doorways, holding a tall White Mocha Frappuccino with an extra shot.

"How much do you think they're worth?" Becca asked, as the man took a small tube with a little dome on the end out of his drawer. Becca looked at Elle, who just shrugged at the odd stick.

"When did you get them? A gift?" he asked.

They had been a "Push Present." She hadn't known what that was at the time, but Josh hadn't either. Days after Mason was born, someone had asked her what she had received from her husband. Apparently, some husbands thanked their wives for having a baby by giving them a gift, some jewelry usually. A few weeks later, she was opening up a box revealing these two big round diamonds each mounted on a small backing. They were so sparkly and clear. She actually had loved the setting because the diamonds seemed to float, rather than being tacked in with little metal clips.

"Three years ago," she responded. "From my ...husband."

He reached into his cabinet below the glass and pulled out a tray of beautiful diamonds, placing it in front of her. He handed her the small tube with what she could now see had a little light on the end. "Pick one," he said. "Any one."

She pointed at a glittering square in the third row, second column. He carefully removed it from its spot and held it up for her to see. "Touch that end to it," he said, pointing at the wand. She placed the tip in the center and the little light on the other end of the magic wand began to glow. "That's a diamond," he said, with a proud, yet sad expression on his face. He then held up hers, "Touch that end to it."

She carefully placed it in the center of the big circle. The dome light did not even flicker.

"I'm sorry," he said, as he removed the now less than magic wand from her hand. "It is a very unusual setting for a diamond. Maybe your husband wasn't aware..."

"Oh, fuck him!" said Elle.

"No," Becca sighed, "Fuck me."

The closet with the cobwebs (hopefully...)

She was in the closet now, the one downstairs, with the vented doors, that was dark, with what she hoped were cobwebs but knew differently. The flashlight helped some, but it was hard to see what was handwritten once, then again, and again, a long time ago, next to each switch in the fuse box.

This one clearly says "DW." Dishwasher? She flipped the switch, walked out of the closet, up the stairs and into the kitchen to see the light had not yet returned to the "on" position on the dishwasher door. Back down the stairs and into the closet. *This clearly says "microwave."* Flip the switch, walk out of the closet, up the stairs and into the kitchen to see the light was now red on the dishwasher and the microwave clock is flashing.

Do not use dishwasher and microwave at the same time, she noted. She had already figured out the rule to the toaster. Don't use it if *anything* else is on. Sometimes, she stood with no lights on as she toasted Pop-Tarts. It was just easier that way.

Other than that, she was beginning to like her kitchen. Meals were easy for the boys as long as she didn't blow a fuse. She didn't need to run the dishwasher and microwave at the same time anyway. Now, Oliver was asleep while Mason played in the room next door. He pushed his battery-operated vacuum around the room, having a conversation on his phone that he had carefully rested on his shoulder squeezed with his little cheek. *It seems that kids copy what they hear as well,* she thought, as she listened in. "No, I can't make it then." "No, I'm busy." "OK, I'll try." Whoever he was pretending to talk to sure sounded annoying.

She sat with her afternoon coffee looking at her calendar. Jay had asked her out at the now infamous wig party for dinner Wednesday night. She was nervous. A date? Maybe it wasn't a date. Maybe it was two old college friends going out for a drink. But it wasn't. The truth was, she didn't really have too many recollections of them crossing paths in school at all. He had had a girl-friend through most of college. She remembered girls talking about him as someone they would have liked to date, though. She took a sip and looked out the window. The neighbors' birdfeeder was covered with squirrels. "Hey, Mason!" she screamed. "Look out the window!" and the two of them watched the squirrels running up the tree, across a branch and trying to land on the plastic disc filled with birdseed.

The girl in the navy blue rain slicker...

Becca was pleasantly surprised when Jay rang the bell and she saw him in jeans and a barn jacket. She didn't feel like dressing up either, so they simply walked into town to grab a quick dinner before the boys would be home. She was wearing her new platform shoes so she was maybe as tall as his shoulder as they walked down the street. "You told Dana that you don't remember me that much from school," Jay said.

I will kill her, Becca thought, as she tried to think of something to say. "Ya know, I think what I said was that I don't really remember our paths crossing so much. Do you?"

"Yes," he said. "You weren't too interested in me. Clearly, I didn't make much of an impression. We had all the same friends. You don't remember that day I saw you with Joe?"

Now *that* day, she remembered. But what she remembered was Joe. She had met Joe at a party through a mutual friend and had sort of been following him around campus so she could maybe bump into him again. It had never worked. One day, she was sitting on campus when a backpack had dropped in front of her and Joe sat beside it. He was quirky, and she liked that. He was funny, had a big nose, a ponytail, liked cool music. Joe had introduced her to some guy that day. That guy had been with a girl. Was that Jay?

"You clearly don't remember," Jay said.

"You can't be sure that was me, either," Becca argued.

77

"Oh, it was you, alright. We talked for a while."

"OK, then if you have such a good memory, what was I wearing?" she asked.

"A navy blue rain slicker," he quickly answered, with a little smile on his face.

Yeah, she thought, *I remember that jacket.* She was trying to think of something funny to say, maybe that's why she didn't see the sidewalk was just a little bit uneven and didn't lift her platform quite as high as she should have. She didn't fall, but the trip was undeniable. She fell forward and Jay grabbed her arm

"Caught you," he said, another smile on his face as he gloated. "Your toe OK?"

It wasn't her toe, it was the scuff on her shoe that had her almost in tears.

"Told you I knew you."

If you did know me, she thought, *you would know that I would rather it be my toe...*

"Sorry about the divorce. How has it been?"

"OK," Becca said. "It's like I always say, it's really just like before. Same routine, different house. The boys go with their dad a couple nights a week and every other weekend."

"Sounds familiar. Your days must be busy then," he said.

"Well, Mason is in school in the morning so that gives Oliver some nap time while I fix up the house. We pick him up from school, have lunch, go for a ride on Weee Street..."

"WeeeStreet?" he asked.

"Asbury. The turny part in the ravine? That's Weee Street. Mason puts his hands in the air," she said, raising her arms to show how exciting it is. "After that, he typically falls asleep. I drive another 20 minutes or so, then turn back. It's a good nap before we get back home to play."

"Every day the same route?" he asked. "You must get bored."

"No, not at all. It's so peaceful, the houses are so beautiful. A lot of really important houses are there, ya know? I mean, not from builders, they're actually really influential architects like Adler, Van Doren Shaw…"

"Yeah, the houses are pretty there…"

"I've been driving it since I got my license. A lot of the houses are still there, but some have been knocked down. Some ugly ones have taken their places."

"That white stucco one?" he asked.

"Oh, that's still there," she said. "There is this one I have always wondered about, though. Maybe you remember it? I mean, you can't see it. It's hidden by a stone wall? It has windows cut into it? There are tiles, though, or something piled inside them. It's hard to look in," she said. "Right on the lake?"

"Maybe," he said.

"It's for sale. I'm hoping it doesn't get knocked down. I've always wanted to see it. I better hurry, I guess. They just knocked one, you know. The white one with the widow's walk overlooking the water? It's gone."

"I don't know that one."

You're being boring, Becca. He is not interested. Talk about something else.

"Tell me about your girls," she said. "They live close, right?"

"Yeah, I have the same schedule as Josh, I guess. I've been doing this a long time, we've been divorced for a year, but separated for three."

"Can I ask what happened?"

"Outgrew each other. We were too young… This the place?" he asked, stopping in front of the sushi restaurant. "I've never had sushi before."

"Oh. I think you'll like it," she lied, knowing most first-timers find sushi odd at best.

Out of the mouths of cheating, lying husbands...

The evening had been more enjoyable than she had antici- pated, and Becca was kind of sad to see it come to an end. "I know the boys are coming back, maybe I could grab a cup of coffee, come back in an hour?" Jay suggested.

"Yeah, that sounds good," Becca responded awkwardly.

"I'll call first to make sure they're asleep," Jay said as he stepped off the stoop. He climbed into his car and waved as he backed out onto the busy street. A car on the road actually stopped to let him out and, as Jay drove away, that same car pulled in. Josh quickly got out, turning to see the car drive off and Becca still on the stoop.

She could see the boys in their car seats, kicking their feet and waving hello. She walked over to the opposite side of the car and opened the door.

"Who was that?" Josh asked, lifting Mason out of his car seat. He looked over at her in the back seat as she did the same with Oliver.

"A friend," she replied simply.

"You on a date, Becca?" he asked more accusingly than curiously.

"He's an old friend from school, Josh. How was your night?" she asked the boys as the four of them made their way up the driveway towards the house. Becca opened the door and the four of them walked up the steps to the bathroom where Josh would help them get ready for bed. The boys had grown to especially like this time, when the four of them would be together for their bedtime routine. After the boys were given their baths, Josh would read to Mason in his bed, stop in to Ollie's room for a kiss. Then the two of them would silently walk downstairs and she would walk him out. This had been their routine for weeks, but not tonight.

"Who was that guy, Becca?" he asked again at the door.

"He's a friend from school," she repeated.

"I hope you're not exposing them to a lot of people, Becca."

"What does that mean?" she asked defensively.

"A lot of guys. I hope you're not exposing them to a lot of guys. It's confusing for them," he said in a loud whisper. "I would just hope, I would just hope you'd wait, till you know, you knew they would be around for a while."

"Are you serious? Have you introduced them to any girls?"

He fell quiet, then.

"Have you introduced them to any girls?" she asked again, not really wanting to know the answer.

"Becca, it's different," he said, placing his hand on the doorknob.

"How is it so different?" she asked, ignoring her phone ringing in her bag.

"Because, Becca, she's been around awhile, that's why," he said.

Wham. She steadied herself on the shaking ground underneath her. "How long is a while?" she asked, still feeling the punch in her chest. Still trying to breathe in, breathe out.

"A while, Becca. Look, I wouldn't expose them to someone unless I thought they would be around for a while. I'm just asking you to do the same. I won't confuse them. You shouldn't either," he said, turning the doorknob and opening the door. "I'll call them tomorrow."

He stepped off the stoop and walked down the driveway. Becca slammed the door and glanced down at the scuff on her shoe. She reached down, yanked it off her foot and hurled it across the room and against the wall.

Through the window, she could see that Josh had taken his phone out of his pocket before sliding into the car.

That's right, her phone had been ringing. She took it out of her bag and saw a missed call from Jay. It rang in her hand.

"I'm at the corner. All clear?" Jay asked, as she answered.

"Yeah," she said, as she watched Josh drive away.

"So what happened?" Jay asked. "You were in a much better mood a little while ago," he said as he walked in the house.

My cheating, soon-to-be ex-husband has a girlfriend and just took me to parenting school. I also think that maybe we have carpenter ants.... "I think maybe I'm just tired. Can we reschedule?" Becca finally asked.

"Nah, no way. I just spent an hour at Walgreens," he said, pulling out a bottle of cheap wine, a pack of Twizzlers and a still shrink-wrapped DVD of "The Breakfast Club," with the $2.99 sticker still on.

Becca looked sadly down the seven steps to the room where the boys played. She worked her hand slowly through her hair, "The DVD player is downstairs."

"Well, that's awesome," Jay said, as he approached the reconstructed play structure taking up most of the room. He bent down and looked inside, spying the blanket and pillows in it, facing the TV set. "Awesome!" he repeated, handing her the now unwrapped movie and climbing in. He lay on top of the blanket and scrunched up the pillow under his elbows.

Becca turned on the TV and ejected the disc in the player. It was a concert from a musician that she used to see in bars in Chicago but had now found fame as a singer-songwriter for kids. She carefully placed it in its cover and put the shiny new disc in the player. "I'll get some glasses," she said.

"Nah, come here," he said, patting the blanket. She climbed in and lay down next to him as he unscrewed the cap.

"We're drinking out of the bottle?" she asked, smiling.

"Don't be silly, Becca," he said, as he took a Twizzler out of the bag, bit off one end, then the other, and placed it in the bottle neck.

"That sure is classy," she said, taking a sip through the makeshift straw. They lay together in the dark, under the colorful panels, sipping the sweet wine through a candy straw. As the music played at the end, and the "criminal" shot his fist up into the air, Jay pushed the hair away from her face and gave her as sweet a kiss as any 16-year-old could ever dream of.

Just a minute later she heard the crying starting from upstairs and quickly slid out of the tent and ran up to Oliver's room. She lifted him up, gave him a hug and held him close.

"It's OK, Oliver," she said, placing him down for a diaper change and a kiss on the toes. She carried him downstairs and brought him into the kitchen, taking a bottle out of the fridge and placing it in the new bottle warmer. Jay came up the stairs just then, and his and Oliver's eyes met.

Oliver smiled and reached out for him.

"I would just hope you'd wait, till you know, you knew they would be around for a while…" she heard in her head.

"Jay," she said, "you should go."

In the morning she came back downstairs to see her shoe lying on the floor and the mark it had left on the wall the night before. *Things are much clearer in the light of day,* she thought, and she went downstairs to throw away the empty bottle and sticky sweet straws.

Miss Peggy with the silver hair...

Becca was sitting in a tiny blue, plastic chair with her knees bumping into the small scale table. She could see Mason through the window that looked out over the playground. He was wearing his winter coat, finally zipped up. *Clearly, Miss Julie or Miss Peggy had gotten him to do that,* she thought, as she remembered their struggle trying to zip the coat that morning. Becca had dropped Mason at the playground then and had walked around the school for a bit while waiting for this meeting. She could see Miss Peggy, now standing near Mason over by the climbing structure, with her hands in her pockets; and she watched as the director of the school came outside and gestured to Becca in the window. Miss Peggy looked relieved to come in from the cold and gladly switched, now leaving the director to supervise. The silver-haired teacher smiled at Becca and waved as she walked towards the building.

That was how she and Mason had been able to tell his teachers apart—Miss Peggy with the silver hair, Miss Julie with the yellow.

Miss Peggy had asked for this meeting today, and Becca's stomach hadn't been the same since. As she watched out the window, she could see Mason playing with another child and the director standing nearby. *Was Mason dangerous? Hitting? Biting? Oh my god, was he biting?*

"Hello, Miss Gold," the sweet lady with the silver hair sang. "Thank you so much for coming today. I hope it wasn't too much trouble."

84

"No, of course not," Becca said, rocking the handle a bit on the carrier Oliver was sleeping in.

"I know it's tricky with the littler ones. How old is Oliver now?" she asked.

"Three months," Becca said.

"Wow, three months. Mason talks about him quite a bit. He is in many of his pictures and stories," she said, now reaching into a blue cardboard folder. Miss Peggy began placing the drawings on the little table. "We are doing a lot of dictation these days. The children draw a picture and then we write their words. Mason really enjoys it."

Becca looked at the many pictures. Two taller figures and two smaller. She picked up one of the pictures. *Mommy and Daddy and Me and Oliver eating pancakes and milkshakes*, was written at the top.

"Many of his pictures are of your family. Once in a while, he has a picture with just a mommy or a daddy. He has told the other children that he has two houses. When the other children ask why, he shrugs his shoulders and becomes a bit withdrawn. How are things going with Mason at home?"

"We talk about how Mommy and Daddy have different houses now. We call it Mommy Time and Boys' Weekend Yea!" Becca explained, now picking up a picture of the four of them floating in the middle of the page. Two taller people standing in the middle and a smaller one on either side.

"We just wanted you to know that we are here for Mason and for you. We have a social worker who consults with us. She is wonderful if you need any advice. She gave me a list of books that she has found helpful about young children and divorce. I hope I'm not over stepping, I just thought maybe these could be helpful in starting a conversation with Mason, maybe answer some questions. That's all."

Becca looked at the list in front of her. They were stories about mommy and daddy animals getting a divorce, getting separate homes. "I'll think about it," Becca said, feeling even smaller than usual.

"You may find that just drawing with Mason and writing his words will lead to conversation, as well. He has a terrific vocabulary and his imagination is so wonderful. If he does dictate to you, make sure you write *his* words. We get so tempted to change their words and their grammar, but we don't. It's much more interesting to get their points of view and ideas," Miss Peggy said, handing her yet another picture, this one mommy, daddy and a yellow-haired boy near a rectangle, possibly a bed.

"Can I keep these?" Becca asked, pointing at the papers covering the table.

"Take a few," Miss Peggy said. "We'd like to keep some for his portfolio. At the end of the school year, we like to give the children a binder of their work."

The children were beginning to enter the building now. Becca could hear them in the hallway hanging up their coats and empty backpacks in their cubbies. She looked down at a sleeping Oliver in his carrier and quickly grabbed some of Mason's drawings from the table. "Thank you, Miss Peggy. I'll think about these books, too," Becca said.

"And our consultant? Would you like to speak with her?" she asked, hopefully.

"Yeah, sure," Becca said, looking at the fat mommy, daddy and yellow-haired boy. *This is Mommy and Daddy and Me at the beach making sandcastles and eating popsicles*, Mason had dictated. The mommy was standing with the little boy. Becca noticed the rectangle in this picture too, in Daddy's hand. She wondered if Miss Peggy or Miss Julie had asked what it was. Becca knew it was his phone. She remembered this day as well.

Oliver woke up just moments after his carrier was clicked into the car seat base, and the two of them pulled out of the school parking lot. Becca could see that some of the mommies were still lingering. She could overhear bits and pieces of their conversations—details about last weekend, plans for this weekend. "How about the mall, today, Oliver?" Becca asked, as she turned left at the exit rather than right. She turned on the radio and listened as the first few notes of a Nick Lowe song played. She remembered the album cover—him pushing the letters of his name, the L falling to form a word in the name of his album, like a crossword puzzle. She knew the words and sang along as she made her way to the mall that still didn't open for another 15 minutes.

"THIS SPOT SAVED FOR PARENTS WITH SMALL CHILDREN," the sign said. These spots are lifesavers, she thought, as she pulled in and turned to talk to Oliver. "I'll just get your stroller and we'll be on our way," she said. She hopped out of the Jeep, ran to the back, pulled out his stroller and slammed the door shut. Oliver was all smiles as she reached in to grab him out of the carrier and the two of them rolled through the parking lot just as the security staff was unlocking the mall doors.

There were a lot of mommies there with their strollers as well. Some of their kids were visibly uncomfortable as they went for their rides, obviously wanting out, kicking their feet and stretching out their backs. Becca made her way around the mall, finally stopping at the bookstore. She grabbed the list from Miss Peggy out of her pocket and began walking around the Young Readers section. Cows, piggies, a drawing of a young child, supposedly by a young child. She sat and read the stories, which were all pretty much the same. Daddy cow or pig and Mommy cow or pig weren't going to live together anymore. Baby cow or pig would have two homes. The other one, the young child, also had a mommy and daddy living in two homes. He had a suitcase and was smiling. They weren't awful, but they weren't great. "Which one, Oliver?" she asked, holding them in front of him. His fingers seemed to somewhat point to the piggies and she placed the other two books back on the shelf.

The two of them continued their walk around the mall, heading into the toy store as Oliver clearly was in need of a diaper change. So much easier, she thought, than when she had both boys with her. She rolled him into the family bathroom and, as she placed him on the changing table, the conversation with Miss Peggy went through her head...

Many of his pictures are about his family...

Once in a while, he has a picture with just a mommy or a daddy….

He has told the other children that he has two houses…

He shrugs his shoulders…

When she finished changing Oliver, she buckled him into his stroller once again and they headed off into the store. There were so many colorful boxes with colorful plastic shapes inside, but that wasn't what she was looking for. She turned at the aisle with the craft supplies and grabbed some paper and crayons.

What do you need to tell me, Mason? she wondered, as she wiped her tears on her sleeve.

Simply an illusion (OK, fine, it's just a bit about Elle…)

"It's been a little strange at the preschool drop-off. The women I've been so friendly with, they're not so friendly anymore," Becca said, putting the Jeep in park, then turning to check on the sleeping boys. She lifted the scratched flap on her bag and gave a small, closed mouth smile as she did.

"It's because you're a divorcee, and you really shouldn't smile like that, Bex. You're going to get little pockets here and here," Elle said, pointing to the diagonal lines from her nose to her lips.

"Well, I'm not really divorced," Becca said.

"You're gonna be and they're questioning you right now, Bex," she said, smiling at the man in the orange vest holding up the stop sign on Weee Street.

"Questioning what? Like what I did in my marriage to fuck it up so bad?" Becca asked, now scrounging through her bag but taking in just a moment of the beautiful view.

"Maybe, or what they think your divorce might do to their marriages, maybe," Elle said.

"Like what?" Becca asked somewhat incredulously. "Like I'm going to go after their husbands?"

"Or they might go after you. Or they might see it's not so awful to leave your wife because so-and-so did it. Or they are thinking about how insecure they are feeling in their own marriages," Elle offered.

"You've given this a lot of thought," Becca said, finally finding the lip pencil in her bag and folding down the visor to look in the mirror.

"Bex, I don't blame them. I know this is scary for you. It was scary at the beginning of my divorce, too. Of course, at 16 months into my divorce I was less frightened and more wanting to kill Adam, but think how scary it is for the people around us. You were their friend, they liked you and, if this could happen to you, why not them? They don't want their husbands around you, even the idea of you. It's nothing personal," Elle said, flatly.

"Well, they're having some kind of luncheon or something. I didn't get an invite," Becca said, coloring in her bottom lip so she could purse it up against her top one before completing her very particularly crafted handmade cupid's bow.

"A couple little needles and you wouldn't have to do that all the time," Elle said flipping down her own visor to check out her pout in her mirror, as well. "You can join me today with Dr. Bender, downtown. He's not even expensive at all, Bex."

"I'm seeing Dana today, but I'll think about it," Becca said, trying to pout like Elle. It was useless, of course—no one, *no* one, pouted like Elle. "Sixteen months? Did you really say 16 months just now?" Becca asked, only just now realizing.

"Yup, 16 months of filings, fighting and sleeping in the sun room. He fought me for everything. Ev-er-y-thing! Those small MacKenzie-Childs bowls? The checked ones? He wanted those. With the matching plates, water pitcher, serving tray. He wanted it all," Elle said, gesturing with her hand with the syllable of each word.

"What for? Is he really going to use them?" Becca asked.

"No, Becca, he is not going to use them. He was trying to slow down the divorce. Once we settled that, it was the china, the stemware, the highballs, the low balls, the old fashioneds. We decided to split the silverware. Do you know what he did, when after he counted everything out, there was one extra spoon?" Elle asked.

"He let you have it?" Becca asked as she started the car again, the orange vested man motioning that it was their turn to move through the still-under-construction route.

"In return for the butter knife. Becca, it was endless. You'll see. When it comes time to split things up, he'll make it difficult for you," Elle said with a dramatic sigh.

"We've already split everything up," Becca said.

"Really? Well, then you're lucky. He won't slow down the proceedings. You can be done soon," Elle said.

They slowly passed a beautiful ivy-covered house with a stone blue roof. The driveway was older pavers with little grass blades sticking through the small spaces between them. The dad, two kids and a mom, their bikes in a row, each with their helmet on, were leaving for a ride.

"Wow, amazing," Becca said, turning around to catch another glimpse.

"Most people don't have that," Elle replied, as if she knew exactly what Becca was thinking. "You're making a beautiful home for your family."

"Not the house. The family. Riding bikes together. Doing family things."

"You're always doing that, Bex, always thinking things are so perfect all the time. You know, things aren't always as they seem. Even when we were little, you always seemed to think everything was so nice, that people were always going to do the right thing."

Becca knew this was probably coming. When things got bad, Elle took it more globally, instead of taking ownership of it herself. Becca had fought against Elle's cynicism for most of their friendship, being the happy cheerleader to her moody teenager, but, still somehow, they were best friends— through bad haircuts and bad husbands.

"Oh, I love this song," Becca said, turning up the volume, hoping to shift the conversation.

"What does it even mean? That they're attracted or not?" Elle asked. "Can you pick up steel with a magnet or no?"

Becca had no idea. Elle was too practical, as usual. "Not sure..." Becca said, as they were approaching the vineyard house. Becca had been hoping to catch a glimpse of what had been going on behind the fence, so she slowed down. Then, she saw it. It was as if someone had taken a sledgehammer to the fence, creating a dent, revealing the chicken wire and plaster beneath. The stone was simply an illusion. For a moment, it took her breath away. She even forgot to look beyond it.

"That dad, with the big house and nice family? He's having an affair." Elle said it so nonchalantly, without even taking her eyes off the road.

Becca looked out the side view mirror and watched as the four of them grew smaller and smaller. "How would you know that?" Becca asked.

"There's some story that they did it in an elevator. You haven't heard about it? Apparently she's a real gold digger, a real whore," Elle said.

There was silence then as Elle tousled her bangs and scooted her sunglasses back up higher onto her nose.

Becca *had* heard that one.

"Things aren't always as they seem," Elle said, but Becca wasn't listening. She was once again looking out the side view mirror, catching the last glimpse of the plaster grabbing to the wire swinging in the wind.

Or revenge can be served with Hermes, too....

She felt out of place in this store. It was a beautiful building in the city that took up the whole corner but didn't appear heavy because it was mostly glass. There were headless mannequins in the windows, maybe so passersby could try to envision them*selves* in the $10,000 outfits, and that wasn't even including the bag. Josh now only lived a couple blocks away, so after they dropped the boys off with him for Boys' Weekend Yea!, Becca had bee-lined there.

"Why are we here?" Elle kept asking, even as the gentleman at the entrance opened the giant doors for them. The only colors visible in the room of white carpet, white walls and white display cases were the bags. They were displayed along the walls, behind glass panels. So many to choose from, every color, every shade. Finally, there it was, between the Agate Blue and Garnet Red: the Orange Evelyne III. She gaped at its silver and palladium hardware (she had no idea what palladium was but knew the word because she'd been researching absolutely everything about this bag for this moment), outside pocket, leather tab closure, and, most importantly, its perforated leather plaque—two vertical lines, met in the middle by one horizontal—and thought, it looked larger than she remembered. The sales lady unlocked the glass door and removed it from the display. Becca put the strap over her head and rested the bag at her hip. "Angelique" (let's face it, her name was proba-bly Rachel or something) quickly stepped out from around the counter and began adjusting the strap—that was new, by the way, because it's only adjustable on the III, not I or II—to fit her not-quite 5-foot frame.

Becca turned to look at herself in the mirror, gently resting her hand on top of the bag. Her fingers looked so dainty on this 13-by-12-inch beauty, now covering most of her side. Elle stood there, dumbfounded. Becca had never experienced the silent Elle. Was she even breathing?

"I'll take it," Becca said, with a small smile growing on her face.

"What are you doing, Bex? You can't afford this. Just tell her you want to think about it," Elle said, grabbing Becca's old bag and taking her elbow.

"That will be $3,375," Angelique said, as she reached for the credit card already dangling out of Becca's hand.

"Oh, fuck. Fuck, fuck, fuck," Elle whispered as Angelique walked away with the credit card pinched tightly between her fingers.

"No," Becca said. "This time, fuck *him.*"

Then, a quick lunch with Dana...

"Well, we never really danced," Becca explained.

"You were married," Dana said. "How is that even possible?"

"Ya now, it's not that uncommon. I think if you ask most girls my height, they will probably tell you the same thing. It's hard to dance with someone so much taller. I mean, it's not like I could ever rest my head on his shoulder or talk to him. I never really danced with anyone I dated. It just isn't fun. It's actually a lot of work."

"I never really thought about that. So it shouldn't bother me that he wouldn't dance with me at his office party?" Dana asked. She was complaining about Luke already. They had been dating for two weeks now. The holidays were always a tricky time to date, Hillary had explained. Everyone wants to be in love at New Years, well, not exactly. Every *woman* wants to be in love at New Years, that's why the office party was a mistake in the first place. He wanted a date. She wanted to be in love. He wanted to drink. She wanted to dance.

Becca was getting the hang of this now.

"I don't think so. Have you heard from him since the party?" Becca asked.

"Well, of course! We talked the next day. That's when I told him that I thought it was really terrible that he didn't ask me to dance. I told him that I got all dressed up, that I left work early and that I had a big project for the next day…" Dana explained.

"You talk to him since then?"

"No, but it's only been a couple days. Right?"

"Right," Becca replied as she pressed her lips together and nodded. This was typical. Dana would typically morph into the guys she dated, then around two weeks or so, wanted *them* to be more like *her*. They were sitting in their favorite restaurant. The little bit of snow looked so pretty as they looked out the eighth-floor window and watched it fall on the city. The wait had been forever, but it was always worth it for a Fred's salad and martini.

"Allie's party will be fun. You excited?" Dana asked.

"Mmm, I'm not going," Becca said, as she placed her pretty pink drink down. "The whole reason Josh has the boys today and tonight is because I have the boys for New Year's Eve. I got some funny hats and horns. It'll be fun."

Becca looked up to find Dana looking at her from over the rim of her matching glass. "I didn't even think about that. You really can't go? Josh can't watch them? You can't get a sitter?"

"No. Look, I'm looking forward to it. We'll celebrate around seven. After they go to sleep I'm going to get in bed, watch a Bradley Cooper movie, relax. Really, it's all good," Becca said, poking around her salad to get the perfect bite.

"But it's at Allie's! It's gonna be so much fun! Really?" Dana asked again in disbelief.

"Really," Becca said, and she meant it. "Maybe I can meet you all for brunch New Year's Day. Josh is picking them up in the morning. How's that?"

"Not the same, but better," Dana said.

The check came and Becca pulled at her bag hooked on her chair. She gazed at it for just a moment, looking up to see a woman at a table by the fireplace eyeing it as well.

"Elle told me about your shopping trip earlier today. Look Becca, about that bag..." Dana began.

"I know. I can't believe I got it either," Becca said.

"How did you do it?" Dana asked, with a sad look of concern.

"Oh, my wedding ring? The one Josh got from his grandmother?" Becca said, as she took the last little sip of the pretty pink drink. "Turns out those diamonds were real."

Like this wasn't going to happen...

Asbury was closed on her way back from the city. *Do not go past the pet store. Do not go past the pet store...* Becca signaled, slowed down and pulled into a spot. She slowly turned off the engine and sat for a moment before finally grabbing her bag and hopping out. She was getting used to the car now but still fumbled to lock it while she walked up the sidewalk. The dog was in the pet shop window, spinning with his long, black tail elegantly twirling behind.

"Sorry it took me so long," she said to him through the glass, and she pushed the door open as the bell overhead rang.

Just another Sunday morning...

"Open the door, Becca. Now! " Elle was screaming as she pounded on the patio door. "I see you in there! I see your feet! Becca, come on! I'm not kidding! Bex!" She leaned a little closer to the glass. "Seriously, I had a white pants incident. Let me in!"

Becca lifted the green-colored panel of her weekend hideaway, just enough to catch a glimpse of Elle in the window. "Holy shit," she mumbled with her hand over her mouth and slid carefully out, holding Stevie, who, by the way, was not a boy. "You look like you were hit by a truck or something..."

Becca opened the door and Elle ran passed her up the two flights of stairs to the bathroom. She heard the shower turn on, and that high pitch whistle that always seemed to start when it did. She walked up to the kitchen and scribbled on her "to do" list on the chalkboard- *high pitch whistle when shower is turned on.* This was added to *blowing fuses, what is that switch for in the kitchen? and is that black mold in the bathroom the bad kind of black mold?* She heard the water stop and the shower curtain get dragged along the bar, followed by a sound like Elle tumbling a bit. The shower rings had come off the bar. Again. *Price out glass door for shower* she added to her list.

"Do you have anything I can put on?" Elle yelled from upstairs.

"You're like half a foot taller than me!" Becca yelled as she plopped down on the stairway.

"Anything, Becca. Anything at all. Can I use your washing machine?" Elle asked.

Becca glanced at her list. Nothing about the washing machine. "I think so," she said. "Let me see what you can wear." Ten minutes later the washing machine was taking care of the white pants incident. They were sitting on the sofa, Becca's yoga pants looking more like capris on Elle. "These remind me of that pair of pants you used to wear to bar mitzvahs. Do you remember them? Remember when Judd picked you up and swung you around? All the grandmas were oohing and aahing at how cute it was. Why did he do that again?"

"My toe was broken. I was wearing a wooden shoe," Becca said. "I was trying to get out of the family room and my brother wanted the street number for Racine. I tried to get past him and hit the wall."

"That is hysterical," she said. "What is it anyway?" she asked.

"1200," Becca said, sipping her coffee.

"Yeah, you'll never forget that one," she said with a smile.

"So…what happened today?" Becca asked.

"It's so horrifying. We were having a team meeting. Corporate wants more cheerful sales people on the floor. We got shopped. They said that my team looked bored and unmotivated. They didn't approach the shopper at all. Not even a 'good morning.' So, I called a meeting. It was 'How do you act like you're feeling a 10 when you're really feeling a two?'"

"Oh, that's cute!" Becca said, slapping Elle's knee.

"Well, it was going really well for a while. They were all volunteering, and I was writing their ideas on the dry erase board in the break room," Elle said, covering her forehead with her hand. I turned around and they just went silent. It was crazy. Their eyes were really big, well, the ones looking at me. The guys, well, they were trying to look away."

"The guys?" Becca asked.

"Yes, Becca, guys can sell girls clothes, too! They're even better than the girls, really. It's almost like the customers want to be their friends or something. It's a little weird. Anyway, Natalie—"

"The one who always leaves her coffee at the checkout counter?"

"No, that's Tammy. Natalie is the one who doesn't like to touch tissue paper, so she won't wrap up her sales…" Elle reminded her.

"Oh, that's right."

"So, Natalie reaches into her purse and is showing me a tampon. I look down and, well…" Elle was now covering her entire face.

"I haven't seen anything like it since middle school," Becca said. "Why didn't you just buy something from your store?"

"Oh my god, Bex, I would never shop there," she said. "What was that little tent?"

"Sometimes when the boys are away I go in there. It's quiet."

"Isn't the whole house quiet when they're away?" she asked.

"Yeah, it's too quiet. I hate these Boys' Weekends, I really do," Becca said.

"We just need to keep you busy, that's all. You were going to start seeing somebody, right?" Elle asked, apprehensively.

"I have an appointment in a couple weeks," Becca said.

"That's good, Bex. I think that's really good. You should try yoga, too," Elle said. "It really helps me to relax, find my center," but Becca was distracted.

Becca had been learning some lip-reading skills from Hillary, who was convinced that Becca probably suffered some hearing loss from all the loud music she listened to. Today, she tried to practice, but all Becca could see was the over-plump, uneven shape Elle's lips formed with each word, and the red lipstick on her front teeth.

"I don't really have the time," Becca replied, while trying not to stare.

"You'll come with me." (Some trouble making out the M sound there.) "It will be fun!"

"I have so much work to do around here. I really need to paint. I just can't find the right beige…"

The two of them glanced over at the swatches of beige paint still taped to the mustard-colored walls in the living room.

"Becca, they're brown. Just choose this one," she said, pointing at one with a little too much yellow. It wasn't right. The beige in the old house was right; it matched the ottoman. The red flowers on the ottoman matched the chairs. The green vines on the ottoman matched the sofa. She had been trying to recreate the old house here. Mason's green was still the same color as the square patches underneath each of the balls and bats on his quilt. Oliver's room was still going to be the same robin's egg blue as the "A" patch on his. "Or this one, I guess…"

"I'm not coordinated either," Becca replied.

"It helps your sex life, by the way. This one! This one!" Elle said.

"That's nothing I'm worrying about right now."

"Speaking of which…You hear from Jay?" Elle asked.

"He texted me," Becca handed Elle her phone to see.

It simply read: *"Dinner?"*

"You didn't reply yet? How come?"

"I just don't have the time right now." She was peeling the swatches off the wall and placing them on the ottoman, studying them carefully.

"Bex, you're becoming a bit of a drag. You use to be so funny, so witty. I mean, you haven't even said a word about my lips! What's wrong with you?" Elle screamed.

Becca wanted to cry, but was surprised when the laughter came out first. She was wiping the tears away as the two of them laughed hysterically.

"Let's hear it! Let me have it, Becca!" Elle cheered.

But, she couldn't. She just laughed.

"There's lipstick on my teeth again, isn't there? That keeps happening!" she said, taking her finger and trying to brush it off. "You're coming with me to yoga."

Happy New Year!

"Hey, are the boys around?" It was 8:30 and they had been asleep for about 45 minutes already when Josh called. She could hear the celebration in the background.

"They're asleep," Becca said. She was petting Stevie who was next to her, sleeping on the bed, her paws moving wildly. Becca grabbed the remote and froze the screen right on Bradley Cooper's face. She had been enjoying this quiet time. Sipping her lemon drop martini had become a bit of a game, sprinkling the yellow sugar on top ever so slightly for each sip.

"Oh, I'm sorry I missed them. Will you tell them I called and said Happy New Year?" he asked.

Like they'll understand that, she thought. "Sure."

"Will you get off the phone?" It was a woman's voice in the background on the other end. She didn't sound pretty or sexy, just drunk, and with him.

"Sorry. You'll tell them, right?" He sounded uncomfortable, like he had been caught. She felt uncomfortable too, not because she had been caught out with someone else, though, but because she was caught home, alone.

"I'll be there in a second," she yelled up at the ceiling in her bedroom, startling Stevie from her sleep. "I'll tell them," she said into the phone.

"Great. Happy New Year," Josh said.

She looked at Bradley Cooper's face on the screen. "Thanks," she said and hung up. The game was over. She gulped the last few sips in her glass and looked at the TV. She felt frozen, just like him. She looked at her phone and then tapped it a few times on her bathrobe. She had been so cozy in it till just a few minutes ago. She wondered how Allie's party was going and decided to text Dana.

"How's the party?" she typed but deleted it. It sounded too pathetic…

"Having fun?" she entered but deleted it, as well. It sounded too leading, like she would be expecting a *No cuz we miss you* kinda thing…

"Happy New Year!" Perfect. Send.

She watched the bubble pop up and waited. *Nothing. The party is great. Yes, she's having fun…*

Her phone rang in her hand. FaceTime with Dana appeared. She answered quickly to see Dana's face, so huge in the screen she could only make out the edges of the shiny tiara she had semi-balanced on her head.

"We miss you!" Dana yelled. "How is your New Year's? Did you and the boys have fun?"

Becca could hear the celebration there, too. Someone walked behind Dana carrying a tray of martini glasses. Dana ducked and grabbed her crown, then laughed and smiled at someone off screen. "There are some cute guys here from Allie's art class. Some of them even have man buns. I wish you were here. Are you having a good night?"

The tears started to come then. Becca started flapping her hand in front of her eyes. "Bex? What's wrong? What's wrong?" Dana yelled.

"Who's that?" she heard someone ask and suddenly Dana disappeared from view. She could see a bit of the party, well, mostly some feet, and then Hillary's face. "What's wrong?" she screamed.

Becca was waving faster. No words would come. She saw Hillary look around, then start walking through the house. She caught glimpses of people but couldn't make out any faces. Hillary entered a quieter, brighter room, waving someone in behind her. Dana and Hillary both crowded onto the screen. "What's going on!?" they were hollering.

"Nothing. I'm fine. I'm fine," Becca said, finally able to speak. "Josh called, he's at a party with some girl. I don't know what's wrong with me. This is so embarrassing. Ignore me. I'm fine. I'm fine…"

They stood quiet then, looking at each other and then back at the door. People were coming in and they jostled the phone all over. Elle's boobs, Gary's funny looking shoes, Jay's face. *Shit.* Becca put the phone down but could hear everyone yelling. She hopped out of bed and looked in the mirror. Most of her makeup was off now, and she was still in her cozy bathrobe. She ripped it off to reveal her Ramones T-shirt, sans bra, not that it mattered. She pulled her hair in a messy pony and picked up the phone. She held it as far away from her face as she could as she faked a smile and a laugh.

"Happy New Year!" Becca yelled, waving crazily into the screen. Everyone was smiles, except for Hillary and Dana. Elle's look was more questioning, as she squinted, or tried to, to make her out. Gary was blowing kisses. Jay, in the back, answered with a simple wave.

"Happy New Year!" they yelled back. Most of most of them fit into the screen, all of them waving. She hung up and fell on the bed. She looked up at the ceiling and then turned her head ever so slightly to catch Bradley's face, still smiling, still frozen on the screen.

"This acting stuff is pretty hard," she said quietly, as she sat up enough to see the clock: 8:45. "Happy New Year, Bradley," she said, cuddling Stevie into her robe and rolling over onto her back.

Her phone was vibrating next to her on her bed. 10:45. She had fallen asleep. The light of the TV hadn't even kept her awake. *Answer the door,* appeared on her phone. She sat up and once again looked at Bradley's face before grabbing her bathrobe and heading down the hall. She could hear both boys softly snoring as she passed their rooms, then made her way down the seven steps. In the front door window, there they were: Dana, Elle and Hillary, still with their crowns on, holding one up for her. Becca opened the door as they loudly whispered, "Happy New Year" and gave her a hug.

"What are you doing here? You didn't have to come."

"We couldn't have you home watching Bradley Cooper movies all night," Elle said, pulling a bottle of champagne out of her bag. "What's going on?"

"Josh called from a party. He was with a girl. No big deal," Becca said.

"It wouldn't have been if you were out, too, but you were home. We should have been here," Dana said. "What did you do all night, anyway? You didn't watch Bradley movies all night, did you?"

"No. Of course not," Becca said, realizing that the TV was still paused with his face on the screen in her room.

"You're lying," Elle said, running up the steps, the girls following closely behind. Elle pushed the door open to find Stevie still asleep on Becca's messy bed, an empty martini glass and Bradley's smiling face still filling the screen. "What are we going to do with you? You can't spend your nights in this box, with that box. We're getting you out of here," she said as she sat down on the corner of the bed. Hillary and Dana sat too, and they gestured to Becca to join them.

"Ya know it's funny," Dana said, looking into the closet. "I thought you had a lot of shoes, but you really don't, do you?" She hopped off the bed and sat on the floor, opening up the boxes and lifting off the bags and tissue. "These are pretty. I've never seen these."

"I've seen those," Elle said. "In your hands, though, not on your feet. You carried those home after the wedding that night, right?" she asked.

Becca remembered walking down the alley on her toes, sidestepping the puddles, glass and pebbles as they all made their way to their apartments.

"Those really are pretty," Elle said. "You should wear them. Or at least have them out. Why do you keep them all packed away, anyway?" She hopped off the bed and joined Dana on the floor, taking more boxes off the shelves and opening them up to see what was inside. "No way do you still have these," Elle said, lifting the Waffle Stompers out of a paper sack. "Oh my god, the paint, look at the paint! It's still there!" she screamed, flipping them over and pointing at the pink paint still stuck in the treads.

"Guys, leave her stuff alone," Hillary said. "I gotta go check on Lucy. I'll be back in the morning. Happy New Year, all!"

Elle waved without even looking. "They really are little. I'd ask if I could borrow them, but look at this!" she said, holding a leopard print heel in the sky. "These need to come out of their box, too, Chickie. Hey, pretty girl," she said to the shoe, turning it around by its heel. "We're getting you out."

Clunk, Crank, Crank, Crank…

In the first few moments of the new year, Elle was flipping through the fall Pottery Barn catalogue, turning her ice cream spoon upside down in her mouth, leaving it there as she stared at the many different vases on page 26.

"You want to talk about it?" Dana asked somewhat apprehensively. Was she concerned or curious? Becca couldn't tell. Dana asked a lot of questions, all the time. *Was it an interview? Is this research?*

"Not really," Becca said, peering over Elle's shoulder. *Remember to check out page 26,* she thought to herself. *That small, recycled vase is cute.…*

"You must hate him," Dana said, reaching her spoon into the ice cream carton between them. It looked quite a mess in there. Nuts picked out by Dana, chocolate chunks spooned out by Elle and the long strips of caramel scooped out by Becca, left a lot of very melted and mushy vanilla mess.

"I guess," Becca said. "I don't really know how I feel. I think I just can't believe it's happening at all. Like, I'll wake up tomorrow and we'll be in the old house, with the boys, he'll go off to work, he'll come home..."

"That sounds boring," Elle said, turning the page to the holiday items. "That's all you think about? Being with the boys? Him going to work and coming back? Is that all that was going on?"

"You must feel so mad," Dana said. "You took such good care of him, the kids, the house, and this is what he does? He gets bored and leaves?"

"Yeah, I guess so," Becca said.

"You scared?" Dana asked.

"Stop it, Dana," Elle said, looking at her over the top of the catalogue. "You're scaring her."

"It would be OK if you were scared, Bex. You have two little boys, no money, dating is hard."

"Shut up, Dana," Elle said, rolling her eyes toward Becca. "You're gonna be fine."

"I just think it's sad. It would be OK if you were sad too, Bex. I mean, you planned on a future with him and he let you down. The boys, too. You counted on him, and he left you for some girl? How old is she anyway? What does she look like? Does she live in the city? Oh my god, Bex do you think they were sleeping together all along? Do you think his late work nights were with her?"

"Dana, shut up!" Elle screamed.

"I'm sorry, Bex. You just never talk about how you're feeling. Do you feel anything? Anything at all?" Dana asked sadly.

Becca hesitated, trying to find just the right words. "When I used to babysit in high school, I thought that parents were so happy. When the mom came downstairs, she'd look so pretty that the dad's eyes would pop out a little when he saw her. He would put his arm around her, and they would walk to the garage door together. I wondered what they did on their dates. They were at nice restaurants, movies or parties, and I would be doing little puppet shows, reading stories and tucking the kids in."

"Is that how you thought it would be?" Dana asked. "His eyes popping out when he saw you? Romantic dates? The kids all tucked in at home?"

"I did," Becca said, continuing to put her feelings into words the best way she could. "At the end of the night, I'd be waiting to hear the garage door go up. I can still hear it, 'clunk, crank, crank, crank,' because that meant that I was done, and I didn't need to be responsible for anyone else anymore."

Dana looked puzzled. "I don't understand."

"Josh leaving," Becca explained. "It kinda feels like it did when I would hear the garage door starting to go up…"

Just like looking in the mirror, only 15 years ago…no, really!

"Well, so I made cookies," Becca spoke into the phone, glancing out the window.

"Why would you make cookies?" Hillary asked.

"Well, I guess I want her to like me. If she thinks I'm nice, then she'll want the job and be nice to the kids," Becca said.

"She's supposed to want the job. She's supposed to be nice to the kids. She's a BABYSITTER, Becca," Hillary reasoned.

"I hear they're hard to get. Everyone needs one. Some people around here even want more than one. They want like two or three, even. They want some that do this, some that do that… They need backups. I mean it's really competitive around here," Becca explained.

"When we were young it was *competitive* to get a babysitting job!" Hillary said. "I sat whenever I could, for like, two dollars an hour. How much are they asking for now?"

"I think like 15…" Becca said.

"Fifteen! I'll babysit for 15, Becca! Ask me! Ask me to sit!" Hillary hollered into the phone.

A little red convertible with the top up was pulling into the driveway and a young girl with ripped jeans and cropped winter jacket stepped out of the car.

"Where did you get her name, anyway?" Hillary asked.

"The director of the preschool. She used to be a student there, I guess," Becca said as she watched the girl with the large key chain check out the house. "She said I would like her. Look, I gotta go. I'll call you back."

Becca took a quick look in the mirror before answering the door. The girl on the stoop was just an inch or two taller than Becca, but was wearing platform sneakers. Maybe they could have this in common… Becca greeted her with a big smile.

"Hi, Ms. Gold," the girl said in a spritely voice. She sounded like she was right out of an animated film. Stevie ran to her right away, wagging her tail, bumping her side into her leg. "Oh, I love dogs!"

"This is Stevie," she said, pointing to the 3-pound dog, now upside down with her legs in the air as Victoria rubbed her belly. "Thank you for coming today. I made cookies. Are you hungry?"

"No, no thank you," Victoria said, again in a wonderfully sweet voice. "I'd love to meet Mason and Oliver, though. Are they here?"

They walked toward the living room and just then five little fingers wrapped themselves around the corner of the wall. "Who's that around the corner? I see you," Victoria said, now walking on her tiptoes. She, too, then wrapped her hand around the wall to peak over and find Mason with his dinosaurs set up in their green pillow cave. "I love dinosaurs, Mason! Is that a diplodocus?"

Becca stood back and watched as the diplodocus—that's the one with the shorter, sturdier forelegs, by the way—slowly make its way towards the brachiosaurus—the one with the longer forelegs. Oliver was mesmerized at the meeting.

"Ooh, these dinosaurs are amazing," Victoria, said, carefully reaching toward her long bangs and tucking them behind her ear.

This is crazy, Becca thought, listening in on their conversation as she stayed to the side of the room.

"Do you have a triceratops? Those are actually my favorite. Is this your guitar, Mason? I've always wanted to learn to play guitar. What does Oliver like to do? Oliver, what do you like to do?" she asked, taking off her jacket revealing her vintage Stones T-shirt. Oliver sat in his bouncy seat as Victoria tickled his toes, his little feet kicking furiously as he bounced up and down. "Ms. Gold, you can call me Tori. Nobody calls me Victoria."

"And I'm Becca. So, how much do you charge an hour?" Becca asked, anxiously.

"Fifteen, but, Becca, can I ask you a favor?" Tori asked. "Can you pay me with just one check? Once a month? You see, I'm actually saving for this pair of shoes, and I'm terrible with saving money. I mean, I'd probably go and spend it all each week at the record store or something."

Whoa.... Where's the record store?

One more thing to worry about...

Whatever the theme was, it was big, but the invite was simple-

Be here at 7

Dress Formal

See you Saturday

Signed, as usual, with Allie's signature kiss.

The boys would be with Josh that weekend. Jay had texted he could pick her up at 6:15, so as luck would have it, Becca could be there, right after she painted. She had become quite good at it. What was the big deal anyway? Roll out the wall then cut into the ceiling and corners with an angled brush. She would paint Friday night and have Saturday for fun, maybe take Stevie for a walk, then sit in the weed-covered yard.

Becca really hadn't realized a puppy would be like having a baby all over again. Her Boys' Weekend Yea! mornings to sleep in late were now over as Stevie wanted to eat, go outside or even play. Becca had just gotten used to taking up the whole bed and now she had a new 3-pound roommate that she needed to be careful about rolling over onto. And then, of course, there were the hawks. Becca had never considered them before, but after last week, they were all she thought about.

It was the day she had been in the back yard among the weeds, relaxing on Faye's chair. Stevie had been resting quietly at her feet, and Becca was on her iPad placing several items into her Pottery Barn cart. Each time she ordered something, she filled in the same info—name, address, email, blah, blah blah.

It was exhausting, but as luck would have it on that sunny 50-degree January day, she noticed the express shipping alternative. She could fill it all in just one more time, and then they would have her name, address, email, blah, blah, blah, all ready to go. They would even have her credit card number with its expiration date and safety code safely in their protection. In the future, a simple press of a button could now complete her order each and every time.

Becca had just been pondering a password, and looked down at the 3-pound ball of black fur resting at her feet. She began typing S-T-E... when, suddenly, for just a second, the sun was gone. That's when she saw it—the huge stretched-out wings flying within inches of where she was sitting, gliding past her, just missing Stevie. It swooped into the sky and flew off as Stevie jumped to her feet and spun in a frantic circle. Becca had swiftly picked up the frightened puppy and had run inside. *One more thing to worry about,* she thought, *hawks picking up my dog...*

This afternoon, she was once again amid the backyard weeds in Faye's chair, resting before Allie's secretive bash. She only placed a few white mugs in her cart, with Stevie at her feet... on a leash wrapped around Becca's ankle.

Finally, a peek!

"It's always the same story. Everyone always wonders, 'What could I have done differently?' 'I use to be like this, but now I'm like that,' 'I drove them away,' 'It's my fault'" ... Jay said, a little while later, not even taking his eyes off Asbury to glance at her once.

"When we met, I looked different, I acted different. I mean, I was a lot of fun. We went out all the time, tried new restaurants. I became very boring, wanting to stay home and be with the kids," Becca said.

"The truth is, Becca, I actually think those are *your* thoughts about you, not his. Maybe it's *you* that misses the girl you were. Look, maybe you have changed. No, you are absolutely not the girl in the blue rain slicker running around campus. But whoever you are now..." Jay trailed off then, somewhat gesturing an "oh well" with his hand.

"Whoever I am now what?"

"Becca..."

"Whoever I am now what?"

"Becca, look, whoever you are now, I can't sugar-coat it for you, he's not in love with you. If he were, then..." he trailed off, again.

Becca sat quietly, fidgeting with the strap around her ankle. She was getting angry again, angry like that day in the store with the rain.

"What time is it, anyway?" he asked.

"6:30. Look, we really don't know each other well enough for you to be the one to set me straight on stuff, OK? You certainly don't owe me any truths, so maybe just keep them to yourself."

"That's fine. I will. Get out," he said, pulling over on a little side street east of Asbury.

"Are you serious?" she asked.

"This is the house, right?" he asked, gesturing toward the stone wall. "I'll circle the block. Take a quick look, cuz the party is in 30 minutes and the traffic is gonna be hell. Be careful, it's probably a big mess in there."

She looked at him in disbelief. *He remembered the house.* She looked down at her pretty shoes and carefully slipped them off her feet, placing them on the seat. "You are going to come back, right?" she asked.

"Becca, go peek at the house," he said. She opened the door and swung her feet out, placing them carefully on the sidewalk. It was still fairly warm from the sun that day. She shut the door behind her and ran on her tiptoes around the corner. The cars were speeding by on Asbury. She waited for a break in the traffic before she leaned to peek around what was left standing of the wall.

It was gone. The house was all gone.

She carefully wandered onto the lot. There were different piles scattered around. One of wood, one of brick, one of stone. There was a clear marking of where the house once stood. It looked like maybe it had been turned sideways to the street. She looked back and could almost imagine turning off Asbury and onto a winding driveway bordered with trees only to come into the opening of where the house stood. She imagined the pile of stones, all spread out in the driveway, the grand front door opening as people stepped out of their cars. There had probably been dormer windows overlooking the huge lawn where, without a doubt, the family's five children played, running as if in a picture, with the backdrop of the lake. She could see their bright clothes against the blue sky, mom and dad sitting on a bluestone patio in Adirondack chairs, sipping wine and holding hands.

"You're always doing that, Bex," she could hear Elle saying. *"always thinking things are so perfect all the time…"*

For all she knew, the driveway pointed straight into the front of the house that simply faced Asbury. Maybe no children played, no wine sparkled in the sunlight, no Adirondacks, no holding hands. Maybe, they never had children, after years of trying. Maybe he fell out of love with her. Maybe he… She heard a honk then. She could hear Jay's car idling around the corner and slowly backed up towards the street. She looked over her shoulder, back towards the cars speeding by, but took one last peek, imagining their dogs chasing each other as the sun set.

She ran on her toes to the car, opened the door and got in. "Well?" Jay asked. "Was it everything you dreamt it would be?"

She was rubbing the gravel and dirt off her feet. "Maybe."

Allie's big surprise...

When they entered Allie's house, there were boxes everywhere. They were arranged like furniture, stacked strategically to look like sofas, tables and even chaises. Allie had flat boxes of different colors acting as throw pillows resting on the structures. On some of her box tables, she had tall cardboard cylinders with touch lights on top wrapped in packing tape and bubble wrap. She never missed a beat. What was missing was, well, everything.

"I'm so glad you came tonight. You may have noticed that there is going to be a bit of a change around here," Allie said with a smile, ear-to-ear. It was the only smile in the room as everyone knew what was coming, or at least they thought they did...

"I'm getting married!"

Allie went on to explain that he lived at 13 East Chestnut. It was a smaller building in a busier part of town. Lots of shopping, fewer trees, the units were smaller.

The question everyone was thinking was, *Why wasn't he moving in here?*

The answer... she hadn't met him yet.

"It's like magic," she explained. She had heard story after story about single women moving into 13 East Chestnut and shortly after, they meet their husbands. "I moved in yesterday!" She raised her glass and let out a shriek. The men looked at each other silently as the girls raised their glasses. If it were anyone else, this wouldn't work. But Allie? Just maybe....

The girl with the perfect eyebrows...

She had fallen asleep on the sofa downstairs with the TV on, so when the package hit the front stoop late the next morning with the big "thump," it woke her. She quickly covered her eyes from the sunlight peeking through the old curtains and wondered if the delivery man had seen her passed out in the living room. There was a preacher on TV talking about his tree. It had fallen in a storm. It didn't have strong roots. *You need strong roots,* he was explaining. She quickly turned off the noise and stumbled into the darkened kitchen. Stevie was already wagging her tail, switching her feet back and forth with the excitement of what would soon be in her bowl. She figured she would hide in there until she heard the truck drive away, so she poured the water into the coffee maker. She kept miscounting the five scoops of coffee and had to restart the process of filling the filter twice.

Finally, she and Stevie walked to the front door to see a box, poorly taped, on the stoop. She had ordered several more things from Pottery Barn. Was it the brushed nickel bathroom caddy or the linen bulletin board? She shook it, then placed it on the floor. She didn't normally answer the phone until after she had her first cup and the coffee still wasn't even brewing when the phone rang and Elle's name appeared.

She managed to get out a quick "hello" while still covering her eyes.

"Well," she said. "You're home?"

"Of course I'm home," she replied, pressing the button on the coffee maker again and again and again. She glanced up to notice that the clock was out on the microwave. Had she blown another fuse? "Where else would I be?" She shuffled her way down the stairs to the closet with the vents in the doors covered in cobwebs, she hoped. She found "sink" in permanent ink written next to a switch that was flipped the opposite way of the others. She flipped it back and heard the electricity return to the kitchen.

"Dana's birthday party?" she said in a too sing-songy way.

That was in 45 minutes. Just enough time to shower and dress before Hillary picked her up.

"See you there!" and with that Elle was gone. Becca grabbed her coffee and ran to the shower. She was ready just in time for Hillary to pull up.

They pulled up to the building and gave the keys to her doorman. Walking down the hall, they could hear the girls laughing in Dana's apartment. It was a wine tasting party, and mini wine glasses covered the table. Dana's sister was there and she stood behind the table with a rolled-up piece of paper in her hand.

Dana came over with a huge hug. "I wasn't sure you would be able to make it today!" she said excitedly. *Did something happen last night?*

"Gather round, all!" her sister yelled as she waved the paper tube in her hand. "A Sunday afternoon is a wonderful time to learn about wine. I'm so glad you all came here to celebrate Dana. She talks about you all the time!"

"Who is she?" Hillary asked.

"It's her sister, Karen. Don't you remember?" Becca whispered, only half covering her mouth with one hand.

"Oh, my god. She's the eyebrow girl!" Hillary said quietly without even taking her eyes off of her. The three of them had gone to the spa to get their eyebrows waxed when Becca had asked the waxing girl how to get her eyebrows to look the same. The lady had responded that eyebrows are not twins, they are sisters. That's when Dana had jumped in and said, "Yeah, kinda like me and Karen. She's long, thin and perfect, and I'm the thicker one that's too short." They had laughed so hard they had almost peed. Now here she was. *Ok, perfect sister, what do you have there on that piece of paper?*

She gently placed her hand on Dana's shoulder, then carefully unrolled the paper and began to read:

"Today we are here to celebrate you

holding glasses up high to cheer on something new.

I wanted to give you a very special day,

but a classy, sophisticated air didn't seem quite the way.

So, this wine tasting will be just a little less classy,

and the names on the labels, just a little more sassy....."

"Becca! You're here!" Allie whispered loudly. "I wasn't sure you would make it after last night."

That's two...Ok, that's it. "What happened last night?"

Karen was now holding a bottle in her hand.

"Some girls like it rarely.

Some girls all day.

Some girls like it black or white.

Some like "50 Shades of Gray."

Taste....

"Becca, the egg joust?" Allie asked. "You really don't remember?"

"Yummy, huh?" Karen said, with an extra-large smile on her face, pointing to the next bottle for the handoff.

'Some girls like a lot.

Some just a smidge.

Some just enjoy "long romantic walks

To the wine fridge."

    Taste…

Gary loved stories about school, and he remembered them, each and every one. Like performing a lip synch show, exposing her secret about dropping out of the journalism school to her parents mid-semester or their antics during Greek Week their freshman year. Apparently, that was the day he had wanted to revisit last night, and he had wanted to act it out, too.

Back in school, they had been on the same team and matched up as a pair for the "egg joust." This consisted of the fraternity boys placing an egg on their heads and covering it up with a shower cap. A girl would ride on his shoulders, carefully balancing as she protected his egg while trying to smash someone else's. She hadn't even been on for more than a few seconds when someone smashed Gary's. The goo had run onto his face and he had decided to wipe it away. That's when he had let go, and Becca had fallen off his shoulders and onto the ground. For some reason (possibly the third martini?) last night, she had been talked into giving the egg joust just one more try.

"Gary didn't even really have a hold on you from the beginning, Bex, so the horror began and ended quickly," Elle said.

Karen continued to the next stanza…

"Sometimes there's just one.

Sometimes two or three.

It's really up to you:

"Menage a Trois" or "Monogamy."

    Taste… Taste…

"I went up on Gary's shoulders? And fell to the ground?" Becca asked horrified.

"Delicious!" Karen yelled, grabbing the next bottle and finding her place once again on the scroll...

"Sometimes just one
Is a little boring for us.
We can dabble! We've earned it!
Be a bit "Promiscuous"!

    Taste...

"No, silly. You fell into the box. The coffee table box? Right through? You don't remember?" Allie asked loudly.

"Girls?" Karen was looking at them now, her perfect eyebrow going up just a bit...

"Sorry," they each mouthed, from the corner of the room.

"Why not at a concert?
The pool or patio?
Kinda boring in bed!
Why not a "Freakshow"?

    Taste...

Becca started to remember. She had landed in the middle of a huge packing box, the strapping tape coming apart, her butt stuck in between the flaps.

"Do as you please
No matter how unsightly!
It doesn't matter what others think!
You're no "Girl Go Lightly"!

    Taste...

"I will kill him," Becca said, covering her face to hide her now blushing cheeks.

"Enough to make your head spin
Or just to feel sedated.
Or just so you won't notice your thighs
When you're "Simply Naked."

    Taste…

"Gary or Jay?" Elle asked, with a giggle, sipping from her little cup.

"And that brings to the end
Our wine tasting time.
Tipping our glasses together
For one last chime."

"Why would I want to kill Jay?" Becca asked, terrified of the answer.

"And now finally
To discuss something new!
Like men and sex, of course!
You knew this poem was about wine, didn't you?"

"Because of the kiss, Becca. He pulled you out, you tripped on your shoe, you fell into him on the sofa, he kissed you…" Elle was saying, clasping her hands together, looking off into the sky.

Karen had brought eight bottles and penned a rhyme for each one. She was even able to rhyme "Promiscuous" and "Monogamy." The food truck pulled up on cue, grilled cheese and tomato soup. *Who does that?*

"Should we tell Dana that her sister has the perfect arch, as well?" asked Hillary.

"Fuck no," Becca said. The story was horrifying, and Becca wouldn't have believed it if they hadn't all gone into the bathroom then to look at the bruise on her butt. She was angry and did want to kill him. How could Jay have kissed her?

Dana opened every gift but three. Each time she ripped the beautiful paper off a box or lifted something out of a tissue filled bag, she gave Becca a smile. Dana hated opening gifts in front of people, Becca knew that. They had had so many conversations about it, Becca was surprised that Dana's sister didn't know. At Becca's many wedding showers, she had smiled at Dana as well. "Oh, the ladle I wanted! Thank you!" she would say as she reached into a cello bag holding a black, plastic oversized spoon or, "Oh my god, this is so neat," about the salad spinner. It was Dana's turn now and she had graciously accepted the glass bottles of bath salts topped with corks, the mani-pedi gift certificate at her favorite salon and the cashmere skull cap that was actually more Becca's style than hers.

Finally, the brown paper bag with the white tissue paper was up. Dana took off the card and read it aloud. "Happy birthday, Dana! Love, Becca." She reached in and pulled out two small objects both wrapped in bubble wrap. If one looked carefully, one could see the stripes on one and the polka dots on the other. Suddenly, Dana's expression changed, "The salt and pepper shakers, Bex?" she asked.

"Happy birthday, Dana!" Becca grinned.

Dana looked down sadly at the two wrapped stoneware pieces and placed them back into the bag. "Thank you, Becca," she said.

"I think you might be in trouble, *Becca*," Elle said, slyly.

Becca? She never calls me Becca. Shit, she thought. *This is why you should never open up gifts at a party.*

What's in the box?

Becca returned home a couple of hours before the boys would be back from "Boys' Weekend Yea" and had stumbled upon the box that had been delivered that morning. There were no packaging labels. The strapping tape was wrinkly and folded in some spots. She shook the heavy flat box and listened. Nothing. She walked into the kitchen and took a knife out of the drawer. She knelt down on the floor and dragged the edge along the misplaced tape and lifted one flap up, then another and another, then stopped. She could see it now. The white ribbons across the bodice, the pretty neckline.

It was supposed to be buried in the rubble and beams... He must be sneaking into the house, too, she thought. She had played it out a thousand times. She had been looking forward to sharing the story with her friends one day—the story of how she left her dress for the house to fall on it. Now, he even ruined that. She took the box and brought it down to that closet with the vents in the doors, the one covered in cobwebs, hopefully, and placed it on a shelf. He had changed her story, again.

Boys' Weekend, Yea?

She had been packing up the boys' clothes when the commotion started. Two shirts for Mason, two shirts for Oliver, two pants for Mason, two pants for Oliver, one extra shirt for Mason…

Stevie began to bark, doing that funny thing she did—bark, bark, twirl, bark, bark, twirl. She looked at the clock; Josh will be here in 10 minutes for "Boys' Weekend Yea!" He was rarely early. Stevie had her paws on the living room window, the one where her pink bed sat, so she could rest in the sun and watch the squirrels in the bushes next door. The barking grew louder and more frantic, her spins faster and there were two in a row, now three. Mason approached the window, still holding his vacuum cleaner. "Mommy," he was screaming. "Mommy! The squirrel! The squirrel!"

Becca placed the one extra shirt for Oliver down. She quickly glanced into the living room to find Stevie growling, Mason screaming and Oliver, now awake, crying in his bouncy chair in front of the TV. She turned the corner and peeked out the window. Just under the neighbor's birdfeeder, now swinging wildly, was a hawk and, underneath that, a tiny, still struggling squirrel.

"Mommy!" screamed Mason, his face red and covered in tears. "Help him, Mommy! Please!" He was stomping his feet now, grabbing onto the curtains. The hawk didn't move.

Becca didn't have time to slip on her shoes and simply dashed outside in just her socks. She stopped on the driveway and looked at the hawk. "You let him go!" she screamed. The hawk turned its head and looked in her direction.

"Let him go!" she screamed again, this time picking up a large stick. The hawk fluttered its wings just the tiniest bit. Becca moved towards it, carrying the stick. "Let him go!" she screamed. She was walking through the lawn now. Her socks were covered in mud, each step, a "squish." The bushes were in the way, but she thought maybe a surprise attack would send it up flying, and it did. As she ran toward it, the hawk grabbed hold tight of Mason's furry friend and lifted up off the ground. She could hear Mason shrieking inside as she watched the squirrel, looking at her, being carried off down the street. She took a few steps backwards. *Stevie can never go outside again*, she thought, as Josh's car pulled up in the driveway. He rolled down his window as he approached her, still standing in her muddy socks holding the stick, Mason still screaming inside.

"You won't believe what I just saw!" Josh said. "A hawk, carrying a squirrel, flying down the street! It was unbelievable! Like out of a movie or something!"

"It was Mason's squirrel," she said, realizing that she was standing in mud armed with a stick. "He likes to look at them out the window." Resigned, she tossed the stick and turned to Josh. "I'll finish getting them packed," she said and sat down on the garden bench to remove her socks.

"We're going out kind of nice this weekend," he said. "Can you pack them with something a little more special to wear?"

"I'll see what they have." She walked up the driveway and opened the door. Mason came running out, grabbing Josh's legs.

"Daddy, that bird took the squirrel!" Mason said between sobs. He fell into Josh's arms and rested his head on his shoulder. "Come inside, I'll show you!"

Josh looked at Becca for approval, and she held the door open for the two of them to walk in. Josh took a look around, while still holding Mason, now sniffling and rubbing his nose on Josh's shirt. "See, it was right out here," he was telling him, pointing out the window. She could hear the story being told as she walked upstairs to the boys' rooms, gathering more clothes. Khakis and a rugby, maybe? She came downstairs to find the three of them playing on the ground, Stevie next to Josh, sniffing his face.

She stood for a bit watching. She had never seen this before. *Is this what it could have looked like?* she wondered, as she held the little rugby in front of her, folding in the arms and then down in half. They were talking a little more about the weekend. They were going for ice cream and the zoo. She walked into the kitchen to put the last few things in their suitcase when she heard Mason...

"She's coming, too?" he asked. It stopped Becca in her tracks. "She's nice, Daddy. Sarah and Rachey, too?"

"Yes," he whispered quietly, looking up to see Becca holding the suitcase in the kitchen doorway.

"They're packed. I'll change Oliver and then they're all ready," she said, lifting Oliver out of the bouncy chair and carrying him towards the stairs.

"I'll put Mason and the suitcase in the car," he said, picking up both and heading towards the door. Becca took Oliver into his room and lay him down on the changing table. He smiled at her as he grabbed his toes and rocked just a bit from side to side.

"It's time for Boys' Weekend Yea!" she said, her voice breaking on the "yea" part. She slowly changed him, lining up the tabs just right, pulling the diaper out from the elastic part that was tight around his legs. She wondered if Josh took the time to do this on Boys' Weekend Yea! Or maybe *the girl* did it. She was beginning to wonder a lot about what was going on during Boys' Weekend Yea!

This is the story of when I buy……

It will make me feel better, she thought, as she turned into the parking lot. Tori had said that the record store was small, but as Becca walked into the tiny space, she couldn't imagine that anyone much bigger than herself could even maneuver around the large record rack in the center. The albums were divided just as they had been when she was young, A-Z but, of course, the more popular bands had their very own plastic dividers labeled with their names. Some were new, but many were used. The used ones were more interesting. A girl named Andrea had written her name on the cover of one by Wings; it was in pen down the lady's leg. *Bummer*, Becca thought, that it had been defaced as she grabbed it from the stack. The pile grew quickly after that—two by the cool lady in the black cape, one by the guy with the long blonde hair that sang with her, one with the space ship (or was it that Simon game? She still didn't know). The eight-legged heart caught her eye, and she quickly put it on top of her collection. As she left, carrying the albums, she did feel better; it *did* make her feel better…

She picked up an Illinois Entertainer on her way out. The magazine used to be bigger and glossier; now it was more like newsprint with more matte black and whites than color pictures. It still had all the listings of all the shows in the city, all the old venues as before, and maybe a few new ones. On Lincoln and Lill, Lillian's was still hosting shows. This Saturday, In Big Trouble at 8; That's Taylor's, at 9; and Izzy Loves to Spin, at 10:30.

The pictures next to their names had been printed terribly, or they all had grown moustaches and their hair was blowing into each other's faces. She could somewhat make out the lead singer in the middle. She hadn't seen him, or them, in years. She just happened to be free Saturday night, too.

The rules...

There are some things that she had learned from her brother that you needed to know about going to shows.

First, if you are going to a show, wear just a T-shirt and jeans. If you're gonna be cold after, bring a flannel. DO NOT *WEAR* THE FLANNEL.

Second, if you are going to wear a concert T-shirt, make sure you know the band. For instance, if you're wearing a Ramone's T-shirt, know all the band members' names and at least four of their songs. Sounds arbitrary, but it isn't. Someone is bound to challenge you: "You don't know them. Name three songs they sing." You'll be able to spit off three and then look like you're able to plow into more by starting a fourth. Then you can stop yourself and say, "That's right, you only wanted three."

Finally, if you're wearing a CBGB T-shirt, you better be able to explain the letters: Country Bluegrass Blues. If it also has OMFUG, you better know it stands for Other Music For Uplifting Gormandizers. Some might argue that it's Other Music Found Underground. Keep your cool, then and go on to explain that a "gormandizer" is a voracious eater of, in this case, music. That will shut them up.

Now, in the case of Izzy Loves to Spin, you just needed to know who Izzy was. Izzy was the lead singer's niece, Isabelle. He used to take her to the park and spin her on the tire swing. She would laugh and say funny things only a 4-year-old would say. These funny little quips would eventually show up in the lyrics of his songs. *Izzy must be almost 12 years old by now,* Becca thought. *She probably prefers to be called Isabelle.*

Walking into a show always reminded her of just how short she really was. People never realized that their beer hung out at just about the same level where her head was. But she had become pretty much the master of zooming through a crowd, ducking the beer-holding height; it was only her friends who slowed her down. She could run the gauntlet from the back of the bar to the stage in less than a minute, but her taller friends had to work around the people like obstacles. Tonight she wasn't looking for the stage, though. Hanging towards the back by tables suited her just fine.

Elle was dressed in a black blouse and jeans and was already complaining that her heels were sticking to the floor. Becca was dressed more appropriately, her Ramones T-shirt featuring Joey, Johnny, Dee Dee and Marky—who, by the way, sang "The KKK Took My Baby Away," "I Want To Be Your Boyfriend," "Bonzo Goes to Bitburg" and "Needles and..." oh wait, that's three already. Her jeans were rolled just the right amount over her combat boots with the slightest bit of skin showing, and her flannel was tied perfectly sloppily around her waist. She could have been any of the others there, although they probably weren't hiding stretch marks under their knotted shirts.

"I'm surprised you wanted to come here," Elle screamed over That's Taylor's cover of "Time After Time." It was a sad version, and the lead singer clung onto the mike stand as if wounded while mumbling the lyrics.

"Let's just stay back here," Becca said, as she took a quick look around and sipped her light beer. She actually hated beer, but that was the look here at Lillian's. Some things just don't change.

That's Taylor's ended with one of their own songs. It was something about wanting some girl back. It wasn't very original or good. They had played long enough, though, so the bar owner had grabbed the mike.

"Izzy Loves To Spin in two minutes, folks," he said, holding up two fingers for those that couldn't hear.

Elle looked at Becca. She shook her head and twisted herself to put her beer on the table behind her. "Izzy Loves to Spin?" she asked, with her eyes opened up wide enough that Becca could actually see the whites of them in the fairly dark room. Becca turned her back on her just in time to see them take the stage.

"Hey guys, sorry we're late. Let's hear it for That's Taylor's!" The crowd erupted with applause for the retiring band. Apparently, they were a fan favorite. "I just got one question before we start," the lead singer said, leaning against the same mike that had just held up That's Taylor's lead singer. "Hey Becca, did you ever marry that guy you dumped me for?"

He broke into Badfinger's "Baby Blue" at that moment. Elle's mouth went completely slack-jawed as she turned to look at Becca, but Becca didn't notice. He was singing their song.

Well, if we're going to be completely honest (OK, fine, it's just a bit about Becca, and you really shouldn't judge...)

It had been the summer after graduation. Josh was backpacking through Spain, and Becca had been taking some courses towards her master's degree while working during the day at Crate & Barrel downtown. Once in a while, she would receive an email from Josh. He was traveling before law school started in the fall. One last fun thing before reality kicked in, he would tell people. Considering she was part of the "reality," that didn't feel so great, but she would smile and let out a small laugh.

In the morning, she would take the bus to work, after work, the bus to school, after school, the El to home. It was a good routine until that Friday. Katie was locked out of her apartment and was heading to the bar around the corner, Lillian's, to find Jeremy; he had the keys and was drinking there with friends.

"Please come meet me here!" she had hollered over the phone. "Jeremy wants me to stay. The music is pretty good, too!" In the background, Becca could hear the crowd singing. Were they singing *me and my red ho*?

"Katie, I'm just on my way home. It's been a long day," Becca said.

"Oh, you think *you're* tired?" Katie responded. "Do I need to remind you…"

No, she absolutely did not. You didn't complain to Katie about being tired. No one was more tired than Katie. It had been four months since she was released from the hospital. Her physical therapy was only once a week. The only reminder of Katie's stroke, really, was her memory, or lack of it. Katie would often tell the same story again and again and again. Elle would say, "You already told us that, Katie!" but Becca would just listen again and again and again. If she didn't have time, she found, "Oh, you mentioned that," to be quite helpful.

In school, Katie had been a whiz at math and Becca just wasn't. Becca had spent endless hours under Katie's tutelage of balancing algebraic equations. It just wasn't happening. "Can't you just tell me how much each letter is worth? I have a great memory! I'll just memorize them all!" Becca had reasoned. Katie had only broken the smallest smile that day. She was always patient reminding her to take the steps slowly. Now it was Becca's turn to be patient, as Katie needed to take her steps slowly now, too.

"I'll be there in a few," Becca said. There it was again, *me and my red soul*? She had heard some pretty crazy audience participation songs, but this was just weird. She hung up and turned towards Lillian's. Sheffield to Lincoln is one block, Fullerton to Lill, maybe a block and a half. Walk faster, she thought. Lots of people were out and about that night. She would have changed to go to Lillian's, but her work/school clothes would have to do. It was her shoes she was worried about—those sticky bar floors. She had never worn her prettiest shoes to one till that night. She walked past Katie and Jeremy's condo, noticing the For Sale sign in the window. They had been together since high school, finishing up college together just months before and now selling their place for something bigger. She passed the corner and could hear the music now.

She was always impressed with witty names. Lillian's was, of course, a play on "Lill ends," as it did kind of dead-end here. Across the street was a beautiful little park. Lill continued one more block west. Their place would probably sell quickly on location alone, then they would move downtown where they both had jobs already. Their wedding was in the fall. Katie's bridesmaids' dresses were teal with a braided trim. Ugly, but it matched her jewel tone theme. After last spring, everyone was just happy to be dancing at her wedding at all, even if it meant dancing in the matching dyed-teal satin pumps.

The band on stage had been playing covers that night. Katie was right, the music was good. Becca stood at the door scanning the crowd before she finally saw Katie towards the front with Jeremy and two other guys near the bar. She quickly slipped through the crowd maneuvering around the many beer bottles in her head-height path.

"Thank god!" Katie had screamed when she saw Becca suddenly appear behind Jeremy. "Let's go dance!" Dancing had always been their thing. Katie's steps were a bit shaky still, but they moved closer to the stage and listened as the lead singer talked about his niece, Isabelle.

"This is one of her favorites," he explained and began singing Badfinger's "Baby Blue." Becca gave a little jump of excitement and cracked the heel tap off her pretty shoe. He had noticed her slipping it off and looking at the heel, no longer covered with the tiny black tip. Becca was too absorbed in the catastrophe to even notice he was watching her. She disappeared out of sight to bend down and pull the tip from between two floorboards. When she popped up with it, she saw him smiling at her. She looked over her shoulder to see who he was directing the cute smile to, but behind her was just a group of guys. She turned back to see him smiling again, this time laughing in her direction.

"He's smiling at you!" Katie was screaming into her ear. "Smile back!"

Becca gave a small smile and began the repair of her shoe, fitting the heel tap back on, in a lopsided kind of way. It was wiggling back and forth; she was never going to be able to wear it home.

"Hey, I got a good one," the lead singer said, just after the last chord faded away. He winked at her and started the first few notes of "Tiny Dancer." Becca could feel herself blushing as the whole crowd joined in. He was cute, maybe about her age. He had a ponytail and that great smile. In college, he would have been just what she was looking for, but now her plan was already in play. She wasn't looking for a guy with a ponytail and a nice smile, even if he played guitar and sang to her. She and Josh would be getting engaged soon. That was, as Josh would say, reality.

They decided it was too late for Becca to go home, so Becca agreed on a sleepover and walked to Katie's after the last song. "He was cute, Bex," Katie had said as Becca brushed her teeth. "He was just the kind of guy you would have gone for before Josh." Yes, he was.

The poster Becca had made for Katie had been leaning against the wall, tucked behind the door. The poster board was bright pink, but she could see some other colors behind it: turquoise, white, maybe a few white. Becca walked over, the toothbrush still dangling from her mouth, and closed the door just a bit.

"Those were all so great," Katie said. "They were so nice to look at. Your poem was great, did I already tell you that?"

"No," Becca said, but Katie had, many times. It was just good to hear, that's all.

"I swear, you guys would come in and not know what to say. It was so weird. I mean, you're my friends. I knew who you were, I just couldn't put the words together, that's all. That day, when you walked down the hall and past my room? I saw you. I knew who you were. I just couldn't call out, ya know? It was *you* who didn't recognize *me*."

Becca looked at the pictures on the pink board, still holding the brush in her mouth. "Yeah, I'm sorry about that."

"Cuz they shaved my head, right? You didn't know me without all of this!" she said, rubbing her new pixie do. The pictures on the board were what Katie called BS, Before Stroke, and in those, she had the long, wavy hair everyone was used to. "I think Jeremy misses it more than I do."

"It's growing back," Becca said, filing through the boards behind the door. Doctors had asked family and friends to make collages to hang on her walls. The hospital room had been plastered with them. Becca had used some pictures from high school, like their prom pics with Katie's shimmering blue eyeshadow and Becca's now infamous, "Little Bo-Peep" dress. Some from college, like when they had visited KU together for the first time. They had gotten lost going from town to their dorm and had finally called a cab. Upon giving him the address, the cab driver had driven them three driveways before letting them out. They had spent that night in the dreary room, eating pizza on paper towels from the bathroom down the hall. A picture of Katie holding the mushroom za was there, too. The oldest picture was of them in their first bikinis, running in circles underneath Katie's Donald Duck sprinkler. Some were more recent: parties at Allie's, Becca and Katie with Josh and Jeremy. Some of Dana and Elle. They had made their own posters, as well.

"It could happen again, ya know. It could. I could die. I mean, what if I die?" Katie asked.

"Katie, you're doing great. Don't even think about that. The doctors said everything is good. Let's not worry, OK?" Becca said.

"It could happen again. It could be worse," she said.

"Or, it could never happen again," Becca said. "Let's talk about your wedding instead."

"You shouldn't be with Josh," Katie said. "He's not right for you, Bex. I mean, does he even make you happy anymore?"

"I'm happy, Katie. I am," she argued.

"Really? I don't even know if I am. A lot of exciting things are happening, but I did think it would be different. It's not really exciting at all," Katie said. "What if my whole life is just like this?"

"Like what?" Becca asked.

"Boring. I mean, we'll have beautiful things. The registry is almost done. I may have to go back and register for more, even. The new place will be great. Jobs are good. But, Bex, it's not exciting or anything. I mean, is this it? My whole life?" Katie asked. "And his mom, she's really a bitch, Becca. You should have heard her the other day. I just had my nails done and I went with blue, something different, ya know? Oh my god, you should have heard it! 'Katie, that color is awful! I sure hope you don't wear that to the wedding. Definitely not to the shower I'm throwing. Ugh, your taste! Who wears that?'" Katie was looking at her hands now. The truth was, Katie had beautiful hands. She could wear whatever color she wanted. Colors only she could make look good. "She's so critical. And I'm signing on for a life of it!"

"She seems nice enough. I've never heard her—"

"It comes out of nowhere. People think I have no filter anymore? She doesn't even have an excuse. I suppose it would be funny, maybe, if it were directed at someone else, I guess," Katie said.

"Have you talked to Jeremy about any of this?"

"He's different now."

"Different how?"

"He's just different... You shouldn't be with Josh," Katie said.

"Yeah, you mentioned that."

That night, as she fell asleep on their leather sofa, the one Katie and Jeremy had bought because they knew, in the future, their kids could never ruin it, Becca thought of the guy with the ponytail, who sang her a song.

One week later, and there still had been no email from Josh in Spain. He had called, once, and had left a quick message about some people they had met in Barcelona. They would be traveling on with them and he would call from their next stop. Becca hadn't even noticed the week had gone by. Busy with school, frustrated by his lack of calling and, most importantly, totally consumed with the man who she and Katie now called, "Ponytail Guy." Izzy Loves to Spin was back at Lillian's that weekend. This time, she would be dressed more appropriately and in better shoes.

"Going to see Ponytail Guy Friday?" Katie had asked at coffee with Elle the day before.

"Who's Ponytail Guy?" Elle had asked, with a smirk towards Becca.

"He's the lead singer of Izzy Loves to Spin," Katie had said, rolling her eyes up to the sky and fanning herself with the Third Coast menu. "He's hot. He likes Becca."

"He does not," Becca had said, somewhat fishing for more. She had been a little nervous about going to the show. Playing with fire was exciting but dangerous, she knew. "He's in a band. They all smile at all the girls. That's how they get us to come to the shows."

"I'm in!" Elle had said. "Maybe he'll smile at me!"

He better not, Becca had thought.

And it all started out not so innocently at all... really!

Friday night, Izzy Loves to Spin had ended their set around 1. Becca, Elle and Katie had stood outside the bar having a heated argument: What would be better right now, French fries or pancakes?

"Well, of course pancakes," Ponytail Guy had said, as he walked out from the alley. "Where are we going?"

"We're going to Tempo," Elle said, changing from her French fry vote to the breakfast-24-7 place rather quickly.

"That's the other side of town," Becca said, without calling her on it.

"That's right by my place," he said. "Let's go."

"That's right by your place too, Becca," Elle said with a wink.

"Did I ever tell you about the time I took the El and missed my stop?" Katie started to say as they climbed up the stairs to the train. "I was trying to go to the library..."

"Right, and you missed it and kept going around and around," Elle said quickly, finishing the story for her.

They each took a seat, Katie and Elle across from Becca and Ponytail Guy, his guitar case standing between his legs. "So what did you think of the show tonight?" he asked.

"It was great," Elle said. "You know, Becca knows all about music. Ask her anything, really, anything."

"Not everything," Becca said, feeling embarrassed and shooting Elle a stink eye.

"You like music, Becca?" he asked.

"Yeah," Becca said, as Elle rolled her eyes.

"What do you like to listen to?"

"The older stuff, '70s stuff, a lot of the stuff *you* play, really."

"That's cool. You play anything?"

"No, I don't play anything. I've always wanted to play guitar, though. It's kind of hard cuz I have little fingers." *Shut up, Becca,* she thought.

"I don't know if that matters," he said, looking at her hands, then slowly taking one in his. "They look fine to me."

Becca heard Elle's foot kick Katie's just before she yelled, "Ow!" They got off at the stop and made their way down the steps again. "I can't be out too late. We're going to the caterer's for a tasting early tomorrow," Katie reminded them.

"Yeah, you mentioned that," Becca added.

"You getting married soon?" he asked.

"Four months," Katie said. "I think we'll only do chicken or fish, though. Not too many people want meat anymore."

"You were thinking vegetarian too, I think, right?" Becca asked.

"Right, vegetarian too," Katie said. "Jeremy wants a chocolate cake. It's going to ruin my dress…"

"I thought you were going to talk to him about that," Becca said.

"Right," Katie said, nodding her head.

The 24-hour restaurant was packed, but they managed to get a corner booth and the four of them sat and ate pancakes and French fries for a while. "I like Chicago, still getting used to it," he said.

"Becca knows the city like the back of her hand. Watch this, Becca, what number is Belmont?" Elle asked with a wink.

Becca raised her eyebrows at her. "I have no idea."

"Yes, you do," Elle said. "She knows them all. She'd be a great tour guide, too. She loves all the architecture. Becca, you should show him around the city."

"Sounds good. I'm free tomorrow," he said.

"Look, we better go," Katie reminded them again. "I have an early appointment tomorrow with the caterer."

"Yeah, you mentioned that," Becca said. "I really should be getting home, too."

"So," Ponytail Guy started... "Katie, she doesn't have too much of a memory, huh?"

"Short-term is pretty bad, sometimes," Becca said, walking next to him towards his apartment. "She had a stroke a little while ago. She's actually doing very well, considering."

"Really? She OK?" he asked.

"Yeah, of course."

Ponytail Guy pointed to the buzzers and the short list of three names that was hidden in the wall. "This is me." The comic book store below his apartment still had people inside. "I can grab my car, drop you home? Or do you want to maybe come up for a bit?"

Becca looked down at her perfectly appropriate bar shoes. "I probably should get home," she started.

"Yeah," he said. "You mentioned that..."

He opened the door to his apartment, and she apprehensively peeked inside. She was not supposed to be here, she knew, but she was curious about how he lived. Josh certainly hadn't been curious about her and what she was doing. He would never need to know.

It was a small studio, just enough for a sofa and table on one side and a bed on the other. The kitchen was tucked away in the corner, and on the counter she could see a box of cereal, a carton of milk and a big plastic red bowl. *"Me and my red bowl"* started in her head. Now it made sense!

"So, pick that one up over there," he said. There was a small guitar in the corner leaning against a laundry basket full of clothes. "Sorry about the mess. I don't usually live like this." It was clear that he did; his mess was actually very organized. His dirty clothes in a basket, and his breakfast ready to go. "Have you played before?"

"No, never. I've always wanted to, though," she replied, picking up the guitar. It was much heavier than she had expected and it banged her ankle as she swung it up. He gave a little laugh and gestured for her to sit down across from him on the sofa. The two of them sat with their guitars between them. She tried to keep her eyes on the guitar but could feel him looking at her.

"You do have little hands," he said, looking at them slowly strumming the strings.

"Well, if they were big I'd look pretty goofy so..." *Oh my god, shut up, Becca*, she thought.

He reached for her left hand and placed it on some strings, then picked up her right hand and held it in his. He looked at her and slowly dragged her hand down the strings making an awful sound. "Just like that," he said, then let go.

This isn't going to be easy, she thought, *and learning to play guitar isn't going to be either.*

For the next four weeks, Becca didn't miss Josh, nope, not at all....

Not exactly an audience participation song...

"I wrote this song for an old friend of mine who just happens to be here tonight. This one's for you, Blue." It was a ballad, dare she say, a love song? Elle looked at her, covering her smile with both hands but removing them once or twice to hit the table she was sitting at.

This rhyme scheme wasn't as clever as his older stuff. Didn't matter. As Becca clasped her hands together in front of her chest, he looked right at her.

And that guy who's far away

That guy you wait for everyday

That guy who's your reality

That guy who's going to replace me

Well, you could have mentioned that...

Just a few months ago, that line would have been funny, but not now. It wasn't his fault, though. How could he know? How could he have ever known?

They say it might snow…

Becca had been getting her nails done that morning. At nine months, she was ready to burst and couldn't reach her toes. She couldn't decide between Ballet Slippers and the one just a shade lighter. She needed to hurry home for an engagement party for Josh's friend, so the manicurist had finally chosen for her. The luncheon was at noon, but the sitter would be there in just an hour. They had been discussing what she would wear when the noise overhead started.

"Oh my god! What is that?" Becca had asked.

"Helicopter!" the lady had screamed back pointing to the sky. "For the hospital!"

"Is it always so loud?" Becca had asked, wanting to cover her ears, but not being able to with the Ballet Slippers still tacky.

"Sometimes," she had answered, and started putting the quick dry coat on.

Becca and Josh drove to the party in silence that day. They stood next to each other during the speeches, shared cute stories about Mason, wished the couple all the happiness in the world. Then, her phone rang in her purse. "Katie" was on the screen. "I'm sorry," Becca said. "Just a minute," signaling to their hosts. "Katie, I can't talk right now, I'm at a party. Can I call you back?"

"Becca, it's Jeremy. Katie's had a stroke. It's bad Becca. It's bad," she heard Jeremy say in a shaky, quiet voice. "Call everyone, Becca. Call everyone. And Becca, get here. Get here fast."

The ride to the hospital seemed endless. She dialed numbers and gave info to everyone she could think of. *Where was Elle? Why wasn't she answering her phone?* She checked her texts for a response but ended up just scrolling through and finding the one that Katie had last sent:

Sat. Oct 3, 11:58 PM

The deer caught up with its family. I knew you would be worried :)

That's right, the last time she saw Katie was the night with the deer. They had talked in the car. Katie had made her make that promise. Ugh, why did she have to go and promise that anyway?

"Katie Kaplan," she heard Josh say to the woman at the front desk. The lady in the blue blazer scrolled through her computer screen, scanning for the name.

"I'm sorry, no Katie Kaplan here," she said.

"Katie Marx," Becca heard herself say.

Once again, the lady scrolled through the computer screen in front of her. This time her shoulders went up just the littlest bit as she recognized the name on the screen. "CCU. Take that elevator. On the seventh floor, make a right."

She heard Josh say thank you and the two walked quietly to the elevator. They weren't talking or holding hands. It was a quiet and lonely ride up. When the elevator door opened, Becca saw lots of people waiting around. She slowly recognized some of their faces. Some stood up when they saw her, like Marnie, a friend from middle school, Alyssa, a college friend.

"Becca, I can't believe it," Marnie had said. "I just talked to her yesterday. She was fine, Becca. She was fine." Marnie was crying on her shoulder now, hugging her and trembling. "Jeremy is with her. He came out here a little while ago. He said that she woke up this morning with a headache, Becca.

She said her head hurt and..." Marnie was getting the words out through her sobs, but Becca's mind clung to "headache" and "woke up this morning." She had been awake. She had known. Katie had been awake and had known what was happening, and it was everything she had been afraid of.

Becca could see the swinging doors over Marnie's shoulder and slowly let go of her to walk towards them. The little vertical windows in the doors allowed for a peek down the hall and to the nurses' station. There was a man leaning over the desk. He straightened up and turned around. It was Jeremy. He started walking down the hall to the doors. He held the hair off his forehead with one hand; his cell phone dangled from the other. He opened the door and could barely get the words out.

"Becca..." was all he could say. He grabbed her arm and pulled her down the hall. They passed just a few rooms before he abruptly turned and lead her into a small glass room with a machine that was keeping a steady beat. She could hear air, going in, going out and then, finally, she looked at Katie, lying on the bed, connected to the tubes connected to the machines. She had always had the prettiest hands. Becca reached out and took one.

"Katie?" she whispered. She leaned closer, "Katie?" she managed to say louder.

"Becca, she can't hear you. She just...her head hurt. She said she had a headache. I called as fast as I could. The ambulance got to us so fast, so fast, Becca," Jeremy said, sitting in the chair behind her, his head in his hands.

Becca stood on her tiptoes and got right up to her ear, "Katie!" she screamed.

"Becca," he said, without even looking up, "she's gone."

A short while later, Becca pressed the arrow pointing down for the elevator as Katie's mother-in-law was walking towards her down the quiet hall. She had always been sweet to Becca, making her wonder why Katie had felt uncomfortable with Jeremy's mom. Becca felt her hand on her shoulder.

"Becca, I'm so sorry. I know she was a good friend to you. She really loved you, Becca. She really did."

The elevator beeped then, and the doors slowly opened; Elle stepped out quickly. She had run from the parking lot in her nylons and was now walking in ripped stockings holding her shoes. Her hair and makeup were a mess, an Ellington visitor badge, stuck at an angle on her untucked shirt. She saw Becca and knew right away. "No," she said. "No, Bex, no, no, no."

Becca couldn't get the words out. She opened her mouth and then she heard it.

"Elle, you got so fat! What happened to you?" It was Jeremy's mom, standing over her shoulder. Elle's eyes went huge as she fell into Becca's arms. Becca looked up at the sky.

"*Katie, did you hear that?*" she thought, and hid her laughter in Elle's hair.

It had snowed the night before. The sun shone through the curtains, and Becca rolled over to look out the window. Fresh snow was falling off the branches and onto the walk in front of their house. Becca closed her eyes and shielded them from the sun. Josh was up with Mason watching TV. She sat up and dangled her feet off the side of the bed. She looked at the outfit she had taken out the night before. Gray sweater, plaid, wool skirt, black booties, still in the box with the block letters on top.

She was reading the texts on her phone.

"I can't believe it snowed," Elle said.

"I'm wearing boots. Can we drive together?" Dana asked.

"I'll wear tights," Elle tapped in.

"Josh!" she yelled, "I don't have tights." She heard her voice. What a stupid thing to say, she thought, as she got out of bed and touched the hem of the skirt. "Josh, I don't have tights!" she yelled again, as she saw him standing in the doorway to their bedroom.

"I can get you some," he said. "What time do you need to be there? Becca?"

She was still holding the hem of the skirt, looking out the window. Katie had liked the snow. Becca remembered walking on campus, helping each other as they slid on the icy hill by the Chancellor's house, holding the fence as they made their way down the twisted path. By the time they got to their house, they were wet and shivering. Today, Becca would help Katie in the snow.

"10:15," she finally mumbled, and walked into the bathroom, slowly clicking the door shut behind her.

One more try with Ponytail Guy...

He was surprised that she had two sons, not about the divorce. He still lived in the same apartment. It may have been a different laundry basket, but it was definitely in the same place. He had several guitars lined up on stands against the wall now. The sofa they had been sitting on was just as uncomfortable as it had been years ago. There was a real life waiting for her at the end of Boys' Weekend Yea, but she was 22 again in this moment. It was like old times, like things hadn't changed at all.

"You hungry?" he asked from the kitchen, with a crunch at the end. She could see his shadow approaching on the curtains. He was cradling something big in one arm and holding something rather dainty in the other.

She knew that sound. She turned around to see Ponytail Guy in his sweatpants and ripped Foreigner T-shirt, a spoon in one hand and the red bowl in the other. She figured the bacteria in that old, red bowl would be enough to quarantine Mason's entire pre-school, and the amount of sugar that he was consuming in there would make a horrifying visit to the dentist. No, he hadn't changed at all. Not the slightest bit.

Trouble was, she had.

Set an intention, breathe...

Becca drove down the windy street to the beach. The city had done a renovation just last year—a new cedar walkway with matching benches, a lagoon and, most importantly, today anyway, a building for the community to use. They had parties here, book clubs, children's activities and, every Saturday and Sunday at 8:45, yoga. Elle was waiting outside, sitting on one of the new benches, specifically built to help you sit with proper posture as you gazed at the lake.

"Let's go!" Elle called out and grabbed her perfectly rolled yoga mat. She looked great in her yoga pants and matching jacket. "You ready, Bex? Oh, you're gonna love this. You really are."

Becca stopped in her tracks when she saw the stunning new building. The perfect glass cube sat right on the sand overlooking the lagoon. Past that, just the beautiful lake, then, the sun.

Elle found a spot towards the front of the room and gestured for Becca. She began unrolling her bright green mat and Becca followed. Becca's was brand new from the store. When she went to lay it out, it was still holding its rolled-up shape. Becca looked at it with the edge rolling in. "Does it matter what side I use?" she asked.

"No, the mat is your space. Whatever you want to do. Up to you," Elle answered, walking to pick up foam blocks from the corner. Elle sat on one and tossed one to Becca who followed suit, joining the others in meditation looking towards the water.

"Good morning. As we return to our mats today, let's clear our minds from the virtual storms we all certainly have," the lady in the Lululemon instructed. "—our kids, our jobs, our spouses, our friends, our parents. Breathe… and hands to heart. Let's start with an intention. Remember, an intention isn't something you have, it's something you give…"

An old, new playground…

Stevie couldn't be outside off leash anymore since the day with the hawk, squirrel, mud and stick, so once again, Becca stood holding Stevie's leash as she lay on the front lawn watching the cars zoom by. When the large truck pulled to the side of the road at her neighbor Marc's house, she watched as three men piled out, one with a clipboard, the other two dressed for messier work in their already stained shirts and cargo pants.

"Hey, Becca," Marc called, taking the clipboard from the nicer dressed man who was now off chasing the other two, clearly with directions.

"What's going on over there?" she asked, gesturing to the truck.

"I'm getting rid of Danny's playground today. He's getting older, and I could really use the space," he said, pointing towards the backyard.

"Where's it going?"

"Dunno. They're taking it apart and taking it away is all I know. You guys want it?"

"Seriously?" Becca asked, hopefully, imagining Mason standing at the top of the slide and speeding down with his hands in the air.

"Hold on," he said, gesturing to her and running into the backyard. Becca turned to look back into the house. Oliver, still playing on his blanket and Mason, drawing pictures at the dining table, now doubling as a craft table. Those Brady Bunch windows really gave a great view, she thought. Stevie was up now, smelling something in the hedges that hid their house, somewhat, from the street and finally getting ready to pee. "Becca," Marc said, startling her a bit. "They can bring it right over and set it up if you want. It's $125 for the assembly, though. That OK?"

She looked back at the boys once again. "That would be perfect," she said. The nicer dressed man with the clipboard appeared then, and the three of them walked towards her backyard.

"*There's* Danny's bat. Sorry, Becca. I can't get him to put anything away," he said, quickly picking it up off her lawn and then using it as a walking stick as he followed into Becca's backyard.

"Right here?" she said to them, pointing towards a shady area of weeds. "I'd like to surprise the boys. Is it pretty easy to set up?"

He gave a thumbs-up that Becca quickly returned, then she picked up Stevie and walked toward the front with Marc. "How much for the playground?" she asked him.

"Becca, you're doing me a favor. This is actually a bit of an investment for me. Thanks for taking it," he said. Becca returned the thanks and carried Stevie into the house to find the boys still busy at play, Oliver banging something plastic into something else plastic and Mason hard at work.

An investment?

The noise was beginning in the backyard, so Becca picked up an album, put it on the turntable and let the sound cover the noise from the construction. "What are you working on there?" she asked Mason.

At school, the children were still drawing pictures and dictating their stories to the teachers. Mason's drawings were clearer now. Becca knew she had long hair, Josh didn't, and Mason was bigger than Oliver. The dining table had been covered in construction paper, crayons and lined paper for weeks. Now, Becca could make out a small figure next to tiny yellow gobs on the ground.

"It's the day at the zoo," Mason finally said. "When I'm done, you can write my words."

She looked out the window to see the two men carrying more pieces across her front yard and disappearing into the back. She had forgotten she was still holding the album cover in her hand and looked down at the pretty lady in jeans and loosely ribbed, over-sized sweater. She was sitting on a window seat with one knee bent exposing her bare foot, her other must have been keeping her balance on the floor. The sun was shining on only half of her face through the tapestry-like curtains.

"I'm ready, Mommy," Mason said, handing her a crayon and a lined piece of paper. "Ready? OK, so this is me at the zoo. I'm running, chasing ducks, and you and Daddy are behind me, and the rain is coming, and you're saying 'Mason, we need to leave it's gonna rain!'"

Becca sat completely still, the crayon didn't even tremble in her hand. "Do you remember our day at the zoo?" she asked him.

"Yeah, Mommy. Now write, K?" he said, pushing her hand, slightly.

"So, this is me at the zoo…." he began again. She started writing, carefully, remembering to not change his words or sentence structure, just as Miss Peggy had explained. *This is how Mason saw it,* Becca reminded herself—*as a beautiful day—don't change his view.*

You can't judge an album by its cover...

She was following along with Allie's students as they wound around the galleries, stopping at select paintings before unfolding their stools to sit down. These lectures were meant for classes only, so, if they wandered into a room and a security guard was watching, Allie would either give her a subtle signal or simply give her the spiel that meant it was time to scram. "This class is for registered students," she would say to her curtly. "If you're interested, go register. We would love to have you join us!" Then, she would wink and continue her speech. Today, they were in the American Artist's wing viewing "Arrangement in Gray and Black Number 1." Allie jerked her head to the side, gesturing to the security guard standing in the corner. With that, Becca moved toward the wall and began to read the stenciled lettering next to the painting.

Despite Whistler's intentions, the reception of the painting could not be divorced from its sitter, and it was soon better known as "Whistler's Mother"... Becca read it again, trying to figure out exactly what that meant. People simply could not think of it as anything else? Would that mean that the identity of the painting, even though the artist wants it to be one thing, would actually be determined by others? Given, the title was easier to remember and kinda catchy, but is that really how this works? Would others decide if she were "Becca Gold" or "Josh's Ex-wife?" She assumed she would hold both titles now, regardless of how she felt. Maybe it would be up to the others, as well. She could hear Allie lecturing behind her. "His range of palette is so small, but he does so much with it…"

How did they stand so still for so long? Becca wondered about the people on the canvases. Didn't they get anxious or have something to do? There was a tired-looking woman staring back at her from the wall. "Mother and Child" by Gari Melchers, she read off the plaque. She was clearly working class, dressed in brown with threads sticking out of the seam on her shoulder. The baby she held was staring at her, too. The woman looked tired, but still had beautiful eyes. Maybe she was young, maybe she was just remembering when she was.

"This class is for registered students. If you're interested, go register. We would love to have you join us!" Allie called over, as she winked and mouthed "Sorry." Becca took her cue and stepped into the hall. They probably had a picture of her up in the break room by now. ALERT: LOOK OUT FOR THIS PERSON, with her picture underneath. They would probably be charging her for a lot of lessons by now.

There was another lecture in the exhibit down the hall. The people were taking off their shoes and socks and lining them up against the wall, stepping up onto an art installation and then walking on the paths of pebbles or the sand surrounding them. They were being told to be participants and explore. The docent waved for her to join, but Becca remembered how badly she was in need of a pedicure and walked past. Instead, she found an installation that reminded her a lot of the structure she and Mason had built in the house, the one she sometimes fell asleep in on Boys' Weekend Yea!

"It's a maze," the guard told her. "You can go in," and she gestured to the entrance. There were speakers overhead that seemed to be turned to a radio station playing disturbing stories as she approached red, plastic curtains hanging in front of her. She separated them carefully and walked through to the next box where she found purple ones just three steps ahead. She parted those to find green, stepped ahead and parted those to find blue, parted those to find a … dead end. It startled her and she turned around to go back but stopped herself. She touched the wall. No, it wasn't a dead end, just muslin fabric that looked like a wall. She parted the first layer, then the second, to find purple velvet drapes a few feet ahead. They were heavier to pull apart, but when she did, she looked ahead to see another set. As she stepped forward, they closed behind her and the cube got dark. She quickly took five steps and pulled the next set apart. She was back in the light again. There was a shelf on the wall with a pitcher of orange juice and stack of cups.

What the hell was that? Becca thought to herself as she made her way down the corridor. She waved and smiled at the guard who was already sending more patrons into the first curtain. She walked to the Modern Wing to wait for Allie, sat in front of the silly picture on the wall and took out her phone. *I'm at the Twombly,* she texted.

You're becoming a bit predictable, Allie texted back. *I'll be there in five.*

Becca looked around a bit before snapping a picture of the splatters and gobs and dashes in front of her. She was still looking at the screen when Allie appeared, taking the phone from her hand. "So, what did you see?" Allie asked in a sing-song voice.

"I went through a maze of colorful curtains," Becca said. "What does it mean?"

"What does it mean to you?" Allie asked.

"Ha ha," Becca said, looking back at her Twombly.

Allie was scrolling through Becca's pictures when she saw the picture from the photo tour—the chipped curb, the rusted legs of the mailbox, the wrapper stuck in the sewage grate. "What's this?" she asked.

"That's from that tour with Dana, that SnapChicago thing."

"What's architecturally significant about this?"

"Nothing."

"Feels lonely," Allie said. "The way you shot down is cool. Makes it feel kind of small. What were you thinking when you took it?"

"My camera just kind of went off there," Becca lied. She looked at the phone so long that she could almost see the petite figure in the black dress and pretty shoes, her chin resting on her hands.

"You could delete it," Allie said.

"I probably should."

"Unless it means something to you, of course," Allie said, a curious tilt to her head. "Does it mean something to you?"

"Nah," Becca said, taking the phone and placing it back in her bag, without deleting it.

"You could paint something like this," Allie said, staring thoughtfully at the large canvas in front of them.

"I could never do this. It would look silly, like kids' artwork or something," Becca said, without taking her eyes off of it.

"Some people said that about this, too," Allie said, putting her teacher's hat on. "There are a few drips and splatters and an occasional pencil line. There isn't anything to these paintings, but the director of the Art Gallery of New South Wales explained it pretty well. He said, 'Sometimes people need a little bit of help in recognizing a great work of art that might be a bit unfamiliar.' Maybe you like it cuz it looks like that Pile of Rocks album cover…" Allie was saying. "Colors, shapes, letters. You see that, right?"

Becca could see some resemblance. "Rockpile. It's Rockpile. Not Pile of Rocks."

"Right. Rockpile. My class loved that CD assignment, by the way. I should show you their work. Really interesting how they chose to express themselves, portray themselves. I never would have guessed that some of them saw themselves like they do. I explained your album cover for Scrappy and told them all about your songs and how you felt they described you. How I never would have seen it at all. How that makes it a *self*-portrait. Your view of you. Not my view of you."

"You don't see it at all?"

"Certainly not the title, Becca. Of course, those things really happened and they made you who you are. It tells your story. It does. But the title, not so much. Look, maybe when you were younger you had a wild side. A self-confidence about you, but now you always seem to think too much about what others are thinking. To me, scrappy means someone who is really determined. Someone who finds a way to get what they want. In a creative way, of course, not a mean way. Like an ass-kicker, I suppose. Someone who doesn't let others get in their way. I could be wrong. What does it mean to you? I guess that's what really matters anyway."

Becca sat looking at the canvas in front of her. "Like what you said, I guess."

"Well, does that sound like you? Don't get me wrong, Becca, I love you no matter what, but you are not scrappy. You are not kicking anyone's ass. You're playing it safe. Where are you going? What do you want to do? You're not evolving; you're kind of just standing still. This is a chance for you to set a goal, recreate yourself. You *could* be scrappy, Becca, you could, but you would have to let go a bit. I know change is scary for you, but maybe you just need to embrace it, that's all. Cuz your life is changing, Becca, no matter how hard you stomp your foot."

Becca silently wiped the tears away. Allie had seen right through her. No wedges or highlights were going to disguise who she really was. "I'm scared, Allie," she said, clutching tightly to the slats of the bench beneath her.

"Don't be scared, Becca. You have us." Allie reached out and placed her hand on top of hers. "Little known fact: Sometimes Twombly would sit on his friends' shoulders, that way he could reach the top of the canvas and paint a continuous line across as his friend carried him."

Becca stared at a line towards the top of the painting. It was one long swoop, no break, just black and smooth, getting the littlest bit fainter as it continued to the right. "That sounds terrifying," she said, resting her chin on her fist.

"It means he let his friends help him, Becca. It means he trusted his friends," Allie said annoyed.

"I know that's what you meant…" Becca said smiling. "Can we just sit here for a bit?"

"Yeah, Bex, but just for a bit. Can you drop me at home before you go to Dana's?"

"I'm terrified to go there, by the way," Becca said.

"I don't really blame you," Allie agreed.

Those damn salt and pepper shakers….

Becca could see the salt and pepper shakers displayed in the glass cabinet. "They look pretty," Becca was saying, looking at the collection under glass. "Maybe you should take them out and put them on the table. They would be so pretty out here with your other things."

Dana was walking out of her kitchen, carrying two Diet Cokes. Becca reached out for one, then noticed the look on Dana's face. It wasn't one she recognized, and her hand shook a bit as she took a glass. Dana sat down with a sigh, holding her glass in her hands, rolling it in her palms. "Becca, how could you get me those?" she asked, as her shorter, wider eyebrow raised up slightly.

"I thought you would like them. You don't like them?"

"You don't think it's ever going to happen, do you?" she asked, sadly. "You don't think I'm ever going to get married?"

"What?" Becca asked. "Dana, what are you talking about?"

"You know that I'm going to register for them. You know that I plan on getting everything for MY WEDDING. Why would you get me these *now*?"

Becca felt like a deer in headlights. She carefully licked her dry top lip and measured her words carefully. "Dana," she said cautiously, "I really thought that you would just like to have them now. That's it. I promise."

Dana was looking at the pieces in the cabinet. "I might never get married," she said, sadly. "I'm 32 on Tuesday. You've been married, Elle has been married. Katie was married…"

Becca was cringing now. "Those aren't the best examples, Dana. That is setting the bar very, very, low…"

"But you have the story, Becca. Don't you see? Josh, although a total asshole now, once was romantic. He told you how wonderful you were, that he wanted to spend his life with you, he got down on a knee, he took your hand…"

"And he said, 'This is what you wanted, right?' one afternoon at his apartment. And he wasn't on his knee, he was sitting on our green sofa eating chips and salsa. Dana, you have the wrong idea."

"OK," she said, through a small smile. "But it's a story to look back on and share with people. I want to tell a story about my proposal one day. I want to call all my friends and have all of you look at my ring. I want to plan my wedding, get a dress, choose your bridesmaid dresses, register, have parties and showers and plan a honeymoon."

"I get that," Becca said. "But it really is such a small part of it all. I mean, after the party is over, sometimes, the party is over, ya know what I mean?"

"Yes, of course," Dana said. "But I still want to go to the party in the first place. I want someone to tell me that I'm wonderful and that he wants to spend his life with me. I want him down on a knee holding my hand. I want to say 'I do,' when he asks, not 'yes.' I want it all, Becca. Do you understand?"

"Yes," Becca said. "I do."

Getting a little help...

Becca found a parking place after 10 minutes of weaving in and out of the lot. She had no idea it would be so busy, especially on such a cold day. Who knew so many people in town did this anyway? She only hoped it would be worth the $15 she would be paying Tori towards those shoes.

Becca pushed open the door and the cold air blew in sending some papers flying off the end tables in the waiting room. A single leather sofa was placed against the wall. No coffee table, but two other chairs on the opposite wall made it feel cozy. It didn't lend to conversation, though, and no one there was talking. Not the lady on the sofa with the magazine or the one sitting behind the counter.

"Hi, I'm Becca. I have an appointment at 4?" she said quietly.

"Yes, I have you right here. Would you mind filling this out while you wait?" the woman asked as she handed Becca just one piece of paper. "Goals" was printed simply on the top of the page. The questions were easy, and a simple check in the "Yes" or "No" boxes wouldn't take long, especially because only one was more like "Only one time" and the rest were all "No" anyway. She sat with the paper in her hand looking at the word Goal, then quickly scribbled those three little words.

A young man walked out of a small room in the back and called her name. His brown, curly hair seemed perfectly balanced on his head as he peeked around the corner.

"Come on in," he said and waved her to follow him down the hall. Each of the small offices looked alike, with two chairs facing each other in each one. "So," he said, sitting down and gesturing to the other for her to do the same, "You want to learn to play guitar?"

"Yes, yes I do."

Kerplunk...

Becca got the time wrong and ended up sitting on those benches that help you to have good posture. There was sand at the bottom and she didn't want it on her butt for all to see in class, so she took her foot and swiped it away as best she could before slowly sitting down. Her legs were just an inch or two too short, but it made all the difference—the bends in the bench simply did not conform to her small frame. She couldn't lean back, so she leaned forward, her legs stuck out straight as she felt the damp sand on the seat of her pants.

People were already up and about, walking the path and collecting sea glass. Some people were cleaning up the litter thrown about in the sand. There were no kids out at this time, building sandcastles or even playing on the recently constructed playground. She wondered about the boys on their "Boys' Weekend Yeas." What did they do all day? What did they eat? Did they miss her? Did they ask for her?

It was only 8:25. Elle wouldn't be there for another 20 minutes. She told herself to relax and enjoy the view but, of course, that was impossible. Nothing could ever help her to relax, it seemed. She watched a duck slowly swimming in the lagoon and felt a little sad. Where were the other ducks?

Did he mind being alone? She told herself that the weather would be getting warmer soon and they would all be back. She wondered what this place would look like in the snow. More people were showing up now with their rolled-up yoga mats. Some, carried them just under their arm, some on a strap or in a bag. Most were women, but now there was a man approaching the path. He was carrying his mat on his back. She figured he had about four percent body fat. He was one of those people who had no fat in his face, making it look very angular and dull. Maybe supplements? *How does anyone get that skinny and that strong at the same time?* she wondered, as she watched him enter the glass building.

Five minutes till class. *Where is Elle?* She took her phone out of the perforated side pocket of her bag and checked for a text. Nothing. She had recently, as a joke, changed Elle's contact to Late Lady and scrolled through to call. One ring. Two rings…

"Hello?" Elle asked.

"You almost here?" Becca asked.

"OMG, Becca," Elle said with a sigh between the M and G.

Becca could hear how startled she was. Had she woken her? "Where are you?"

"I'm… *stop it…* I'm in bed. I totally forgot. I'm so sorry," Elle said only partially into the phone.

"Elle, I don't want to do this alone," Becca whispered into the mouthpiece, watching everyone walking through the lot.

"I'm sorry. I'll make it up to you. I promise," she said, hanging up in a hurry.

Becca grabbed her mat and started heading towards her car when the teacher yelled to her, "Let's go! We're starting!" She made a huge wave with her hand, and Becca reluctantly turned and walked to the little glass box. "You're Elle's friend, right?" she asked.

"Yes. Becca," she said, signing her name on the list.

"She's not coming today?"

"No, she's busy."

"Well, you'll have a great time. I find sometimes I do my best work when I'm alone," the smiley instructor said, handing her a purple foam block.

"I'm beginning to think that, too," Becca said as she lay her mat down in the only spot left on the floor, the one right next to "four percent body fat guy." He was stretching out differently than everyone else. His stretches seemed, well, a bit more stretchy—reaching further, bending more.

"OK," the instructor said. "Let's start with an intention. Make up one of your own today. Think about something for here, right now, or something for the week. We'll start at heart," she said, leading everyone, palms together, placing them on her chest, almost as in prayer.

"My intention is to make it through this class," Becca told herself as she raised her head tall and pushed her bottom into the floor. *"And to kill Elle..."*

Downward dog to lifting right foot behind, slightly bent. "They say if you put your head upside down, your worries, your problems, fall out," the teacher explained in a calm but cheerful voice. Everyone got a chuckle with that. Several even had to place their right foot back down and try to find balance again. She knew she would be shooting her leg down, forward and through to her shoulder soon, ending in warrior—was it "three" pose?

There were about 16 of them today, their mats almost touching and their blocks getting mixed up, but Becca recognized some faces from last week. It was funny, but no one really talked to each other. They stayed on their mats, followed directions and once in a while shared a laugh. "Here is something to think about," the instructor said, as she walked around the little glass room. "Ram Dass says, 'Early in the journey, you wonder how long the journey will take and whether you will make it in this lifetime. Later, you will see that where you are going is HERE and you will arrive NOW... so stop asking.' Can you imagine? What if, right now, what if, you are right where you are supposed to be? I mean, what if there were 100 percent chance that you are right where you are supposed to be?"

That would be a problem, Becca thought, standing at monkey pose in the second row, *and that Ram is as bad at math as I am, because HERE and NOW, my head is just inches away from "four percent body fat" guy's ass.*

The hour session always ran a bit long and, then, of course, they all lay down on their mats listening to the waves for a while. That was usually the hardest part for Becca, the just relaxing part. The instructor had only adjusted Becca's form once today, and it wasn't during pigeon or plank, but at the end, while she was lying down with the sun shining on her face. The instructor had gently pushed Becca's shoulder down to the mat. Becca could see how that would have been funny to Elle, and she had cracked a small smile herself. It had always been easy for Elle to let go.

When the last of the class had rolled up their mats, Becca took a quick look around to see if anyone on the beach was looking, then she quickly walked over to those benches that were good for your posture. She sat, then swiveled on her butt to rest her thighs against the slanted back, slowly uncrunching to rest her back on the seat and let her head fall down towards the ground. She listened closely to see if her problems falling out might make a sound. A "kerplunck" per chance? Maybe as they hit the sand?

221 points...

"So, Becca, what brings you here today?" the lady in the knock-off Eames chair asked. She wasn't wearing glasses or holding a notebook or resting a pencil above her ear or anything. Was she a real therapist? Becca always figured they would look a little more educated and polished.

She was wearing jeans and strappy heels with a Boho-looking blouse. *This is who Miss Peggy with the silver hair thought could help?*

"Well, my husband is having an affair, I'm getting a divorce, I just moved into an old house, and one of my best friends died," she answered coolly.

The lady was quiet then, studying Becca as Becca avoided eye contact, staring up at the lights in the ceiling. "Do you know what this means?" the woman asked.

She did. Becca had added it up a few times: Divorce was 73 points, change in residence 25 points, death of a close friend, 37. She couldn't find out how much the affair was worth. She decided 86 seemed appropriate. "It means that according to the Holmes-Rahe Statistical Prediction Model, I have a 50 percent chance of a mental health breakdown in the next two years."

"No, Becca," she said, crossing her legs in the other direction and leaning forward. "It means, if you can get through this, you can get through anything."

The music festival...

Becca watched them every day. They usually started around 3:30 or so, usually in pairs, but sometimes in larger groups. Mostly, they were young, twenty-somethings, give or take. They all carried folding chairs on their shoulders. Sometimes they folded up like umbrellas and fit in bags. Sometimes they simply folded in half and had a strap. There were coolers, too. Those were either on their backs or in little carts or wagons. By 6 o'clock, there were fewer of them and her street returned to normal, but until then, her front window overlooked the parade of people and traffic entering the music festival by her house.

When she was younger, the orchestra and lesser-known pop groups performed, but now it was quite a draw with more popular bands playing. It brought younger, louder fans to the area and they stayed for hours listening to music just feet away from her backyard. She had thought about walking over there, bringing Faye's chair, some snacks, setting herself up on a blanket to listen as well, but instead she set up in her backyard while the boys were sleeping quietly upstairs. She brought the monitor outside with her, placing it alongside her things. If the wind *did* blow just right, she could hear every word to every song and shared in the applause of the crowd. Sometimes, though, the wind blew the wrong way and she couldn't hear a thing. She would make the several trips back into the house or garage then, returning Faye's chair, blanket and dinner to their respective places, waiting for next time. Someday, she thought, she would carry that chair on her shoulder, her dinner and wine in a bag and take the walk over to the festival.

But it just isn't cool....

This is much harder than it looks, she thought, as she tried to wrap her little hand around the neck of the guitar. Stretching her little fingers and pressing them on each string was crazy. Either she couldn't reach the string she wanted or couldn't press it down hard enough when she did. But it did look so cool. Just like she thought it would. She felt especially cool pulling it out of the back of her Jeep, slamming the trunk and throwing it over her shoulder.

No one has to know I suck at this, she told herself as she walked into her third lesson. Rich was waiting for her and walked her into the same little room. She pulled the guitar out of its case and picked up her pick and proceeded to have the same conversation as the week before.

"My hand is too little, I can't reach around to press the strings hard enough…"

"Electric guitars are smaller. You could reach around, press easier…" he said, again.

She knew that. That wasn't the plan. The plan was an acoustic guitar thrown over her shoulder. Period.

"Here, try it," and he offered her a shiny, awkwardly shaped guitar already plugged into the large amp in the room. "And try tabs, like I showed you. The lead singers always play tabs, not chords."

It rested easier in her lap. It was lighter and did seem to fit her hand easier, just as he had said. Reluctantly, she looked at her sheet music on the stand in front of her. She pinched the little pink pick in her hand and pressed on the first string in the second fret and plucked. 2-2-2-0-0-0-3-3-3-0-0-0, and the sound came out. She moved to the second string, slid her hand up and down the neck. Rich joined in and together, they played. When it was over he looked at her.

"I'll take it," she said, even though she knew it wasn't how it was supposed to be.

But if your roots are too strong,
it can really fuck things up…

It was obvious to everyone by now. Not only to those that came inside her house, but by simply walking past, people could see what was going on. Becca was obsessed with Pottery Barn. Inside the house, every throw, pillow and frame. Outside the house, the many empty boxes waiting at the curb for the recycling truck on Mondays. Sometimes, she would hide the packaging in her garage till early on Monday mornings. She would then strategically drag it all out quickly to the curb so the chatting mommies wouldn't see her on their walks before the sun even came up.

It had started out innocently enough. She liked an apothecary jar and bought it on a whim. She filled it with coffee grounds. That was the first. The second had candy, the third, gum, the fourth, potpourri and finally, the fifth, the big one, had photographs of her and the boys. She knew it was crazy. Every lamp, mirror and basket. Everything. It seemed harmless enough at first, but now she was looking at big-ticket items like sofas and consoles. She had even received a nice email with a "special thanks for being a top customer." *Maybe no one will notice if I stop now,* she thought, as she took the last sip of her afternoon coffee from one of the white mugs from the PB catering collection.

"Look, Becca, some people come into your life for a reason," Allie was explaining on the phone. "Some people come into your life because they just happen to be in the same place as you at the same time. You can never really be sure. I moved out of my incredible place just to live in this tiny box. I've met some people, but who knows? Maybe my husband was the guy I just sold my place to," she said.

Becca was sitting on the side of the green sofa that didn't have goldfish crackers smushed into the edges. She had been looking at two white, slip-covered sofas from Pottery Barn on the iPad, placing them into her cart to get the exact price after tax and shipping. Well over $3,000 made the sofas an impossibility, of course, but she couldn't help but imagine what the downy white pieces would look like in the room. Stevie was lying next to her, sleeping with her little feet running quickly, maybe after a rabbit? Maybe from a coyote?

Becca always found it easier to use her landline to talk with friends on these relaxing days. Mason was playing with his dinosaurs, Oliver banging on the different activities in his light-up SuperSaucer. In that moment of peace, she turned herself upside down, placing the back of her legs over the back pillows, her back on the seat and her head upside down over the front. Her hair fell around her face as she gazed out the window while holding the phone to her ear. "That guy was married," Becca said, remembering the guy who couldn't wait for Allie to move out. He had even had the audacity to try to negotiate that she leave the Baby Grand as he couldn't think of anything else to place on the landing either.

"Yeah, but who knows for how long?" Allie reasoned. "It's funny, Becca, but I did actually meet someone…"

That's when Becca saw the large green cloud in the sky. She quickly up-righted herself, scooting her body around to a sitting position, still clutching the phone. The sudden movement woke Stevie, who jumped up quickly and stepped on her iPad before knocking it to the ground. "What the hell is that?" Becca asked as the cloud moved faster and faster towards the house.

"What the hell is what?" Allie asked.

Crackle, crackle and with that, the phone died.

The noise outside was deafening. What was it? It sounded like a train. The sky opened up and the torrential rain began. Her cell phone started buzzing. The town alarm went off.

"Mommy!" screamed Mason covering his ears. "What's happening?"

"Mason," she yelled. "Hurry!" She grabbed his hand and picked up Oliver just as he was flopping the plastic pages of a read-along book. "Come, Stevie!" she screamed and the four of them ran down the seven stairs and stood in the hall. *No windows,* she thought, *get away from the windows.* She turned in all four directions to see the green sky surround the house. She grabbed the doorknob to the closet that was covered in cobwebs, she hoped, but probably weren't, and opened the door. "Mason, help me!" she said, and the two of them proceeded to grab and throw everything from inside into the hallway before she placed the three of them in and climbed inside after them. She closed the door behind them as Stevie barked and spun in circles and she held the crying boys in the dark little room.

It sounded as if the train was right over them, now. It was so loud she could barely hear the boys crying. "It's OK, it's OK," she heard herself saying as she held them tightly. The storm lasted only moments, chugging overhead; then, it was gone. She could once again hear their crying, Stevie's barking. "It's OK," she said, slowly standing up, holding Oliver on her hip and grabbing Mason's hand. She opened the door, peeked out, and slowly the four of them stepped out over the suitcases, photo albums and old toys.

"Mommy!" Mason hollered as he looked out the playroom window and into the backyard. The tree above their used, new playground was broken in two, one half resting on the plastic yellow slide he had played on just hours ago. They climbed up the seven stairs to the main floor and Mason released her hand as he ran to the living room windows. "Mommy!" he screamed again, as he saw the sidewalk slab now standing vertically in front of their house. She could see people outside and placed Oliver down.

"Stay here," she said to them, as she made her way to the front door. Stevie barked and spun in circles at the window as Becca walked outside.

166

"You all OK in there?" a neighbor yelled, as Becca carefully stepped onto the puddle-filled driveway.

"Yes!" Becca called back, keeping an eye on the boys through the window, both with their hands on the glass, looking at the destruction. "What was that?" she asked, noticing the flooded street.

"A microburst!" the neighbor yelled back. "It's like a thunderstorm on the ground!" The street was dark and quiet, not even a hum. "You lose power, too?"

Becca turned around to her quiet house. "I think so!"

"You got a back-up battery for your sump pump, right?" she asked.

"I do! I do! I have one!" Becca shouted back, a little more excitedly than necessary from the look on the lady's face across the street.

"That's good! Look out for the flooding!" and the lady walked a bit further down the street. "You all OK in there?" she could hear her asking next door. Becca turned to run inside and saw that the tall tree that shaded their yard was now lying flat across hers and Marc's yard.

"Mommy! Was that a tomato?" Mason asked, as she walked back into the house.

"It was a microburst. It's a storm on the ground," she explained.

"It turned the sidewalk!" he said, eyes opened wide in disbelief.

"Yeah," she said, flipping the light switch off and on. "We don't have electricity," she said, almost to herself. "Phone isn't working," she said as she pressed the green button but heard nothing. She looked at the boys, knowing that soon the house would be dark, that dinner would be cold. "How about we all sleep down here, tonight? We'll open up the sofa bed, OK?"

"Yes!" Mason grinned, as he turned to run upstairs and gather his things. It was 5:30. The fire trucks and police car sirens were now filling the quiet sky.

Dinner was cereal, yogurt and fruit. "Breakfast for dinner!" Becca had sung out when she placed it on the floor. They ate by the light of Oliver's still lit up SuperSaucer. Thankfully, Becca had a week's supply of batteries in the drawer nearby. After a fun toothbrushing in the dark, they had all changed into their pajamas and opened up the sofa bed. Becca put on the sheets, blankets and pillows, got their loveys then lifted each in.

The four of them lay together on the opened sleeper sofa: Becca in the middle, Mason cuddled into her side, Oliver already asleep, sucking his thumb on the other, and Stevie between her legs. "How about another story?" Becca asked. Mason had been into writing his own lately. He would dictate his stories about pirates and space to Becca, then he would draw his pictures on the many pages.

"Let's write about the microburtht," he said.

"Microburst," she said stressing the s. "Put your tongue behind your teeth, Mason. Sss...'"

"Microburst," he said thoughtfully. He hopped off the makeshift bed and Becca held the flashlight so the light shone on him as he traveled to the craft table. He grabbed a large piece of construction paper and held it in the sky. "Where are the scissors, Mommy?"

"No paper with lines, huh?" she asked.

"I don't see any," he said, moving the pieces of paper on the table in the dark.

"OK, bring that over, we can use that one," Becca said and once again, she shined the flashlight to create a path back.

Mason grabbed a handful of crayons and walked the lit path before sliding in next to her. "Mommy, how is a microbursssst different than a tomato?" he asked.

"It's a tornado, not a tomato. Did you think a tomato was going to fall out of the sky?" she asked smiling at the possibility.

"Yeah, a big one!" he said.

"Tornados are like wind in a funnel," she tried to explain. The wind goes around and around, motioning with her finger. "Kind of like in the shape of the party hats we got, but upside down."

Mason looked at her blankly. "A big party hat in the sky?"

"No, not exactly," she said, grabbing one of his crayons and holding it above the paper. "Kind of like this. It starts at the bottom, slowly spinning and spinning and it goes up and up," she was creating a loopy funnel on the page. "Then it gets faster and faster..." drawing the loops quicker and larger.

"What does a microburst look like?" he asked.

"Best I understand, the winds kind of hit each other on the ground. Some wind comes from this way and that way and this way and that way," she explained as she drew the lines coming towards each other.

"And they blew up the sidewalk?"

"I think maybe the tree between our yard and the neighbor's pulled it up. Its roots were underneath it and when the tree fell, it lifted up the sidewalk with it," she said, drawing a big rectangle with lines underneath.

"Why was it green?" he asked.

"I don't know about that. It came in so fast didn't it?"

"It did," he said, grabbing a green crayon and coloring all around. "It knocked that tree on my slide!" he said, drawing a stick figure tree lying on a bumpy line.

Becca stared at the picture by the light of the flashlight.

"Should I tell you the words now, Mommy?"

Becca stared at the swirls and lines and gobs. "Sure, Mason. Go ahead."

"So a microburtht came to our house and it was loud and it rained and the sidewalk blew up and my playground might be broke but it's OK cuz we're together and we're safe and we had yogurt for dinner and we get to sleep together on the pull-out sofa like Friday Night Movie Night but it's not," he said in one breath. "Did you get all that, Mommy?"

Becca had only just finished writing about the playground but then slowly started *but it's OK cuz we're together and we're safe...*

Once upon a time, there was a girl with perfect eyebrows...

It couldn't have been any worse. They met in a revolving door. She had two bags and one large box from Crate & Barrel. He was standing outside waiting to be picked up by a friend when she was on her way out slowly walking through. People were entering, going a bit faster. She lost her footing. When she quickly stepped out, he grabbed her elbow. The story goes that his friend got there and he waved him on. He carried the box all the way to her apartment. Six weeks later they were engaged.

I guess that's just how it goes for girls with great eyebrows, Becca thought, but she didn't tell Dana that. Becca really couldn't think of anything to say. "Look, that sucks. I'm sorry," was all she could come up with.

"You know the worst part? I'm maid of honor! I throw the shower, the bachelorette party, I make the speech..." she rambled.

"You're going way too fast. There's plenty of time to think about all that," Becca reasoned.

"No, they figure why wait? We're looking for a dress Wednesday so they can pick a date!" Dana yelled. "This is happening, Bex! It's really happening!"

It was Dana's worst nightmare. Her little sister was getting married before her. And it was happening, really happening.

"She wants us all to wear black. We went to the dress store and we all picked out dresses. It was awful."

"Black sounds easy," reasoned Elle. "You can always…"

"If you say I can wear it again, I will fucking kill you." Dana was sitting on the bench with her hands clasped between her knees. She hadn't even taken one bite of her spring roll.

"You gonna eat that?" Elle asked as she snatched a piece away with her chopsticks.

"I'm supposed to be planning her shower. She wants it at my apartment. She wants people to relax and talk, not be at long tables eating. And you just know she expects me to plan something great." Their entrees came about then. Her pad Thai, no peanuts or cilantro, easy on the oil, was steaming in front of her. "I have to have these girls in my home? They're married or pregnant or have kids, and I need to entertain them?" She rested her chin on her fist; in her other hand, she held her chopsticks and tapped them on the table.

"If you're not gonna eat it, can I taste it?" Elle asked as she poked her chopsticks into Dana's plate again. "What about shoes?" she asked as she was slowly bringing a long noodle down to her mouth. "Black shoes?"

"Yes, black shoes."

Becca ate nervously. "You have a nice place. What are you thinking of for a theme?"

"Oh, you should ask Allie, she has the best themes." But no one had heard much from Allie since her move across town except Becca. This was not the time to divulge the fact that the apartment magic may have already starting working for her. "What's up with Allie anyway? She meet her husband yet?" Elle asked.

Dana stopped tapping and looked up with a curious look on her face.

"I don't know. I'm seeing her Saturday." Her phone rang then and she reached inside the orange messenger bag leaning against her leg. It was from Jay. "Lunch?" appeared on the screen.

"I still can't believe you bought that, Bex," Dana said. "You're crazy. Look, maybe I should be happy. I mean, look at you, you marry your college sweetheart, you have two babies and he gets bored. What the fuck is that about anyway?" Dana asked.

Becca slid the phone back inside and pulled the bag just a little closer. "Just lucky, I guess," Becca said as she carefully picked up a slippery noodle between her two sticks.

Elle reached over and speared a piece of tofu off Dana's plate. "Are you gonna eat this, or what?"

"It's because she's been married," Dana said. "That's why Elle can't relate."

Becca and Dana were walking to the car. "I've been married. I have kids. You think I can't relate?" Becca asked.

"You're different," Dana said. "You know that. I know you guys have been friends forever, but you don't really have that much in common, ya know?" They were at the car now, sliding in, narrowly missing stepping in the puddles.

"We have a lot in common. We grew up together. We know everything about each other," Becca argued.

"So, you know she's having an affair with that Joel guy?"

"Yes, I do." No, she didn't.

"And you think that's OK? Everyone knows! He has kids, Bex! Three kids! You know his wife, and you think that's OK? You think that's OK?" Dana screamed.

The phone rang then. Becca fidgeted for the button with the talking face on the dashboard. "Hello?" she asked.

"I'm in love!" screamed Allie. Becca didn't look over, but out of the corner of her eye, she could see Dana throwing her hands up into the sky.

Just like magic...

Becca had gotten the scoop from Allie after dropping Dana off. She had met Jackson late one night walking around the building. He was an artist. He showed his work in a teeny gallery in Pilsen. He was a bit older, well-traveled, had a wealthy family.

"When do we meet him?" Becca asked.

"Not yet," Allie said.

"Well, that's great. Ya know, Dana was in the car. I thought she was going to explode when you screamed that."

"She needs to lighten up."

"Her little sister is getting married," Becca reminded her. "It's killing her."

"She'll live. I'm still dropping by Saturday?" Allie reminded, more than asked.

"Yeah, you'll just need to leave by 5," *because there's a birthday party for Mason's friend Andy,* she thought, *and she had promised his mom, Courtney, that she would help since her husband, that Joel guy, had to work. Or so he said...*

Maybe a peek for Courtney, too...

"So, I think the cake over there and the party bags on that table by the door. What do you think?" Courtney asked, as she backed into the rec center room holding boxes in her arms. She pushed the door open and stood with her back against it allowing some room for Becca to slide in with the cake. "Thanks for helping tonight," she said. "Joel will be here soon. He's been working a lot lately. I really should go back to work. That was the deal. I was supposed to go back when they were old enough for daycare. I just like being with them, that's all."

"What did you do? Before the kids?" Becca asked, looking at the meticulously decorated dinosaur-themed birthday cake, mini dinosaurs walking across the top, over the chocolate malt-ball rocks.

"Believe it or not, I was a travel writer," Courtney said, laughing at the irony.

"Any place cool?"

"Every place cool," she said, placing the balloons on the table, centering them just so. "Joel and I traveled everywhere. It was pretty much an all-expense tour of the world, really. He loved it. I think he would have done it forever."

"I don't blame him."

"Yeah, but it's not practical now with the kids. I think about getting back to it. They offered me a little trip to a spa in Wisconsin. He told me to go and he'd take care of the kids, but I feel funny leaving. Oh my god, Becca, here I am talking about me, and I haven't even asked about you and the boys."

"We're OK. The routine has set in. The new place is coming along. They're with Josh every other weekend, so I get some time to work on it. It's actually kind of nice to have them to myself. We have fun."

"Will you go back to work?" Courtney asked.

"I will. It looks like I can stay home with them for a while, though. I took time off work to be home with the kids, so apparently, I can stay home a bit longer. It's called maintenance. Kind of like maintaining the lifestyle we had. At least for a little bit," she explained.

"Some people would say maintaining the lifestyle would include sticking with the marriage. I forget, Becca, what did you do before the kids?" Courtney asked.

"I was a teacher. Just for a short time, though. I got pregnant my first year of teaching, so I didn't teach for long," Becca said.

"Good hours for a working mom," Courtney said with a reassuring smile.

"It wasn't my first choice, but it's OK, I guess."

"And your first choice was?" Courtney asked.

"A writer, for Rolling Stone Magazine. It sounds ridiculous, but that was the idea," Becca said.

"What stopped you?"

"I am 'too shy to be a good interviewer, just an average writer.'"

"Really? You don't seem too shy to me," Courtney said, laughing.

"That's a direct quote from my teacher, Mrs. Rich. She told me that during one of our meetings."

"And?" Courtney asked. "You quit because of that? Wow, Becca. I can't believe you quit because of that," Courtney said, opening another tablecloth. "I wonder if she was just daring you or something, ya know? Like, prove to me you got what it takes, kind of thing?"

"It didn't feel like that at the time…" Becca said, contemplating the idea. "I liked art, too, so I took a lot of art classes."

"What can you do with art?"

"Exactly."

"Well, it sounds like you have some time to think about that," Courtney said with a smile. "Enjoy this time with the kids."

"I am. It seems a little lighter in the house. It was the three of us a lot, anyway, so this isn't that different, really," Becca said.

"I can see how it all happens. Joel and I don't have any time for each other at all anymore. He's working. I'm taking care of the kids. There's no excitement anymore. Sometimes I think I should try to shake things up a bit. Be more spontaneous. I'm just so tired, and he's so, so…I don't know," Courtney said, searching for the right words.

"So what?" Becca asked nervously.

"So, uninterested. Distracted. Look I have put on a little weight. It shouldn't be a big deal, but I certainly don't feel very attractive, so it wouldn't be that surprising if he felt the same way. He's probably tired, too. He works all the time. Late nights. Weekends…"

That sounded familiar. Becca watched as Courtney once again shifted the last goody bag on the table just the littlest smidge to make it line up with the others. It reminded her of choosing the perfect blue for Oliver's room. Staring at the different swatches taped above the crib, painting a few inches of the three closest blues on the wall. Eventually, she would be staring at them blankly, her mind wandering to Josh, where he was, who he was with… Courtney had a far off look on her face now as well. She wasn't looking at the bags anymore.

Becca could hear Jay's voice in her head, "*I'm not going to sugar-coat it for you…*"

"Maybe you *should* shake things up a bit," Becca said, apprehensively.

"Like what?" Courtney asked.

"Maybe," Becca said, counting out the four polka-dotted birthday candles, "you should go and surprise him at work."

*Well, you never know
who you're going to fall
in love with, I guess...*

Normally, Becca didn't like heavy eye makeup. It always seemed to smudge, flake and get stuck in every little line around your eyes, but, on this woman, it worked. Her eyelashes were perfectly winged at the outer corner, turning slightly up in two lines, the shadowed lid growing lighter as it approached her brow, the black liner, a perfectly undisturbed line on the top and bottom lid. She not only looked like Amy Winehouse, but she sounded like her, too. She stood on a small rug that was half covered by the Baby Grand that Allie had purchased to simply fill up empty space in her last place. It was played by a man in a more modern solution to a tux and tails—a pink polyester suit, a soft purple, paisley print shirt with no tie. He wore his straw fedora low on his forehead to somewhat cover his eyes. Together, the Amy Winehouse woman and the piano player covered Cole Porter and George Gershwin, and she sang with the emotion of one with a truly broken heart, looking for answers, comfort or company.

Becca slowly sipped her Champagne, not wanting to even come close to finishing one glass. The bubbly went with Allie's theme, of course, but not with Becca's schedule. She, personally didn't think that Champagne was all that much fun, unless, of course, she compared it to the day after she drank it. Elle wandered over and sat down on the fluffy, white pouf next to her, carefully grabbing Becca's arm to steady herself properly on the mushy, 13-inch-diameter stool.

"This singer is really good," Elle said, carefully balancing her small plate of appetizers. "Allie likes some guy who likes this music, huh?"

"Yeah," Becca said, gesturing with her glass across the room to an older gentleman sitting on the way-too-oversized, white sectional. "He lives in the building."

"*That's* what she moved into this little place for? To fall in love with *him*? He's the artist? That's Jackson?" she asked incredulously.

"Nah, he's just a neighbor. You know Allie, she wants to learn it all. He's been teaching her about music," Becca explained.

"Hmm, so when do we meet Jackson?"

"He's working tonight is all I know."

"Well, why hasn't she introduced us yet do you suppose?" Elle quizzed.

"Maybe we embarrass her…"

"Maybe," Elle said, once again trying to pull her shirt closed while trying not to tip over. "Is Jay coming tonight?"

"Maybe, we haven't really talked since the party…"

"When he pulled you out of the box and…?" Elle asked.

"Yeah."

"You're making too big a deal about that, Bex…" Elle began.

"Maybe…"

Allie was walking back into the apartment with a rather large grin on her face.

"Where has she been?" Elle asked.

"Dunno, but she's never looked happier," Becca said.

"Well," Elle said with a sigh, "that can't be good."

Becca's phone was humming in her bag, vibrating on her side.

I have to go out Can I drop off the boys? They're all ready for bed

"Josh is asking if he can bring the boys back…"

"Well, looks like he will be disappointed then. Sorry, Joshy! Mommy's out!"

Becca could already see Mason, still awake in his pajamas, sagging in the knees, wondering where he would sleep tonight. "Look, I can take a cab," Becca said.

"You can't take a cab home," Elle shot back. "Just tell him no."

"I can't. I could never let the boys think I didn't want them. I'll just go. You stay!" she spoke loudly to be heard over the piano player singing in perfect harmony.

"You know, sometimes I think some of this is sort of your fault," Elle said as she walked away.

Did she hear that wrong? *My fault?* She texted back that she didn't have a ride but, if he could pick her up, he could drop the three of them off. In the elevator, she thought about it again. *My fault?*

"Everything OK?" Sonny asked, pressing the button at his desk, opening the door for her.

"Yeah, Sonny. Why?" she asked.

"I've been working here a long time. Seen people come and go. Allie stands out. And her parties. No one leaves those early," he said.

"Something's just come up," Becca tried to explain, pulling on her cape, revealing the smudge of Beige Calm on her inner forearm.

"You can probably get that paint off your arm with some cooking oil. I just rub it on and wash it off with some dish soap," he offered.

"I'll give it a try. Ya know, she moved here because apparently this is where people come to fall in love."

"Well, you never know who you're gonna fall in love with, I guess," he said with a wink. "Is that your ride?"

She walked outside and saw Mason and Oliver in the back seat of Josh's car. They had fallen asleep. She quietly lifted the handle as someone came up the sidewalk in the dark.

"Leaving already?" Jay asked from behind her.

"Oh, you scared me," she said, jumping and grabbing her bag.

Jay looked in the back seat, then the front. "Have a good night," he said and walked toward Allie's apartment, where Sonny opened the door for him.

Becca slid in next to Josh. *My fault?* she thought again, as they drove through their old neighborhood. *My fault?* she thought, as they merged onto the highway and barreled towards her house. *My fault?*

"Well, you never know who you're gonna fall in love with..." She heard Sonny's voice in her head and looked at the paint on her arm, thinking of his tip to get it off. Sonny. Sonny. Sonny? Jacksonny? Holy shit! Allie didn't even make it past the first floor. Allie's in love with her doorman!

That girl...

"Courtney went downtown to surprise Joel last Thursday night," Elle said, sipping her coffee. "He wasn't at work. She's devastated."

"How do you know that?" Becca asked, trying to avoid eye contact by looking at the other tables in the only coffee house in town.

"Joel told me. He's thankful that she doesn't know everything, but knows he needs to shape up," Elle answered, tilting her head a bit back and forth to catch Becca's expression.

"Why him, Elle?" Becca asked, finally looking her in the face. "There are a million single guys out there. Why a married guy? With kids?"

"First, there are a not a million guys out there, ask Dana. Second, I didn't look for him. He found me. I didn't know he was married at first. We met at a bar. We talked a bit. He didn't mention he had a family," Elle answered angrily.

"You didn't ask?" Becca asked, leaning back in her chair.

"Why would I ask?" Elle answered, leaning back in her chair, as well. "He didn't have a ring. Look, not much happened. It was more of a flirtation. That's it."

"You didn't sleep with him?" Becca asked, squinting her eyes just the littlest bit.

"No, Becca. Did you think I did?" Elle answered, squinting just the littlest bit back.

"Yeah…" Becca said.

"Thanks, Bex. Very nice." Elle's bottom lip started to quiver. "I know people talk about me, you know, but I'm not that bad. I flirt. I tease. I suggest, but I don't sleep with all of them."

"But some?"

Elle tapped the table angrily with her fingernails. "Becca, I would think that you would know that the last thing I want is a guy with kids…"

"Then what are you doing?" Becca asked, leaning towards her.

"I'm just having fun, Becca. These guys, they're looking for someone to have fun with. Their wives are at home. They're boring. They're tired. These guys want to have fun, and so do I! I'm not looking for a relationship, Becca. I'm not stealing anyone's husband."

"Don't you see? You're the girl who *makes* us look boring. You're the girl who *makes* them think there's more out there if they leave!" Becca tried to keep the volume down by clenching her teeth but was screaming under her breath.

"I can't help if they have boring wives at home, Becca," Elle said, moving her hand down slowly in little steps as if to signal Becca to quiet down.

"Don't you get it?" Becca shrieked. "I'm that wife! I'm the one who is home with the kids! Don't you see that? I'm *that* girl! *I'm that girl!*"

"Maybe that's what you're so mad about. That *I'm* the girl who's out. The one who's more exciting. I'm *that* girl! But Becca, I'm not the girl who took Josh. Let's find *her,* Becca. Let's find *that* girl."

He said what?

The Adirondack chairs were normally $249 each but since she was one of their "best customers," she had been sent a code for 20% off one item. There was also another sale going on for everyone else: 10% off a $100 purchase, 15% off $500 and 25% off $1000. $249 x 2 = $498. $498 + x = $500. Subtract $498 from each side. X = $2. She was two dollars short of saving the 15%. That is exactly how Becca reconciled buying the galvanized steel drink dispenser and stand along with a set of six classic acrylic glasses to go with it. That would put her over the top for sure. Algebra wasn't so tricky anymore. She would still need a way to reconcile serving the sugary drinks from her new serving pieces to the boys, but, first to put the chairs together. The message on her machine had actually said that delivery had been scheduled for today, so she had been pleasantly surprised when they arrived a day early.

The toppled tree had recently been removed, and Mason was playing spaceship on their new used playground while Oliver sat on a blanket under the recently purchased market umbrella in the backyard. Becca lugged the two 32-pound boxes to the lawn and cut along the top flap sealed with the strongest glue known to woman.

"Watcha doing, Mommy?" Mason yelled from the top of the yellow curved slide.

"Just putting these new chairs together," she called back to him with a grunt as she ripped the flap off. She could see the glue dried on the cardboard piece was applied in a back and forth swirling motion. *Why would they go to all that trouble*, she wondered, as she carefully tipped the box up and watched the pieces slowly slide their way down from inside and onto the grass. This only momentarily distracted Oliver from his playing before he went right back to mouthing the plastic horse from Mason's farm set.

"When can we make the lemonade, Mommy?" Mason yelled again from the top of the slide.

"When I'm done putting these chairs together," she said, as she unfolded a large piece of paper with the directions and turned it 180 degrees. "We'll sit in them and have some lemonade when I'm done, OK?"

"OK, Mommy," Mason said, turning to climb down the rope wall and lowering himself slowly. "How about a pirate party, Mommy?" His 4th birthday was quickly approaching, and this was his third idea for the celebration.

"Sound good, Oliver?" she asked as Oliver smiled and drooled more on his horse.

Becca gave a big thumbs up to Mason and he returned it with a smile.

She carefully laid out all of the pieces on the grass: the back, the bottom, two sides and two arm rests. The screws, washers and Allen wrench were all still safely in their bag. "It looks like you just connect the back to the bottom and then put the arms on the sides, right Oliver?" More smiling and more drooling. He had had a rough week with the teething. Up late and trouble napping. Late to crawl, but right on time for this, she thought, as she remembered Mason's late nights and restless days.

"Can I help you, Mommy?" Mason asked, as he stood above her now, picking up the bag full of screws and casting a shadow on Becca.

"Sure, Mason," she said, as she carefully took the bag from his hand. "I think we need to put this together first. Can you hold this right here?" She showed him how to hold up the back and she quickly put the screws in the holes, holding the back in place. "Can you stick this in the hole there and turn it?" Mason carefully took the Allen wrench and gave it a little turn.

"This is fun, Mommy!" he said, with a huge smile on his face. Thirty minutes later, the chair was done. Mason climbed in and quickly slid back with his feet flying up in the air.

"How about that lemonade?" she asked him, and the three headed inside. They carefully walked around the littered toys in the room and then made their way past the mess that was still pouring out of the closet.

"Mommy, will we need to go in there again?" he asked.

"I don't think so. We don't usually get storms like that here," she answered as they walked up the stairs, Mason's hand in one of hers and Oliver up on her arm.

"Then why don't we put everything back inside?" he asked.

"I will. I should. You're right, Mason," she said. When they reached the top of the steps, Mason ran off to sit in front of the TV. Becca carefully placed Oliver on the blanket nearby then looked at him as he chewed on the first toy he discovered on the blanket: a big, orange hoop that should have been stacked neatly between the larger yellow and smaller red one on its stand. "Any time you're ready to get goin' on your own, you just let me know," she said to him, giving him the thumbs up. She walked into the kitchen and began ripping into the box that held the galvanized drink dispenser, once again grunting as the flap finally separated to reveal the intricate application of glue. She filled the glass dispenser with water and counted out the right number of sugary, lemony, powdered scoops before stirring it up and placing it on the galvanized stand. *Almost just like on page 28*, she thought. "Mason? You ready for lemonade?"

When she peeked into the living room, she could see that Mason had fallen asleep on the sofa, sitting straight up with his head cocked just a bit to the side. Becca sat down next to Oliver on the floor and began to play with the other hoops strewn around the blanket. She wasn't sure if the bite marks were his or Stevie's and decided a cleaning was in order. She picked him up along with the hoops now all collected on the pole and carried them to the kitchen, dumping them in the sink. She sat Oliver down on the counter and held him around his waist. "What do we do now, Oliver?"

"No," he responded.

"What?" Becca asked, her eyes huge looking at his.

"No," he said, leaning into her a bit as he said it with a smile before sticking his fist in his mouth and chewing.

And that's why some people are guests...

"His first word is 'no'," Becca said into the phone, as she started pouring the macaroni noodles into the boiling water on the stove. "How can Mason's be 'Mama' and Oliver's be 'no'? It doesn't make any sense."

"Becca, you used to hold Mason in your face and say 'Mama' all the time," Elle reasoned.

"I don't say 'no' in Oliver's face, ever," Becca said, stopping the stirring motion as if she couldn't think and stir at the same time.

"Maybe he just hears it a lot," Elle said. "You say 'no' a lot?" she asked, in a voice that sounded like she already knew the answer.

"N... maybe," Becca said, stirring the noodles that were stuck together at the bottom of the pot.

"Say 'no' less, that's all. Next Thursday night get your sitter, OK? We're going downtown. I even got you a cool pair of sunglasses to wear so you'll be incognito at the bar," Elle said excitedly.

"Mommy!" Mason called from the living room, "There's a truck!"

"Every day we have trucks here, Elle. They're removing all the branches, checking the poles and the wires. Mason never naps anymore, and here comes another one waking him up again. I was hoping to get rid of a bunch of shipping boxes at Spring Cleanup but the garbage trucks are picking up everything from the storm instead," Becca said.

"Stop changing the subject," Elle said shortly.

"I don't think this is a good idea. I don't really want to see him or her or them or anything," Becca said, looking at Oliver on all fours in the living room, once again rocking back and forth.

"There's a man in the driveway, Mommy!" Mason screamed. "It's going beep, beep, beep, beep..."

"What are you saying, Becca? Are you saying 'no'?" Elle teased.

Oliver slid one knee just the littlest bit forward. "Five o'clock, OK? Happy hour," Becca asked.

"He's at the door, Mommy!" he screamed, running to the front door with Stevie chasing behind.

"I'll be there with glasses on, babe," Elle said. Becca could hear Elle shout, "Woohoo!"

before she even hung up the phone.

Becca looked through the kitchen and out the window in the front hall. There was a man with a tablet in his hand, waving at Mason and Stevie and smiling at her. She walked to the door and held Stevie back with her foot as she opened it.

"Delivery," he said, "for Becca Gold."

She took the tablet from his hand and reached for the pen. "My delivery came earlier this week. What do you..." Two men were lowering a large white, slipcovered sofa off the truck as the man at the door opened the screen door and slid the washers over to hold it open. "Wait, I didn't order these. Wait, stop, stop!" she screamed, picking Stevie up and running outside.

"You received a call last week confirming delivery, right?" the man asked. They were carrying it up the driveway then turning to make the right angle in through the front door. "Where do you want it?"

"This is a mistake," Becca was saying, over Mason's cheers and Stevie's barking. "It needs to go back on the truck."

"We need to deliver it today. You can schedule a separate pickup if there's been a mistake," the man said. The two men had placed it down and gone to retrieve the second one. "We have everything packed in the truck by order of delivery. There are other items still on it. These are in the way. We need to deliver them, now," he explained.

Becca thanked the men as they left the house and left the two large sofas in the living room. She was dialing the 1-800 number as Mason began jumping from one to the other.

The parking whore...

Becca, again, found Danny's bat in her front yard and started to walk next door with it. Marc sure seemed to have a lot of friends. Every big festival, they were at his place. So many, in fact, they even had to park on the lawn. There must have been 10 cars there last night. Maybe the wind *did* blow just right, into his yard, anyway. Becca needed to invite the girls over. Maybe for the next big show she could break out the martini shakers, make some lemon drop martinis with the matching sugar around the rim of the glasses. *I can serve some appetizers, maybe some cheese, crackers and dips. Maybe it could even be a potluck. We can make s'mores and talk all night whiles we listen to the show. I bet there are a lot of good ones this summer.* She wondered if she could maybe track down just a little bit of pot even…

"How's it going, Becca?" Marc asked as he waved his hand rather awkwardly, but not at her. It looked like a somewhat secret gesture, so she approached him carefully as a car was slowing down in front of his house on the busy street; they signaled and began turning into his driveway. He smiled and waved them in.

"Sorry!" Becca said, "You have company," placing down the bat and turning to walk away.

"No, I don't," Marc said, as the driver walked toward him and placed some bills into his hand. "He's just parking here for the show tonight."

Becca looked over and watched as the man popped the hatchback of his car and began unloading his chairs, wagon and bags. "Can you do that?" she asked quietly, tipping her head towards him to keep it confidential.

"Well, I can, but not really. I don't stand at the street yelling 'Parking!' like that family around the corner. I keep it quiet. I'm on Facebook, Craig's List, I have business cards…"

"Are you serious?" Becca asked.

"Yeah, last weekend almost paid my mortgage. Look, I only have room for one more car for tonight. Do you want some at your place?" Marc asked, taking the money from a man in a Creedence Clearwater Revival T-shirt.

Becca thought for a minute. "I really don't want any trouble," she finally said, nervously.

"Yeah," he said, again gesturing with that awkward wave. Another car driving slowly on the street signaled and began to turn into his driveway.

Becca watched as he parked, walked over to Marc and placed the bills into his hand, then walked back to his car to pop the trunk and remove his things. "Here," he said, motioning for her to follow him to her house. "We're lucky we have these shrubs out in front. Stand about here," he said, pointing to just inside the bushes on her front lawn. He held his left hand perpendicular to the ground, close to his chest, then cupped his right, waving it slowly towards the other.

A car slowed on the busy street, signaled and turned into her driveway. Another followed, another, another. He had parked four cars, three in the turnaround and one blocking hers. Each driver had approached him, handed him some bills and began to unload their cars.

"Where do we go?" one of them asked, his chair in one hand, the handle of his wagon in the other.

"Make a right at the corner and follow the street. The entrance will be on your right," Becca answered. He waved a thank you and he and his date grew smaller in the distance as they walked away.

"You're the third driveway, Becca. Yell, you're the third driveway," Marc said.

"I'm the third driveway!" she called after them.

They turned and, again, waved thank you.

"Make a right at the corner and follow the street. I'm the third driveway!" she offered again and again and again. When the last couple walked away, getting smaller and smaller, Marc appeared next to her.

"Here you go," he said, and placed the stack of bills in her hand. "Have a great night, Becca."

She watched him walk to his driveway and disappear behind his shrubs. She looked at the bills in her hand. One hundred and sixty dollars. *People are paying me to park in my driveway. I am a whore. A parking whore.* She considered the beautiful evenings she had imagined in the yard with the girls. *Fuck that,* she thought as she stuffed the roll of bills into her pocket.

Just an average writer...

"Becca, I can't get Mason to sleep," Josh called to say later that night. "He keeps asking for the book you got him. He keeps saying 'Mason's Book, Mason's Book'. What is that?"

The conversation in the room was loud. She'd decided maybe she could make money and enjoy the concert too, so the girls had come in one car and had parked on the grass to leave room for the paying customers, of course. Becca covered one ear with her hand. "Put Mason on," she said.

"Here, Mason," she heard Josh say, as Mason cried in the background. "Mason, here, it's Mommy," she heard Josh say again.

"Mason! Mason!" she yelled, catching Allie's attention who joined her on the sofa. "Mason!" She heard a soft hello between cries and started…

"A long time ago, before you were around

two people were so happy about the love that they had found."

She could hear Mason's cries becoming sniffles.

"So they had a big, big party, with lots of fun, fun things."

The sniffling had stopped.

"And they gave kisses to each other and they gave each other rings.

And in the years that followed, times were too good to be true. Because with all that love they had and shared, they created you."*

"He's smiling, Becca," Josh said, quietly.

As she went on about his two houses, his two rooms, the adventures of Boys' Weekend Yea! and Mommy Time, she could hear him giggle.

"You see," she concluded,

"At that party, with the rings?

Mommy and Daddy celebrated love and the many gifts love brings. And although they don't live together anymore, their love for each other was true. And with that love, they created, a very special you."

"I love you, Mommy," Mason said.

"I love you, Mason," Becca said. "Good night."

"Good night, Becca," Josh said.

"Good night, Josh," she said, hanging up. The girls were sitting around her now.

"You memorized a whole book?" Dana asked in amazement.

"Well, I wrote it," Becca said.

"You wrote that?" Dana asked again, as Allie stood up and walked into the kitchen.

"Yeah, I was having a hard time finding a book for Mason and Oliver that made sense for us," Becca said quietly.

"Allie? Did you hear that?" Dana was calling into the kitchen. "Becca wrote that! Average writer, my ass…"

Allie had turned the water on in the sink. Becca was the only one who noticed her shoulders shaking as she stood at the counter.

The guy all the girls want...

Becca was walking behind Elle, looking at the colorful carpet beneath her feet. It was almost like a circus tent—red, orange and yellow stripes in a pattern down the hall. It was well worn by the many women walking on it each day. It would probably be removed soon. *He could certainly afford it,* Becca thought.

"We're here," Elle said, holding the doorknob to his office door. The smile on her face reached from ear to ear, and Becca wondered what it would look like in an hour. "Get ready, Bex!" she said, opening the door to the large waiting room filled with women. Most were about their age or so, all of them looking just a tad younger. Elle signaled to two chairs by the window, and Becca walked over to them as Elle approached the desk.

"How are you, Elle?" the lady at the desk asked, as if they were the closest of friends.

Becca sat down and checked out Dr. Bender's "groupies." They were all dressed impeccably, whether it was just off the runway or just off the yoga mat. They were exquisite, really, and their accessories—their shoes, their jewelry, their bags—fabulous. Especially the bags. Dior blue canvas with the retro print, Gucci fanny pack, orange Hermes Evelyne... *Wait, what are the odds of that?*

"He's running a little late. When we get in, we'll get some numbing cream. You won't feel a thing," Elle was saying. But Becca had tuned out and was looking at the lady with the Evelyne a little more closely. The lady was looking at her, too and gave a small smile before turning her bag around on the floor. Becca gazed at the woman, trying to envision the big sunglasses and the heels she saw that day when she was sitting on the curb. She closed her eyes for just a moment and could see her once again, slowly moving her sunglasses down her nose and peering out from above them, "Get your Manolo's out of the gutter, princess..." Yes, it was definitely her. *In all of the plastic surgeon offices in Chicago, I walk into hers.* Becca lifted the magazine just a bit higher to cover her face, hoping the recognition hadn't quite occurred yet on her side. *What is she doing here? She's so beautiful...* Looking around, Becca realized everyone was beautiful—no creases, no lines, all with perfectly formed apple cheeks.

Becca peeked underneath her magazine and spied the lady's bag on the floor, leaning somewhat sloppily against her chair. *I would never put mine on the floor,* she thought, as she leaned her well-structured bag up against her on her chair. Becca's stood taller; it wasn't as flimsy as the lady's with the big apple cheeks. Her zipper was a different color, too—actually a yellow gold, not like the shiny one on Becca's. Since the lady was so much taller, Becca could see that the adjustable strap was set much longer than Becca's and it hung right in front of the perforated dots on the front. There was no pocket. *Omg. There is no pocket.* The Evelyne series I had no pocket, but only the III has the adjustable strap. The lady who "had it all" upon closer look, had fake cheeks ... and a fake bag!

Not everything is as it seems, Becca heard Elle's voice in her head again.

"Elle and Becca," the woman at the desk called with a smile.

"Let's go," Elle said, and Becca put down the magazine and picked up her bag. As she walked past, the lady with the cheekbones lowered her magazine and gave her a smile. She had recognized her, and Becca gave her a smile and a wave. They walked to the door, and the lady at the desk passed them over to the tech to escort them in. They found their room, and Elle sat on the table as Becca took the chair.

"The usual today?" the tech asked Elle, as she approached her with a spackle tool covered in white cream.

"Yes, and my friend, too. She's a newbie, but don't go easy on her," Elle said with a wink.

Moments later, the two of them were covered in white mush.

"So, it won't hurt too bad?" Becca asked, looking into her phone with the camera flipped towards her so she could see her reflection.

"Well, I wish we were going to be numb longer," Elle replied. "When he runs late, I think there isn't as much time for the cream to work. But you'll be fine," Elle said, her smile now causing creases in the spackle on her face.

Becca continued to look at her reflection, the creases in her forehead even more visible with the cracking cream surrounding them. "So, no one will know I worry after this?" she asked, turning her head a bit to watch the horizontal lines even creeping into her hair line.

"Well, if you talk about it, they will. It will definitely seem like you don't…" Elle said. "Look at me. No one thinks I worry. I spent four hours at Ellington yesterday with Max. Can you tell I worry?"

"I didn't know you were there yesterday," Becca started. "Is Max OK?" Elle's brother had been admitted to the clinic for psychiatry patients over a year ago.

"Same. His meds are helping. The facility is great for him. Mom and Dad wanted to see how he was, so I took his picture in his room. It's nice. He's happy. He's *safe* there," Elle said, picking up yet another magazine.

Becca never knew what to say about Max. She had been there that night when they had called the ambulance and the police. She had even helped Elle with all the blood in the bathroom, cleaning off every surface. "Your parents don't see him?" she asked with trepidation.

"Maybe a little, when they're in town. It makes them uncomfortable, though. Reminds my dad of his brother, I guess," she said, flipping through the pages.

"Hello, Elle," Dr. Bender said, walking into the room with a smile and his assistant. "You must be Becca."

"Yes," she said, reaching out to shake his hand.

"You want some of those lines taken care of today?" he asked, looking at the same creases in Becca's forehead that she had just been staring at.

"Yes," Elle answered for her. "And her cheeks? I was thinking she might like some filler."

"It would look nice. A little bit just here," he said, pointing just below the orbit of her eye.

"Will it hurt? I heard filler hurts more than Botox," Becca said.

"It will feel like plucking an eyebrow, really. No big deal. After you watch Elle, you can decide," he said, now approaching the needles on the tray. The assistant was standing next to Elle now, rhythmically tapping her arm, then leg. The needles went in and out quickly. Sometimes Elle's foot would point, flex, twitch. After a few minutes, Elle sat up with an ice pack on her forehead.

"You're up!" she said through the cream and a few little red dots.

Becca stood up and slowly walked to the table, still warm from Elle, and watched as the technician got her needles ready.

"So, Botox up here," he said, pointing to her forehead. "What do you think about a little filler for those cheeks?"

Becca looked over at Elle, who was still smiling with an ice pack now on the side of her face, giving her the thumbs up. "Really, it will just feel like a little pinch. Your face will seem younger, fuller. It will seem like you worry even less."

"OK," Becca agreed, as she leaned back while the assistant began tapping rhythmically on her arm. *The lady's bag is a fake, the cheeks are fake, the look of no concern was clearly fake...* "Ouch!" she heard herself say as the first needle went in. *Sure seems like more than a pinch to me.*

Write your own story…

"So, why did you marry him?" she asked.

Becca was a bit taken aback. "I guess because I thought I was supposed to."

"Did you love him?" she asked. "No judgment. You just didn't say that you did. I'm just wondering."

I didn't say that I loved him, did I? Becca thought about it for a minute. "Of course, I loved him. It's just more that I figured that was the plan. We talked about getting married, he proposed, we got married. It just seemed like that was the way it was supposed to be."

"So, it wasn't romantic; it was more of a done deal, let's say?"

"Yeah, I didn't want to let him down, I guess. It sounds silly now, of course, because he didn't have any problem on going back on *his* end of the deal," Becca said, angrily.

"You sound mad."

"Sometimes I think about if I hadn't married him. I mean, I followed through, I said yes, I made a family with him. I looked out for him. But he didn't seem to have a problem letting me down. He didn't look out for me."

"Maybe you should have been looking out for yourself a bit more, too. It's OK to be a little selfish, Becca," she said.

"That's what my yoga teacher says my mat is for," Becca said.

"Tell me about it."

"She says that it's my time and my place to be selfish. On the mat. We're not supposed to think about stuff going on off the mat. We set an intention. It's like not something you have, but something you give. I'm still trying to figure that part out, really," Becca said.

"You'll have to let me know when you figure that out. What else do you do?"

"Reach, balance, breathe. If it's hot, I wipe my forehead with my shirt..."

"Reach, balance, breathe, be selfish. Sounds like good advice to me. Do you enjoy it?" she asked.

"Yeah, Elle made me go. Now I go even when she doesn't. Which is fine because my instructor said that sometimes she does her best work alone," Becca said.

"I wonder why that is. Why is it easier to do her best work alone?"

"Maybe because no one is watching you, or you're not watching anyone else, I guess. There is this one guy in my class. He has probably 4 percent body fat. He likes to do headstands and stuff when the rest of us are just in these little balls. I mean, some people do put their elbows on their knees and balance, but he goes all the way up."

"And?" she asked.

"Well, I think it makes people uncomfortable. It is kind of a beginner class. We all look at him. It's as if he wants attention or something, you know? 'Look at me! I can do a headstand!' Or something like that," Becca explained.

"But that is *his* mat, right? *His* space? *His* time to be selfish? He might not be thinking about any of you at all, right?"

"I suppose so."

"I wonder, Becca, how that would feel. To just do something you feel like doing, not worrying about others looking at you or you wondering if you're doing it right," she said. "Just being a little selfish."

"Only think about myself?"

"Well, no, Becca, but maybe invest more in yourself. You are important, Becca. You can make decisions that are beneficial to you. You know? Come through for yourself? Don't let yourself down. Do you think you could be comfortable with that?"

"I have kids," Becca said, confused.

"I'm not saying only look out for yourself. I'm saying that you shouldn't worry about changing a plan that someone else has made. We all have our own story. Write your own. Do a headstand if that's what you want. Don't worry that someone doesn't want you to or that they might judge you. Write your own story," she said.

An unexpected introduction...

"So, you like to hang upside down?" the man asked.

Becca had been sitting backwards and upside down on the benches again after class, waiting for the "kerplunck". She righted herself a bit, holding her hand up to block the sun shining in her face. She could see the toned, hairy legs but couldn't make out his face until, chivalrously, he stepped into the sunlight, blocking the bright rays.

"I watch you in class. You're a gymnast, right?" he asked.

"Nope," Becca answered. She got this all the time. It was her legs. She had short, strong legs. Clearly, she had to be a gymnast... to guys anyway. Women would think she ate candy. They would be right.

"Then a skater?" he asked.

"Nope," Becca answered. She got this all the time too. She was petite. Clearly, she had to be a skater... again, to guys only. Women would think it was difficult for her to find proper-fitting jeans. They would be right about that, too. She looked around the beach to see that most of her class had left already. He was reaching into his pocket, then pulling out a card.

"Look, I think we could have fun tomorrow. Give me a call," he said. He waved and walked down the path to the parking lot.

Is that really what's out there? she wondered as she sat up on the bench. She turned to look at him as he once again gave a wave, not an ounce of flesh moving on his 4 percent body fat frame. *You like to hang upside down?* That's his line? Elle wasn't kidding. Dana had it right, too. The pickings were slim, she thought, as she placed the card in her bag.

Sunday morning at 8 o'clock she was standing in the rain in front of a yoga studio holding her baseball hat on her head. He had said 8 o'clock. *Where is he?* she thought as a car drove by splashing a puddle onto her shoes.

"Becca!" she heard behind her. It was Mike, aka "4 Percent Body Fat Guy," poking his head out of the door of the adjacent building. "Over here! Not that one!" he was yelling.

Becca ran over to the nondescript door, sidestepping the puddles on the sidewalk. She ran into the lobby, took off her soaking hat and began stomping her shoes on the rug.

"You sure move like a gymnast to me," he said, smiling. "Come on. We're late," he said, motioning to the stairway. "I think you'll like this. It's a little unconventional. I started after my last breakup. It's been helpful."

Already telling me about his old girlfriends? Red flag, she thought, removing her shoes and stepping on the mat made of rocks. She looked back in horror as one of the stones came loose and stuck on one of her now bare feet. She quickly pulled it off, placed it back and looked around to make sure no one else had seen. The room was empty, only the contraptions hanging on the walls caught her eyes. Straps, straps, more straps. The yoga teacher appeared with an armful of mats and began to unroll them. Mike and the other three people in class quickly stood at each one as the director greeted them, and

Becca followed. The instructor had an accent; Becca couldn't quite place it, but it was totally fitting to the woman with the perfectly toned everything.

"Behind you is a purple strap, please just release the carabiner," she said.

Norway? Becca thought, as she watched the others unclipping the metal ring and seeing the two holes in the strap become one.

"You should be able to step in now," the instructor said, as she dropped the loop on the floor, placed her feet inside and lifted the strap up to her waist. The rest followed suit, dropping it on the floor, placing their feet inside and lifting the strap up to their waists, as well. The teacher was approaching Becca, though. It was obvious what was about to happen and, as usual, Becca readied herself. "Let's just shorten this," she said, sliding the buckle over, making Becca's strap about a third the length as the others. "Now," she said, and Becca dropped, slid and lifted.

"Now," she spoke to the group. "Lean. It will hold you. Don't be frightened. It can hold up to 300 pounds."

Becca observed the four others leaning forward, their straps becoming taut between their waists and the wall. Becca leaned just a bit and felt the resistance. Mike smiled and gave her a thumbs-up.

"Let go of the strap," she said, looking at Becca. "Really, it will hold you."

Becca looked around to see her classmates, all standing with their feet hip-distant apart, bent over with their arms out to their sides. Becca slowly leaned and lifted her arms.

"A sense of falling would be totally normal here," the teacher explained. "Relax, lift your heels, go up on your toes," she said in her calming *Finnish?* voice.

Becca lifted her heels and dangled with her arms out to her sides, her toes digging into the mat beneath her. *A sense of falling would be normal here,* she told herself, as she floated above her shadow on the ground.

"Breathe and trust," the instructor said, as she walked to each, moving their legs, their feet and arms. She stopped at Becca. "A bit more pigeon-toed," she said, moving Becca's feet even further apart. Becca quickly grabbed the straps and placed her feet down flat. "Breathe and trust," the teacher repeated, pulling Becca's hands from the straps.

Becca could see Mike floating next to her; his eyes closed as he hung effortlessly in the harness. *I could never be that relaxed,* she thought as the teacher finally called for them all to lift up. The next exercises were similar to her yoga class, just the tension of the strap made it more challenging. She missed the music, too. All those '70s songs were so inspiring. The small room on this rainy day was quiet; all that could be heard was the conscious breathing of her classmates on the straps and Becca's nervous giggles as she tried to keep up.

"OK," the teacher said. "I need you to step inside backwards now. The strap should fit tightly across your bottom," she explained, using one of the students as an example. The teacher worked the strap down the student's lower back and across her bottom until her feet were suddenly on tiptoes and then, suddenly, off the floor, in the sky and wrapped around the straps hanging from the ceiling. Mike once again gave Becca the thumbs up, then quickly turned upside down himself. The instructor flipped the other two and quickly approached Becca, who was already grabbing tightly with her toes to the floor.

"Let's put this around here," she said, placing the strap around Becca's butt. "Lean back," she said. Becca slowly went onto her toes and leaned as the instructor gently held her back. Her legs quickly sought out the straps and grabbed them tightly as her hair dragged on the floor. She placed her hands down on the mat and looked around at the others, floating upside down, hands at heart. "Lift up your hands," the instructor said.

Becca couldn't tell up from down and quickly held tighter to the floor. "When you're ready," the instructor said, as she walked to check the form of the others, calmly, beautifully hanging in stillness. Becca searched the upside-down room, trying to orient herself from floor and ceiling. Her brain whirled. Her heart raced. *Breathe and trust,* she told herself. She thought of the horizon at the lake and tried to imagine that where the wall met the floor was where the sky met the water. She could feel her racing heart starting to slow. "Crunch up," the instructor said. "Use your core and pull."

The other four bodies quickly righted. Becca could even hear as their feet hit the mats. Her classmates were now leaning against the wall. She could see her instructor's feet walking towards her. "Crunch up, Becca," she heard her say.

"I can't. I can't tell up from down. I can't. I can't!" The panic was there again. She even spun a bit while trying to right herself.

"Becca…" she heard Mike say.

"She's got this. Becca, breathe. Tighten your core. Bring your nose to your belly. You got this," she heard the *Nordic?* voice say. Becca tried again and again. Sweat dripped off her forehead and fell onto the mat between her hands. "Slow down. Concentrate. Becca, bring your nose to your belly…"

Becca took a deep breath, brought her nose to her belly and the room quickly tipped. She grabbed the straps tightly and watched as the room righted itself.

"Good job," the accented voice said. "Unbuckle now."

Becca's hands shook as she pressed the clip in and released the strap. She placed her back on the wall and lined up with her classmates

"Good work, today," the instructor said. "Namaste."

Mike approached Becca slowly. "It gets easier. Come on. Coffee is on me," he said, handing her the still wet baseball cap.

"I'm never doing that again," Becca said, sipping coffee in the busy coffee house. They had managed to grab a sofa to sit on, and the warm fireplace wasn't far away.

"I said that, too. The first time. I only started a couple of months ago," he explained. "After my last breakup."

Someone should tell him how unattractive that is, to talk about his ex-girl-friend, she thought. "I'm actually getting divorced," she offered, seeing if he would take the bait.

"Really? I'm sorry to hear that, Becca. Really, it's rough. I know," he said sadly. "We were together for four years. I'm really still just trying to get used to being alone."

Well, that didn't work. "Yeah, I try not to talk about it too much," she said. *That should do it,* she thought.

"Really? I can't help but talk about it. It's who I am right now. It's all I think about," he said, looking towards the door.

Becca turned around to look as people walked in and out. "So, you started hanging upside down?" she asked.

"Well, sort of. I was spying. I wanted to check out who was replacing me. I was following the new guy and he was taking a class like this one, so I walked in. He was hanging upside down next to me. He was cut and ripped. I mean, he was in amazing shape. I figured, if that's what it takes, well, I started doing yoga. I didn't used to look like this. This is new. It feels good, though," he said.

"My friend wants me to go check out my replacement," Becca said. "I'm sure she is everything that I'm not."

"Well, Kevin was certainly everything that I'm not," he said sadly.

"I always wonder what Lauren even wants with Josh. I mean, he has kids. My friends have told me that it's slim pickings out there. Either guys are married, or jerks, or…"

"Yeah, they are. Billy disappointed me. I never would have thought he would have left me like that…"

"… or gay…." she heard herself say as Mike took a napkin to wipe his first tear.

A picture, an association…

It was the felt hat. The jeans were simply boy-cut. The belt was plain and barely visible under the loosely tucked-in button-down shirt, its sleeves slightly rolled and pushed up past her wrists. It was the hat. People throughout the gallery were looking at Allie because of the hat. She stood in front of the large canvas and asked her class a simple question. "What do you think?"

Most of her students stood quietly, holding their notebooks against their chests, maybe mouthing the end of a pen or pencil. Allie made eye contact with Becca across the room, stuck out her tongue and loosened the imaginary noose around her neck. "Anything?" she asked. "What if I shared with you that of all of the works here, this is my least favorite? Would that surprise any of you?"

Two or three hands went up just then. "Why? Why does that surprise you?" she asked, pointing at a girl in rolled-up boyfriend jeans with striped tights underneath.

"Because it's so beautiful? A mother bathing her child so thoughtfully? Holding her so tightly so she doesn't fall, but cleaning her feet so lovingly? How the child is so trusting and relaxed in her mother's arms?" she asked, rather troubled.

Allie turned then, facing the canvas, her sloppy jeans and hat in full view of the class behind her. "Anyone else want to share any thoughts?" she asked. "Does it maybe bring back a memory of your mom? Bathing you? Loving you?" Allie asked. Many hands went up then, as Allie turned around. "Art can provoke many feelings and memories. I'd like each of you to give it some thought. Find a painting, a sculpture, anything really that provokes a memory and write about it for Monday. Ask yourself, how does it make me feel? Why does it make me feel this way?"

The students walked away, still holding their notebooks to their chests and their pens or pencils resting between their lips. Allie turned once again towards the Cassatt hanging in front of her.

"I thought you liked 'The Child's Bath,'" Becca said, now standing next to Allie, looking at what Becca had always thought was a beautiful moment and feeling remarkably taller after being stretched in the little room that morning. "One of your least favorite? Really?"

"It's not the work, Becca. It's the memory associated with it. That's the idea," Allie said. "Is there a painting here that you maybe don't love, but always remember?"

"Yeah," Becca said. "The one with the rock. I think there are people around it? Like it fell out of the sky or something?"

"By Josh Blume," Allie said.

"Maybe," Becca said.

"So, out of all of these, why that one? Why do you remember that one?" Allie asked.

"That's the million-dollar painting. My brother and I played Masterpiece once and he had that card in front of him for most of the game. I chose a lot of paintings to take from him but never that one, cuz I thought it was scary. At the end of the game, we added up all of our paintings. I can still remember him slowly sliding the white clip off and showing me the million-dollar card underneath..." Becca said.

"So that's the million-dollar painting..." Allie said. "Is that a good memory?"

"Well, no. He won." Becca pointed back at the Mary Cassatt painting. "Does this make you think of your mom? Is it a bad memory about your mom?"

Allie was remarkably silent. "No, I kind of think of you, actually, alone, bathing the boys, lonely, not knowing where your husband is," she said in a trembling voice.

Becca's eyes grew larger, and she stared at the woman in the portrait. The lady's hair was in a bun except for a tiny wisp or two, her striped dress looked cumbersome and maybe too warm for inside. "She doesn't look so sad or lonely to me," Becca finally said.

"Well, you didn't either," Allie said, sadly.

Becca looked closely at the lady again. "You got it all wrong, Allie. She's happy. No, her husband isn't there, but she's happy. She is with her child. It is peaceful. It is tender. She knows her child loves her," Becca said, taking Allie's arm. "She knows she does her best work on her own."

"I hope so," Allie said. "Don't you just want to punch him sometimes? Don't you just want to…I don't know."

"I *am* supposed to spy on Josh and see the slut he's been sleeping with. Elle and I are going to go kind of incognito to this place I found on his receipts," Becca finally said.

Allie was still looking at the mother and child in front of her. "Oh, that's a good idea," she said. "What are you going to wear?"

"Elle is bringing sunglasses. I don't know, yet."

"Your combat boots, Bex. You should boot-up."

"I should, shouldn't I?"

"Definitely," Allie said, through a growing smile.

"You really moving in with Jackson, huh?" Becca asked.

"Yup."

"It really is like magic, isn't it?" Becca asked.

"Well, we better hope so," Allie said. "I'm subleasing to Dana."

The parking whore's bitch...

He had said 5:15 and he was right. The cars slowly inched along the busy street, sometimes coming to a complete stop. Marc was standing on the sidewalk just a few feet away, looking down at his phone as, one by one, oncoming cars turned on their signals and pulled into his driveway. Remarkable. He didn't even need to look up. Becca stood just behind the hedge, keeping one eye on the street and one eye on the house. Oliver in his SuperSaucer, Mason drawing at the table, and Stevie spinning and barking at the window.

Marc looked up towards Becca and held up five fingers. *Was that minutes or cars?* she wondered, as yet another car signaled and turned in. She turned once again to look at the house. Oliver flipping the plastic pages on the saucer, Mason now on his knees on the chair, reaching for a crayon and Stevie... where was Stevie? Becca slowly stepped backwards, peering into the house. She could see Stevie's tail wagging wildly, just beyond the fireplace. The mustard curtain was stretched from the pole to her mouth. Within seconds, she could see the pole flying off the wall and onto the floor. Becca ran up the driveway and opened up the front door to find white plaster chips on the tile, the pole still connected to the mustard curtain and the mustard curtain still connected to Stevie's teeth.

"Stevie! No!" Becca screamed, as she reached down and picked up the now very satisfied dog. Becca ran outside holding her, watching as the traffic went by.

"Becca, where were you? I sent three cars your way!" Marc was shouting from his driveway.

"I had to get my darn dog," she said, holding Stevie up and away from him. Suddenly, an oncoming car rolled down its window.

"Aw! She's adorable!" the woman in the red Beetle gushed.

"Thanks," Becca said.

"Do you know where there's parking for the show tonight?" she asked.

"You can park here," Marc said, now standing next to Becca, pointing into her driveway.

"How much?" she asked, still smiling at Stevie.

"Forty dollars?" Becca asked.

"It's not a question, Becca," Marc said quietly into her ear, elbowing her in her shoulder.

"Forty dollars," Becca said.

The woman turned on her signal and began to pull into the driveway. Marc waved her in, showing her where to park. Becca stood at the sidewalk, watching her slowly pulling into the turnaround.

"Becca! Get out there!" Marc yelled. "Hold up the dog!"

Becca ran to the sidewalk and held Stevie up. Windows lowered, "Aws" were said, turn signals blinked. Three minutes later, her customers were either unpacking their trunks or greeting their new 6-pound friend.

"Not a bad night," Marc said, handing her $200. She hadn't anticipated the two cars on the lawn, but looked at the bills in her hand and simply side-stepped around the black Corolla by the boxwoods.

"Marc, I have to give you something," she said, holding out $40.

"Nah, no worries. On slow nights, though," he said, patting Stevie's tiny head as her tail wagged wildly, "bring her to my house. What are you gonna do with all that loot? Something crazy, I hope."

"Yeah, crazy," she said, walking back to the house. She walked in and over the mustard curtain lying on the tile.

"Mommy, can I tell you my story to write for me now?" Mason asked, as she put Stevie down and picked Oliver up. She sat down next to Mason, placing Oliver onto her lap and reached for a crayon. "This is me and daddy and Oliver and Lauren and we're at the ice cream store…"

Becca carefully wrote each word. Mason picked up his work and carried it to his room. He already had many pictures in piles up there, some for Mommy's house and some for Daddy's.

Becca picked up her iPad, already opened to the Pottery Barn page. Cart (8 items), with the picture of the white canvas curtains in the upper right corner, this time, carefully clicking *Check Out as Guest*.

Scrappy returns…

"So, this is where he goes," Elle said, glancing around the room. There were lots of men standing at the bar, a few sitting at the tables. Becca supposed that at one point, this place was full of men dressed in their suits from work on Thursday nights, but now they came straight from their casual work places and their clothes reflected it. Some in khakis, some in jeans, but all of them in rolled-up long sleeves. Some were heavier, taller, thinner, shorter, but they all looked the same to Becca. Mostly, she was surprised at the number of them that had shaved their heads. It did explain part of Dana's challenge, she thought to herself, as Dana wasn't interested in anyone who didn't have a full head of hair, preferably dark brown and curly. "He could really blend in here. We better keep our eyes out."

"Keep our eyes out?" Becca asked, smirking.

Elle tried to hide a bit behind her menu. "Becca, you know what I mean. I swear, if you don't make this fun for me, I'm leaving."

"Fine, eyes out," Becca said, looking around the place. Thursday nights seemed to be the new Friday, she thought. She wondered how late they would all stay. The boys were with Tori. She was going to have to spot him in the next 45 minutes. At $15 an hour, she gave herself until 7:30. Tops.

"You sure he comes here, though?" Elle asked, now positively checking out the other guys as well.

"This place has been on his receipts a few times. I'm not sure. Ya know, I'm not feeling right about this. We should go," Becca said, while starting to fidget with her bag.

"Becca, we came all the way down here. The kids are fine. Just a little longer," Elle said.

"What if he *does* show up? I don't... What will I do?" Becca asked, nervously.

"I don't know. I guess you'll figure it out."

Becca's heart raced as she glanced around the room. The 25-foot floor-to-ceiling windows let in all the sun that still shined at 6:45. She could see women entering now. Some walking over to the men who had been there for a while, some staying in their group of girls. Her hand shook each time she raised her drink to her lips. This was a bad idea. "Elle, I gotta go," she said, stumbling a little off the high stool.

"Becca, come on. Sit down. He probably isn't even going to come here tonight. Let's just sit and finish our drinks. Then we'll go. Relax..." Elle said, as she squinted, tipped her head just a bit and sighed. "Becca, he's here."

"Where?" Becca asked nervously. "Where is he?"

"He's walking in the door. Looks like he's with another guy. A little taller, dark hair. Dana would like him," Elle said.

"What's he doing?" Becca asked urgently.

"I told you, Becca, he's walking in the door. Now he's shaking someone's hand. Oh, now it's like that man hug thing. He's fake laughing now. They're saying goodbye. Oh my god, the guy gestured to his friend, 'I have no idea who he is…'" holding her palms up, shrugging her shoulders.

"I want to leave," Becca said.

"I'm getting us two more drinks. Tori's on me. This is better than anything on TV tonight," Elle said, waving her two fingers in the sky, then pointing one at herself and one at Becca. "Oh, here he goes again. He knows this guy, too. He's loosening his tie and leaning up against the bar talking to him," she said leaning back.

"I really don't feel well, Elle. I want to go," Becca said, holding her purse on her lap.

"Well, you can't because he's right by the door. Get comfy, Bex," she said as the server placed two more martinis on the table.

Becca's hands were shaking as she took the phone out of her bag. She called home and Tori answered on the third ring. "The boys are great!" she said. "Of course, I can stay another hour." *I would too,* Becca thought as she figured the babysitting tab.

"He sure does talk to a lot of guys, Becca," Elle said, starting her second drink. "Here, he's tapping someone on the back. Guy turns around, shakes his hand. Blah, blah, blah. Guy leaves. He's alone, now. Looking around, looking around… He's waving at someone. It's a girl."

"And?" Becca asked.

Elle watched quietly. Becca could see the anger growing in her face. Finally, she looked back to Becca. "Maybe we should go."

"What's happening?" Becca asked, covering her mouth with one hand, holding the stool with the other.

"I just think we should go," Elle repeated, taking out her wallet and laying some bills on the table.

Becca straightened her back and slowly turned around. She saw him now, leaning up against the bar, his arm around her. She was about average height, average weight. Her short brown hair was cute, exemplifying her larger chin. She was dressed in black, matching bag and shoes. It was worse than Becca had imagined. There was nothing, absolutely nothing exceptional about her at all. Becca had thought she'd been traded in for a new model; this woman was so ordinary, she could have been standing next to her at the grocery store yesterday. Becca turned to see Elle looking at her pensively.

"Yeah, let's go," Becca said, feeling unsteady as she hopped off the stool. She threw the strap of her bag over her head, crossed the strap in front of her and rested her hand on it. She and Elle walked towards the tall glass doors as the sun was setting.

"Becca, I'm so sorry. I don't know what to say..." Elle said, turning towards Becca only to find her gone.

"Hi," Elle heard from the bar, and turned towards the familiar voice. "I'm Becca, Josh's wife. Can you please be done fucking my husband by eight? Our boys love a good night story right after their baths. Thanks!" Becca was shaking her hand.

Ass kicked.

A picture, and a new association...

"Bex, that was amazing! Fucking amazing!" Elle said, following the street as it bent along the river. "I mean one minute you're behind me and the next, I'm like 'Where's Bex?' and there you are! Standing at the bar with that girl, shaking her fucking hand!"

"Can you turn left here?" Becca asked.

"Yeah, sure. I mean, Josh was right there behind you, so you couldn't see, but he had his hand up on his forehead," Elle said, putting her hand on her forehead. "Like, oh my god, my wife is here!"

"Another block," Becca said.

"Yeah, sure. You should have seen his friends. They all had their hands on their stomachs like they had all just been kicked in the gut, or lower I guess. Did you hear them all groan? I mean, Bex, you destroyed him! Demolished him!" Elle was screaming. "The girls are going to be so proud! I'm so happy I was there! Amazing, Bex. Fucking amazing!"

"Pull over here," Becca said as she took out her phone and handed it to Elle.

"Who should I call?" Elle asked, looking at the screen.

"No, I need a picture," Becca said, running across the street. There it was, just like it had been that night, that day, in the picture on her phone.

"Of what?" Elle asked, looking at the quiet, rather abandoned street.

"Right here," Becca said, sitting next to the rusted legs of the mailbox on the chipped concrete curb.

"Yes, I remember this!" Elle said. "Yes!"

Becca lifted her boot onto the sewage grate.

Stomp.

Click.

So, that's how you remember...

She still had no notebook. How did she remember everything? Did she ever get clients mixed up? *Maybe today she'll mistakenly ask me about my troubles at work? About my teenage kids?* Becca thought as she sat across from the Boho chic lady in the fake Eames chair. "So Becca," she said, "I was thinking about your 221 points. We covered maybe 180 of them so far. I'd like a chance to talk about the last 40 or so."

Becca could feel her heart beginning to race. Those last 40 points hadn't been talked about, not with anyone. "OK," she said, stretching her neck and trying to sound in control.

"You said that you had lost a friend recently," she began. "What was her name?"

"Katie," Becca answered quietly.

"Katie," she said back. "Can I ask what happened to Katie?"

Becca's bottom lip began to tremble as she tried to answer. No words would come.

"Was Katie sick?"

Becca shook her head.

"Was Katie in an accident?"

Becca waved her hand and shook her head no again.

"Becca," she said. "What happened to Katie?"

The words still wouldn't come. Becca flapped her hands to stop the tears.

"Becca, let's talk about Katie. Just tell me something about Katie."

"She was my friend," Becca finally managed to say.

"And?"

"And she died," Becca answered.

The Boho chic lady was looking up at the ceiling now, as if just the right words were somehow printed on the ceiling tiles, between the small square lights. "I bet it would be nice to have her here right about now?"

"Uh huh," Becca said.

"Was she a good listener?"

"Uh huh."

"Did you share a lot with her?" she asked.

"Uh huh," Becca said.

"Did she know you were unhappy in your marriage?"

Becca looked at her, exhausted.

"She give you any good advice?"

"Don't marry Josh," Becca said.

"Hmm. Wow. She knew a lot then, I guess. Was she married?" she asked.

"Yes," Becca said. "To Jeremy."

"How was their marriage?"

"Not great."

"Was she happy?"

"Not really," Becca said, looking away.

"That's sad," she said. "You talked about this stuff, I assume."

"Yes," Becca said.

"You probably miss that, then."

"Yes."

"You ever think about what she would say now?"

"Yes."

"What would she say?"

"That she's glad he's gone, probably," Becca said with a small smile.

"Really?" she asked.

"That's what we talked about the last time we were together," Becca said, looking up at the same square lights.

"Tell me," she said, smiling.

"We were in front of my house. She was dropping me off and we were sitting in her car finishing up our Diet cokes and hot fudge sundaes," Becca said, drifting back to that night.

"Interesting mix," the lady said.

"It always made sense to us… Anyway, there were four deer in front of my house. A mom and her babies. We pulled into the driveway and sat there quietly for a while, watching them eat. They must have heard a noise or something because all of a sudden, they looked startled. One ran in one direction while the others ran in the other. I was worried about the mom finding her family. Katie knew I was crazy like that. We sat in the car talking a little more. She told me not to worry, that I worry too much, that the deer would find her way home," Becca said, finally looking her in the eye.

"Did you ever see the deer again?" she asked, hopefully.

"No, but I know it caught up with the others. When Katie left, she had seen them all run down the street together in line, so she texted a little while later to tell me," Becca said, looking at her shoes.

"Wow," she said. "Becca that is special. Very, very special."

"Yeah, I haven't told anybody about that," Becca said.

"Why not?" she asked.

"I don't know," Becca said. "Just feels like maybe it was supposed to be just for me and Katie to know or something."

"It's a nice memory," she said.

"Yeah. Katie had been running her hand through her bob. You know, I could still tell how surprised she was when her fingers reached the end of her hair. It was the speed of her hand moving through it. Katie still expected her hair to be longer. Her fingers seemed to slip off the ends of the strands instead of working their way through past her shoulders and twisting a handful, like she used to," Becca said, running her hand through her own hair now.

"She lost her hair?"

"They shaved her hair. Every time. Every time she had a stroke, they shaved her hair," Becca said.

"How many times were there?" she asked, sadly.

"Four. I reminded her every time that it would grow back. When we were little, she kept her wig on a stand and we would use it to practice French braids."

"She liked French braids?"

"Yeah. She didn't always wear it, though. Like when it was hot outside. Kids can be mean, you know. I remember one day some boys were teasing her when we ran under her Donald Duck sprinkler," Becca said, now looking out the window.

"How old were you?" she asked.

"Six. I told them to go fuck themselves," Becca said, remembering that day.

"At 6?" she half smiled, curious more than startled.

"I learned a lot from my big brother. Yeah, that was a good day," Becca said smiling, recalling the exact day her brother taught her how to use that word. "That night in the driveway with the deer, I told Katie that next summer, I'd get a sprinkler and she'd come over and we'd watch Mason and Oliver run through it like we used to. It would be like old times."

"Nice plan," she said.

"That's when she started in again with the 'What if I die, Bex?' stuff."

"She was worried about dying?"

"She asked that a lot."

"And what did you say?"

"I'd say, 'Stop asking that! You're doing great. The doctors say you're doing great. It's gonna work this time. It won't happen again. It just won't,'" Becca recited in her perfectly practiced answer.

"Becca, did you think she would die? Was it a surprise for you? I mean, her first stroke at 6? Three others?" she asked.

"I didn't think she would die," Becca said.

"So, this *was* a bit of a surprise for you…" she said.

"Yeah," Becca said quietly.

"So, that was the last conversation you shared, then?"

"Yeah," Becca said. "I mean, no. We talked some about Josh, about Jeremy. That's when Katie said, 'Let's promise to be happy next year.'"

"Becca…" she said.

"She had a stroke two weeks later," Becca said, her voice cracking a bit.

"Becca…" the lady said again.

"She didn't get to be happy next year," Becca said through the tears that were finally falling. "She didn't get to be happy…But I promised her I would."

Let's get to your goal…

"What's that?" Becca asked.

"That's a junior guitar. You can also call it a three-quarter. It's smaller. I thought maybe you might like it," Rich said.

Becca looked at the tiny guitar resting on the stand in the corner of the room. It looked like it could be one of Mason's. She could already see him standing in front of the TV watching her Eagle's concert DVD with it strapped across him. It was so small, he could probably even turn it to his side to take a bow after each song ended.

"You said you wanted acoustic," Rich said, reaching into his pocket and taking out a folded piece of paper. It was the form Becca had filled out on that very first day. Placing it down on the table in front of him, he pointed his finger and read along, *Goal: Play acoustic guitar.* "This is a great option. It's smaller, lighter, the neck is slimmer. There is a bump in the back," he said, while spinning it around. "It will sit a bit further away from you. You'll need to reach around a little. Try it on." He picked up the tiny guitar by the neck and held it in front of her. She reached out rather reluctantly.

"People will definitely make fun of this," Becca said, placing it in her lap.

"You shouldn't care what people think," he argued. "Let's get to your goal."

She reached around.

"I told you the bump on the back might get in your way a bit. Work around it. Keep reaching," Rich told her.

She pressed down on the first string.

"The strings are going to be harder to press because they're steel; your last ones were nylon. You'll need to push harder. And the frets are shorter. Where you're used to pressing in three, you might find you're in four," he explained.

She pushed down harder and could feel the fine steel line imprinting on her fingertip.

"Even harder, Becca," he coaxed her.

She pressed and strummed. Finally, the sound she had wanted. She adjusted her fingers before starting again.

"Don't think so much. Your fingers will remember," he said.

But it sounded wrong.

"Shorter frets, Becca. Less space to move around in, that's all. You just need to get used to the change. You know what it should be like. You'll find it," he continued. "This will work."

She stopped for a bit and looked at him. "You're only 23?" she asked.

"Yeah," he said, picking up his guitar to play the melody.

Give yourself a break. There's a bump. Work around it. Reach further. Push harder. Don't think so much. You know what it should feel like. You shouldn't care what people think. You just need to get used to the change. Let's get you to your goal.

"You sure know a lot for 23."

"I've been doing this for a long time."

"Becca, you going to play?" he asked.

"I guess I'm a bit nervous," she said.

"You know, it's not going to be perfect," he said, "but it will work."

And she hits it out of the park...

Becca was back on that old commercial street again, her new acoustic junior guitar lying in the trunk. She parked and sat for a minute watching the nets swinging in the wind from an open garage-like door, before finally getting out. She approached the man at the counter cautiously; he was wearing a shirt that matched the sign outside: Baseball Bootcamp.

"How can I help you?" he asked as she finally walked all the way in.

"I'd like to try your batting cage," Becca said.

"You ever use a batting cage before?" he asked.

"No."

The lesson was short. Stand here, put your bat there, hold the bat just a few inches up the neck, raise your right elbow high, stand with your legs shoulder-distance apart and slightly bent, watch the machine. He put the helmet on Becca's head, gave it an extra tap and left her alone inside the small baseball field. She stood alongside the home plate and swiped her Baseball Bootcamp card through the scanner. Fifty balls for 20 bucks. He had explained that balls could come at her as slow as 35 mph or as fast as 75. That she could set the height herself, but that he'd be happy to help if she had trouble.

He was out at the ball machine now. "OK, stand right there," he said, as she heard the cranking from the machine as it readied the first ball.

The few times she actually made contact with the oncoming balls were more painful than she ever could have imagined. The reverberation in her wrists, forearms then shoulders took her aback. She stepped out of the batter's box and watched several pitches go by before going back on deck. *Take that, Josh! Take that, it's not a self-portrait! Take that, you're just an average writer!* she thought each time she heard the crack and watched the balls fly away.

When she was done, she brought the helmet and bat back to the counter. She reached in her pocket for the card.

"Save it for next time," the man had said. "You can reload it ."

"I won't be needing it," she said, as she left it on the counter.

Becca drove home, pulling into the chalk-covered driveway to see Mason and Tori coloring, Oliver chewing on a plastic ball. She once again grabbed Marc's son's bat from the front lawn. "Tori, you can stay outside for a bit?" she said, marching into the house. She greeted Stevie with a scratch on the belly as her now 7-pound friend followed at Becca's heels. She walked through the living room towards Mason's work bench and noticed how he had carefully placed each tool in its place earlier in the day. She reached for the goggles hanging by their elastic band, then walked up the seven steps. At the top, she flipped the switch that sent the ceiling fan spinning in circles. She snapped the elastic on the back of her head and pulled the tiny plastic lenses over her eyes, picked up the bat and, holding her bat just a few inches up the neck, raised her right elbow high, stood with her legs shoulder distance apart and slightly bent, then she took four good swings and took that fan down.

The phone started ringing in Becca's bag. She ran down the stairs and reached into the perforated pocket, taking off the googles to see Hillary's number on the screen. "What's up?" Becca asked. There was silence on the other end, then, she heard it, breathing, gasping, crying... "Hillary! What's wrong? What's wrong?"

"It's...it's," Hillary struggled to get out. "It's, it's... Lucy..."

"I'm leaving now. Give me 30."

Namaste...

"Let's start with an intention. Something that will keep you in the moment, help you to be present. Something that you can take off the mat, that will guide you, through your day, each day. Maybe it is something you can even share..." the instructor started that Saturday morning. "Remember, an intention isn't something you have, it's something you give..."

You keep saying that.

"Maybe it's to find a way to be thankful for everyone in our lives. They all add something to our lives that we can be thankful for."

Becca placed the foam brick under her butt and considered this intention, listening to the calming music coming from the overhead speakers. *Not everyone*, she thought. "This is your time," the instructor continued. "Relax, go back to child's pose if you need a rest. Breathe out with the release of your back, in with the tightening of your muscles. Look at the horizon and reach." All of them reached forward, leaning in, raising their left leg behind them. She followed their lead, reaching out, straightening her back and lifting her leg. She looked at the horizon, the beautiful sun just above the water.

"Oh look, here comes a deer," the instructor said in a peaceful voice. It walked right in front of the glass, stopping to look inside. Becca lowered her leg and their eyes met for a moment. "OK, leg down, reaching high…" It tipped its head a bit, as if it were trying to figure out the little glass box with all the silly creatures inside, then, it looked away and slowly made its way, all alone, peacefully down the beach. "OK, downward dog," and everyone placed their hands down on their mats, bending at the waist, all that is, but Becca. The 4-foot 10 yogini stood tall as the others folded. Becca raised her right hand in the air, forming a circle with her forefinger and thumb. She lifted her left leg, bent at the knee and reached around with her left hand to grab her foot. She bent at the waist and reached for the horizon. "Beautiful dancer's pose, Becca, just beautiful…"

Gorilla pose, pigeon pose, child's pose. One hour later, Becca was lying on the floor, the instructor passing out blankets to cover up with. She was relaxed. Not since, well, ever, had she felt so relaxed. "Let's go back to our intention…"

OK… Thank you, Josh, Becca thought, *for cheating on me, leaving me with two babies and no money. Thank you for dumping me so I don't need to waste my whole life with you.*

"Namaste," the instructor said.

"Namaste," Becca chimed in with the class.

No, not the Adler...

She had done it. She had finally taken her intention off the mat. Tracy would be so proud but, more importantly, Becca was proud of herself. *What do I do with this?* she wondered as she steered down Wee street. The sun was still rising in the sky above the beautiful homes, each a little less hidden now with the leaves slowly disappearing from the trees. She felt giddier than even after purchasing shoes or her Evelyne, sweeter than any 16-year-old's kiss. *What do I do with this? An intention isn't something you have, it's something you give. Everyone should feel this,* she thought. *This freedom, this calm, everyone.* She could see a Jeep coming towards her in the oncoming lane. Becca readied her two fingers on her right hand, as her fellow Jeeper came into view. She raised her two fingers with a smile and thought, *You get an intention.* But it wasn't even just for the Jeep people. As each car passed by, she thought, *You get an intention! You get an intention! Everybody gets an intention!*

A few blocks ahead, a construction worker was waving his flag to the right, turning her off of Asbury and onto Elm. She hadn't been down this street in years. She remembered taking it only a few times as its bridge went over the railroad tracks and led to the nearest gas station. She recognized many of the houses, either from her drives or gazing at their photos in her beautiful coffee table book of North Shore houses. She had actually stuck her own photos of some of them in the book's jacket, pictures she had taken as a teenager from the passenger seat on her many drives with friends. Most of the houses had sprawling front yards, walled or gated for privacy. Up ahead, she could see thin brown pickets held together by wire tipping at an angle by the street. The orange, plastic mesh was there, too, and she watched as a flatbed truck backed into a driveway carrying an excavator on top. *Another house will be coming down soon*, she thought sadly, as she slowed behind a convertible with its radio playing loudly. She had remembered a Tutor, some colonials. This area didn't have any tract homes; whatever the house was, it was no knock-off, mid-century modern getting hit by the wrecking ball today.

As Becca drove slowly by the mayhem, she could see the beautiful entry-way in the center of the home, setting a balance for the six windows. The dormer windows surrounded by chimneys on either side. The entrance court was now packed with construction trucks.

No, she thought, *please, not the Adler.*

"Becca, I'll call you right back," Elle said, a little while later.

"Elle, don't hang up!" Becca screamed frantically.

"What's wrong?" she asked.

"It's just that, it's just that," Becca whispered into the mouthpiece, "Elle, I'm only allowed one phone call…"

If you could only have seen the inside…

"So, you ran into the house." Elle was trying to make sense of it as she drove Becca back on Wee Street.

"I didn't, I didn't run into the house…" Becca started to say.

"You were in the house, Becca, in the house!" Elle argued.

"OK, yes. Yes, I was in the house. I was in the house, but inside the entrance. They're going to knock it down, Elle! They're going to knock down that beautiful Adler! Doesn't it make you sick? It should make you sick, sick that they're going to just smash it like that, Elle!"

"It's old," Elle said.

Becca sat quietly next to her in the passenger seat, watching the street lights shine on all the beautiful homes that still stood, for now. "If you could only have seen the inside," she said. "The entry floor? It was amazing, black and white tile with a breathtaking eight-pointed star in the center…"

"Sounds like you got past the foyer," Elle said with a smirk.

"Just a bit," Becca admitted. "You know, there were these doors past the foyer that lead to a garden out back."

"You know that you made the news?" Elle asked.

"I did? For what?"

"Well, originally, the story was that a kid was seen running into a house moments before it was going to be demolished," Elle said, smiling. "People were terrified."

"A kid?" Becca frowned.

"Well, later, the newscasters changed the story to 'a small figure,'" she said, now laughing. "You get a mug shot?"

"No," Becca said, pointing to her car, parked just where she had left it, just past the Adler. There were people holding signs and pamphlets, standing in the driveway, as they approached. "Right here is fine."

As Becca climbed out, the group descended. "You're the lady who was arrested, today?" one of them asked.

Seriously? Say no, Becca, she thought, *say no.* "Yeah," Becca said, grabbing her keys from her bag. "Look, I didn't mean any trouble…"

"Trouble?" another one asked, holding out her hand. "Today, you saved this house for one more day. We're here from the Historical Preservation

Committee. We've been petitioning to save this Adler ever since the demolition date was set. It's so important that people know how architecturally significant this house is. How important all of these houses are. We're hoping to bring attention to these communities, maybe using Asbury as a guide, explaining to the population the importance of the architecture, the history," she went on. "Do you know much about these houses? About the street? We thought maybe we'd create a guidebook? A memoir? A love story, even? Anything to bring awareness of its beauty to others."

You're too shy to be a good interviewer…

You're just an average writer…

"Yeah," Becca said, "I might know a bit…"

Beep, beep, beep (again...)

"Mommy! The truck is here! The truck is here!" Mason screamed excitedly when the truck backed into the driveway, the lights flashing with its constant beep, beep, beep, as the man waved it in.

Becca looked out the window and turned towards the sofa Mason was now jumping on.

"Mason, stop!" she yelled, just as he raised his legs to fall on his bottom. He rolled off and onto the floor, getting on all fours and looking up to smile. "You going to miss it?" she asked him sadly.

"Nope," he said, throwing his arms on the cushion and resting his chin on top.

The man was at the door now, clipboard in hand, about to ring the bell. Stevie saw him in the window and proceeded to bark and spin, bark and spin in the window. The man smiled and put his hand on the window near her face, smiling at Stevie as she went through her routine. Becca picked her up and opened the door. "Hi," she said, gesturing to the living room, "They're all ready to go."

Once again, the screen door was opened and the washers were scooted on their hinges to hold it open. He waved at his two helpers who quickly ran to the stoop, covered their feet with white cloth elastic footies and hurried in. They lifted the larger sofa, turned it 90 degrees, stood it up and walked it out. They returned again and repeated the process with the other.

"Miss Gold, I just need you to sign here," he said, gesturing to the men to finish the job.

Becca took the pen and signed quickly before passing it back and getting a tighter hold on the still barking Stevie in her arms. The men left and the one with the clipboard scooted the washers back, allowing the screen door to close. "Thank you, Miss Gold," he said as he tipped his hat, stepped off the stoop and started down the driveway.

Becca put Stevie down to run wildly to the front window. She barked and spun as the men climbed into the truck. The man suddenly stopped mid-step and ran back towards the house. Becca met him at the front door. "Sorry," he said. "Your receipt for the donation," and he handed it to her through the crack in the door.

She looked into the living room and watched as Mason attempted a summersault on the Pottery Barn sofa, knocking some of the fluffy white pillows to the floor. She walked over to the wall with the many different beige paint swatches taped on it and began to peel them away.

"Look, Mommy!" Mason shouted, and he put his arms up to either side and dropped on the soft and inviting, easy-to-clean, machine washable slipcover.

Bobby Friedman (sigh...)

"I've met everyone there is to meet," Elle explained. "I actually think I might start duplicating soon. That's a real concern, you know, that I'll be out on a date and we'll get to talking and I'll realize I've already heard his story before," Elle was saying, as she sat on the new white slipcovered sofas. She was drinking a pink Moscato, very sweet, like candy. It was in a tall glass, but she had filled it up to the top. Becca watched carefully, almost leaning forward as Elle took each sip.

"You couldn't have met everyone. You sure you don't want to go sit at the table? At the island?" Becca asked nervously.

"No, I'm good here," Elle answered, now pulling up her knees, resting her elbows on them with the glass tipped a bit more. "And I hate my job."

Machine washable, machine washable, Becca reminded herself each time Elle shifted and the pretty pink wine flowed from one side of the glass to the other. "You could quit?" Becca suggested.

"And do what?" she asked, looking at Becca with a rather hopeless look on her face. "My rent is going up, even. Can you believe it? I move to the suburbs to save a little and now it's not even worth it. At least in the city I could get rid of my car. Gas, repairs, insurance, oh my god, I would love to just get rid of it. And the women here don't like me. They all think I'm after their husbands. I was eating at the pancake house the other day and there was a group of them talking and looking at me from another table."

"What were they saying?" Becca asked.

"Well, I don't know, but it looked like maybe they were talking about me sleeping with someone's husband," Elle answered.

"What does that look like?" Becca asked, almost kidding.

Elle steadied her drink, smiled and tilted her head a bit down to the right, before slowly coming up into character. She was raising her left eyebrow, only a bit of course, and looking at Becca, up, then down, then up, then down. "A little like that," she said.

"Yeah, they're talking about you sleeping with someone's husband," Becca said. "You have a lot going on right now, but do you know what that means?"

"That if I could get through this, then I can get through anything?" Elle said.

"No, actually I think you have a 50 percent chance of being institutionalized in the next two years," Becca joked. "Ya know, I thought about what you said."

"About what?"

"My part, what part I played," Becca said.

"In what?".

She took a deep breath and pulled at a loose thread on one of the pillows. "In my divorce," she was able to get out.

"What the fuck are you talking about?" Elle said, her eyes huge as she tipped her glass a bit more.

"At Allie's? You said it was my fault," Becca said.

Elle frowned, well, as much of a frown as her professionally injected forehead would allow, then said, "Your fault that he gets away with so much, Bex. The part about how you let him get away with so much, like calling you to drop everything and get the boys. Shit, did you really think that I meant..." Elle started laughing then. "Wow, you must have really been pissed at me. Did you really think... Well, I hope you didn't waste too much time thinking about it. Your marriage was doomed from the beginning, you know that."

"Why do you say that?"

"That's not what love looks like," Elle responded, very matter-of-factly. "I wasn't in love with Adam. You know, I joke a lot about marriage, divorce, dating, men, but not love. Love is different. Love is wanting to hold someone's hand. You remember my parents, how in love they were. When Dad was sick, Mom would hold his hand all day. There was nothing else she wanted to do more than hold his hand."

"I remember," Becca said.

"So, tell me, what was your part? Let's hear all about how you messed up your marriage," Elle said.

"I was in love with someone else," Becca replied, looking down at her feet, remembering Pony Tail Guy. "Not that it would have or should have resulted in something. Not that I feel that way now. But I shouldn't have married Josh when I felt that way then."

"I think I'm *still* in love with Bobby Friedman," Elle said.

Becca smiled. She remembered Bobby "Fwiedman," as he was called back then. In the third grade they had been placed in a speech class with two other kids. Two Rs and one S, besides her. Ironically, the speech teacher's name had been Mrs. Seager—"Mrs. Seaguh" to Lauren and Jeff, and "Mrs. Theager" to Becca and Bobby. The four of them had grown up together on the same two blocks and thought it was kind of funny to meet up Wednesdays after lunchtime in the little room overlooking the blacktop basketball court outside.

Becca remembered the day that the fire alarm had gone off as the four of them sat around the little laminated wood table waiting for Mrs. Seager/Theager/Seaguh to show up. After a few minutes, the alarm turned off and Mrs. Seager walked in to find the four children with speech impediments sitting in her room. She had asked them not to tell anyone about the mixup and, after that day, there was always candy on Wednesdays. "Thkittles" for Becca and Bobby and "Twizzlahs" for Lauren and Jeff.

"Even with that huge space between his teeth? Didn't he move away when we were in fourth grade or something?" Becca asked.

"Yeah," Elle said.

"Ever hold his hand?"

"Just once," Elle said, (sigh).

Finally, she changes the story....

Finally, it was Mason's 4th birthday. They had ultimately decided to have a costume party, and he had already changed his mind about his costume several times. A cowboy, a dinosaur, Superman. Becca kept starting to work on making one before he moved on to another idea, so she decided to wait till the last minute. Oliver was easy. He was a pumpkin. Pumpkin pajamas, orange hat.

"A astronaut, Mommy! I want to be a astronaut!" Mason yelled, as he took huge, slow-motion steps around the living room. Bedtime was soon and they had been reading one of his favorite books. "Look, Mommy, like this," and his little finger pointed to the man in white with the helmet and mask. "And this, Mommy! The *ockseegen* tank. Please, Mommy! Please!"

"OK, Mason. When you go to sleep, I'll see what I can do," Becca said.

With that, he walked slowly up the stairs with his big, gravity-defying steps and she carried Oliver behind. The boys fell asleep quickly and Becca set to work on the costume. She opened up the pantry and found her martini shaker and examined it carefully. Perfect. It could make the perfect *ockseegen* tank Mason was so excited about. She did a quick look through the closets and cupboards, finding different materials for the helmet, suit and boots. She put on the album with the pretty lady in the window seat on the cover and sat quietly on the floor piecing together the perfect costume for Mason.

The next day at the party, Becca studied Josh carefully. His thumbnail was stuck between his teeth and he was biting down on it rhythmically. His head was cocked just so and one eyebrow was noticeably higher than the other. Was he noticing how big Mason was getting or, just perhaps, was he recognizing those satin white stripes wrapped around Mason's legs?

A change of heart...

It was her lawyer. Eleven months and thousands of dollars in and finally, finally the day was here. *Let's just get this over with*, Becca thought, as she answered the phone. Audrey explained that the documents that she did have were in order, but there was a "glitch."

"Is *glitch* the legal term?" Becca asked. Becca listened closely, but Audrey's explanation took longer than it should have. "What do you mean he isn't sure he wants to continue with the proceedings?"

"Becca, he's here with his attorney. I'll have him talk to you. Hold on," Audrey said, apparently passing over the phone.

"Becca," Josh started.

"What's going on? Why aren't you moving ahead with the divorce?"

"Becca, look, I made a mistake. This isn't what I want," is all he could reply. "Can we just talk? Please, Becca, just talk?"

It had been all she had wanted to hear for nearly a year—*It was a mistake, it wasn't what he wanted, he wants to talk... Maybe he had missed the girl in the blue rain slicker, too. And now that she's back...* "Josh, it's like you said, you thought it would be for the best, and you were right. Let's finish this. The kids are fine. The hard part is over," she said, hanging up the phone, her hand shaking just a little.

She could hear Mason in the next room. He was holding onto his new plastic guitar, standing behind his microphone, all primary colors to match his new drum set and keyboard. "The hard part is over!" he sang.

First side, third song...

"Congratulations, Becca!" Audrey said into the phone when she called back a few minutes later. "It's final. You're divorced."

"He signed the papers?" Becca asked.

"He did. It was sad, though, Becca," she said. "He was sad. OK, go celebrate and, Becca, really, congratulations."

Becca stood in the kitchen holding her phone. *That's it?* she thought. The house seemed so quiet, like it was on pause or something. She walked into the living room to find Mason holding his guitar. She picked hers up as well.

"You gonna play too, Mommy?" he asked.

Becca pulled her sheet music out of the pocket in her guitar case and flattened the well- worn piece of paper on the ottoman. She thought of the pretty lady, sitting on the window seat in her comfy sweater. She balanced the guitar on her leg, picked up her pick, reached around the bump and began. "I learned this one last week, Mason. Want to hear it?"

"I'll play too," he said, standing tall with his guitar.

Third string, second fret; second string, first fret (twice), third string, second fret; second string first fret; second string, third fret (twice), second string, first fret....

It was working. She heard it.

Four cappuccinos...

They were sipping cappuccinos in their old coffeehouse in the city. Becca would pick up the boys from Josh at 4. It allowed a nice chance for some catching up.

"How's Jackson?" Elle asked.

"His gallery is having a show in two weeks. You'll all come," Allie said.

"He can get the night off?" Elle asked with a wink.

"Funny," Allie said, breaking off the burnt cinnamon from her scone and placing it on Becca's plate.

"Where's North?" Dana asked, her gaze and attention buried in her notebook.

"1600," Becca answered.

"So, where's Elm?" Dana asked confused.

"Just south of it," Becca said, picking up the burnt part that Allie had slid over to her.

"Well, so how far is Wells from Dearborn, then?" Dana asked, running a finger down her floral notebook, now turned over and flipped upside down, on the table.

Becca tapped the table with each word: "Franklin, Wells, LaSalle, Clark, Dearborn…"

"You're so weird," Elle said to Becca, as she waved to the waitress for another cappuccino.

"So, that's kind of far… How about Oak and State?" Dana asked, putting the tip of her pen in her mouth.

"1000 and 0," Becca said.

"Will there be lots of doormen there?" Elle asked.

Allie threw the next burnt piece of cinnamon at Elle's head.

"So, that's close to 836 North Clark…" Dana reasoned, jotting down more notes.

"Four blocks," said Becca.

"That's some scary shit you got there, Bex," Elle said, tapping her index finger to her head. Then she turned to Allie. "Will he hold the door for us there, too?" she asked, picking the cinnamon out of hair.

"I'm sure he'll hold it for you and whoever's husband you come with," Allie answered, with the white foam from her Cappuccino still on her upper lip.

Becca's phone rang. She saw the familiar name on the screen and answered. "Hello… Yes… Are you sure?… Thanks for letting me know. I'll be there."

Congratulations! It's a girl!
And a girl! And a boy!

Becca dropped a few chicken nuggets on the floor that were quickly devoured by her now 8-pound furry pal, as she rounded the corner back into the living room.

"I helped Natalie pick out an outfit for her interview," Elle said, reaching for a still hot nugget. "You wouldn't believe what she was going to wear. You ready for this? She showed up at work asking me if she could leave just a few minutes early to be downtown at 4; then she reaches into her backpack and pulls out jeans, an old blouse and old pumps. She said, 'Don't worry, I can change in five minutes!' Can you believe how unprepared she was?"

"What's the interview for?" Becca asked. "Does she want to try something new?"

"No, I told you, Bex, she's applying to a program at the Art Institute part-time. For fashion design? Remember?" Elle asked, sounding very annoyed.

"No, Elle, I don't remember that at all," Becca said, surprised by Elle's reaction. "Ya know, I wish I had known. I could have talked to Allie."

"Oh my God! Tell Allie! That would be great!" Elle said, handing Becca her phone. "Text her. Make sure they keep an eye out for Natalie Moore," Elle said, excitedly.

Becca held Elle's phone in her hand. "She interviewed yesterday? In jeans, an old blouse and old pumps?"

"No, of course not," Elle said. "I picked out something much more appropriate. She wore that."

"From your store?" Becca asked, while texting Allie,

Look out for a girl named…

"No, Becca, of course not," Elle said. "I have told you a million times I would never shop there."

"Well, from where then?" Becca asked, still typing .

Natalie Moore.

"Neiman's," Elle said, matter-of-factly.

"How could she have ever afforded that?" Becca asked,

She interviewed yesterday for your fashion school.

"Well, I paid for it," Elle said. "Text that she has a good eye for fashion. Been working in the business since graduation."

"You paid?" Becca asked, looking away from her phone and turning to Elle.

"It was more appropriate. Really boho chic," Elle said, pointing back at the phone.

"That must have cost you a fortune."

She has been working in the business…

"It did. Hopefully, she gets in. I rehearsed some questions with her," Elle said, watching every letter Becca typed. "She seemed ready. I've been talking to Tammy a bit, too, about her plans. She was thinking she would just get married or something. Can you believe that? I mean, do kids really think like that anymore? I told her she needed a plan. We're going to look into the managerial track with our company. I thought I could give her more responsibilities around the store."

"That sounds like a good plan," Becca said,

since graduation.

"Yeah," Elle said, a bit distracted. "I worry about them, Bex. I mean, what exactly are these kids going to do with their lives anyway? I mean, Ben, he'll do OK. He's a little flighty but this job was always just a step towards being a buyer. He'll leave, though, and go to New York. I wish he would at least consider Chicago, though. You know? Closer to home?"

Home? Becca tried to hide the smile growing on her face. How could she have missed it?

"Maybe," Elle said, "he'll at least come home for the holidays."

"Maybe," Becca said.

Natalie is one of Elle's kids.

You never know what's going to be inside...

"I guess it's a good thing he's out of work," Hillary said, pulling the wagon behind her.

Becca pushed the double stroller down Asbury next to her, slowing as they approached the beautiful home, hidden by the repaired brick wall.

"If he hadn't been there, we never could have gotten Lucy to the vet in time," Hillary said, turning to see the now 13-year-old poodle cuddled in a blanket, enjoying the ride.

"Will she walk again?" Becca asked.

"Not sure," Hillary said. "Your brain can relearn, I guess."

"Yeah," Becca said as she stopped and took a good, long look at the mortar that surrounded every stone. She finally reached out her hand and followed a seam that looked to be smoother and lighter than the others.

"You won't find it," the man in the jeans and white T-shirt said, startling all of them.

Becca shortened the leash as he approached the stroller and Stevie began to growl.

"You're looking for the repair we did? You won't find it," he said again, busying himself, loading up his truck.

"I drove by awhile ago. There was an opening right around here," she said, gesturing to a small portion of the wall in her reach.

"Actually, it was right around here," he said, dragging his finger along the mortar that now filled the seam that had been opened up that day. "But, thanks. You need work done? Here's my card," he said, handing her a small rectangle with cracks on it. "Still trying to think of a catchy name. Right now, just me." "Me" was Steve. His number was out of the area code. He came quite a way to get this done.

"No, I mean, I do, but this house is... My house is nothing like this..." Becca stammered.

"Yeah, this one is pretty spectacular. I was surprised she called me. I saw that new house going up down the street. That's a huge deal. That new wall they put in front? The white stucco one? I tried to get that job. Turned out sort of ugly, but that's what they wanted. Nothing like this," he said, once again touching the old stones, perfectly fitting together. "You got a wall you need fixed?"

"Several. I have a sunken-in patio. Like you get with split levels? The walls are all cracked. It's awful. It's way different than this," Becca said.

"The more I work, the more I find they're all about the same, really. I was thinking I was going to meet this really rich guy, maybe, ya know, stuck up or something. Instead, some guy about my age in a Cubs hat says his mom needs her wall fixed. He hired me in the driveway. You never know by looking at these houses what's going to be inside."

"Did you see the one up the street? The one they tore down?" Becca asked excitedly.

"Nah, just a mess by the time I got a peek. I can look at your patio, if you want. Just call. One year warranty on my work."

"That doesn't seem very long," Becca said, scooping Stevie up to go.

"Look, things happen. If this doesn't hold up, I'll replace it, but things happen," he said, closing up the trunk and walking to his door. "This wall is only as strong as the ground it stands on. A sink hole, tree roots, a crazy driver on this windy street. Some stuff you just can't control."

Becca and Hillary continued down Asbury to the parking lot and then, simultaneously began loading their precious cargo. Becca watched as Hillary gently picked Lucy up and placed her on the blanket in the backseat. Lucy licked her hand sweetly just before she closed the door. "So, anything special planned this week?" she asked before climbing in herself.

Becca placed Stevie in the front and buckled the boys in the back. "Actually," she said, "I got pretty big plans."

"A date?" she asked.

"Nah, just something I've been looking forward to for a while now," Becca said. "An old friend called. It's kind of a big deal. I'll let you know."

On the way home, Becca had the good fortune to be following a school bus and was able to pause behind it. Children were slowly stepping off and walking across the busy street. She took in the view and scribbled a note on her growing stack of Post-Its. The trees were starting to drop their leaves, and more houses appeared through the empty branches. The bus again began its way down the curvy street and Becca followed behind, taking in the colors, the smell, the sounds. The school bus then again turned on its flashing lights, slowed down and stopped with the sign unfolding from its side. Among the trees, she could see painted blue shutters with white trim, the whitewashed bricks and finally, rising up through the few leaves left, the mansard roof. The house, the one she imagined with the little French children, after all the destruction around it, the house was still there.

The pretty girl in the window...

Becca was pushing the stroller through town. Thursday nights offered some fun for kids, and everyone at the preschool was talking about it. Music, pony rides, ice cream and popcorn.

"Steve is getting off the train at 6:30! We'll meet you there!" one mom in a minivan had yelled to another mom in a different minivan.

"Mike is off early tonight. We're heading over at 5:45. Tell Brian!" another had said to a woman in a Volvo as she loaded her kids into her Escalade.

Becca loaded the boys into her Jeep at 6:00 as she had no one she needed to wait for and headed towards town. Parking was actually difficult as so many people had shown up, but she finally found a spot down the street and began unloading the boys from the car into the stroller. She could see that other families had some trouble negotiating the crowd too, and many of the fathers were balancing one child on their shoulders as the moms pushed strollers with another. In town, they stood in groups, mothers talking to mothers, fathers talking to fathers, children running pretty much unsupervised in the fountains that would soon be turned off for the season.

Becca waited in line for the pony rides next to some mothers she had never seen before. They were sharing ideas for their next trips. Family fun places that also had kids' camps so the parents could share some time alone. Mason finally had his turn on the pony and waved as he yelled, "Look, Mommy!

Look!" and Becca waved back. Right about then she smelled Oliver's diaper, always the most difficult time, changing one while watching the other. Becca looked around for a familiar face and did see some of the preschool mommies, but instead called Mason over after his ride and put the boys in the stroller and walked through town towards the only public restroom she recalled with a changing table.

Elle's car was parked in front of Rosebud. *What luck,* Becca thought, as she glanced in the window. Elle was at a table right in front. Becca could only see the back of the man Elle was having dinner with. He was wearing a fairly conservative striped shirt with the sleeves rolled up. Becca wasn't about to interrupt her with whoever's husband this might be. Elle began to wave.

Oliver had since fallen asleep but Mason was awake. "The ice cream, Mommy! The ice cream!" he was yelling.

"Mason, we need to go get Oliver changed first," Becca said, while pointing to Oliver, gesturing to Elle "sleeping" by resting her hand on her opposite shoulder and placing her cheek down on it.

Elle continued to wave, now standing up. Becca pointed to where her watch would be, if she owned one. "Gotta go!" she mouthed.

"Mommy! The ice cream!" Mason was yelling again.

Becca turned towards him. "Not yet, Mason. Later!" She looked up at the window to see the man's back, but no Elle. "Mason, let's go."

"Why won't you come in?" Elle was now asking her, standing with them on the sidewalk.

"Oliver needs a change, Mason wants ice cream," Becca started to say.

"They have ice cream here," she said to Mason.

Mason looked up at Becca. "I need to change Oliver..." Becca started to say again.

"I'll watch Mason. Come in," Elle said, taking Mason's hand and holding open the door. The four of them walked into the restaurant and Becca parked the stroller. "We're just over here, Bex." Elle walked towards the table, Mason in hand.

Becca lifted a somewhat sleeping Oliver and threw her diaper bag over her shoulder. *Now she is with my son and someone's husband,* Becca thought as she lowered the changing table from its hinge on the wall and laid Oliver on top. He cried a little as she started taking off his pants and kissed his feet. Maybe Mason will be done by the time I get there, she thought, as she slowly took off Oliver's diaper. She slowly wiped him, she slowly put on a new diaper, she slowly dressed him. Five minutes later, Oliver sat awake on the table. Becca picked him up, threw the diaper bag over her shoulder again and stepped out of the bathroom. She could see Elle waving her towards the table. Again, Becca gestured to Oliver and mouthed, "sleeping." Elle looked baffled as Oliver lifted his head and smiled.

"Mommy!" Mason called.

That's it, Becca thought. Which Mommy will I not be able to look at this week at school, the grocery store, the park? Becca approached slowly as the man in the striped shirt and rolled up sleeves turned around.

"Well, hello Becca Gold," he said.

The space between his teeth had filled in. "Hello, Bobby Friedman," Becca said.

Sigh…

One girl's trash…

Finally, Spring Cleanup, just closer to fall. The garbage piles were getting bigger every day. The rules were simple: You could throw away anything, well almost anything, on your assigned day. Of the four Saturdays in October, Becca's pick-up day—the southeast section of town—was the first. It didn't give her as much time as the residents in the north, southwest or central, but she was organized and prepared. She had placed the shipping boxes, finally broken down, at the curb, along with the broken pieces of fan and the old curtains and rods. Her many quarts of unused beige paint were drying out in the garage. She had left them open, poured in some sand and had stuck newspaper inside to rush the drying out process, just as had been explained in the local paper.

Many people drove around searching for small treasures, these days. Some just in their cars, others in pickup trucks. Some people collected discards from others for their own homes, others collected scrap to sell. It was kind of sad, actually, a family putting out a bike hoping it would be picked up for a child to ride could easily be disappointed when a pickup took it just to sell for its metal weight instead. Becca watched them each day that week. Someone actually looked at the mustard curtains, only after the metal rods had been driven away by someone else.

That day, heading towards Weee Street, Becca did her fair share of looking as well. There were always plenty of playpens and carriers. Lots of toys, too. There was even a miniature basketball hoop that Mason wanted. He screamed every minute of the ride after Becca said they weren't going to take it home. Then, she spied it, sticking out from the top of a rather tall pile, the littlest bit of Donald Duck's small head, poised perfectly above a 5-foot-tall tube.

And finally…Thank you

So, it wasn't quite as glamorous as she had pictured it would be. Carrying the chair Faye had given her was impossible. With each step she took, the metal frame whacked her ankle. Step, bang, step, bang. Everyone else made it look so easy. Effortless, really. She could see a good place to sit—a nice patch of green just about 100 steps away. The bottle of wine was getting heavy, and she knew the glass she had carefully packed was already in shards next to the julienned veggies and low-fat dip in her diaper bag now doubling as a picnic basket. The brownies were probably in good shape, though, and she kept that in mind as she made her way.

It was louder than she had imagined too. She could hear voices over all the noise. Some people looked at her with puzzled looks on their faces, but she continued her walk in the hot sun and felt excited for the show to begin. Finally, in just the right spot, she unfolded her chair and placed it just so, twisting and turning it to get the best view. She sat down and carefully unpacked her things, watching as some of the men stared at her screwing the bottle opener into the cork. *Yes,* she thought, *I am capable of this,* silently praying she would be successful on the first try since she had an audience. The cork came out with a loud pop as one of the men approached.

She could see the questioning look on his face as he came closer. He was scratching his head now, but making eye contact. With no glass, she took a quick sip from the bottle and placed it between her legs. *I've waited so long for this day, please don't let him ruin it.* Then, it started.

It was so loud. The banging and the booming. When she looked in the sky, she could see the green paint she had so carefully chosen for the kitchen, more gray than yellow, and the robin egg blue paint for the nursery, just the same color as the "A" patch on the alphabet quilt—all exploding like fireworks, really, into the sky. The beams cracked in half, hanging down from what was left of the roof, brushing the floor beneath. Pieces of cabinets that she had never really liked splintered with delightful cracking sounds each time the crane came down then lofted in the dust of the walls of the house.

I'm not responsible for him anymore and, in her head, she heard the "clunk, crank, crank, crank" of the garage door going up. The demolition man was in front of her now. *Say something. Say something witty. Say anything.* Becca pulled the bottle out from between her legs and tipped it in his direction. "Thank you."

Out of the box...

Becca had been able to pack a box, inside a box, inside a box. In fact, when she went to pick up the largest one, she thought there must still be something inside and unpacked the box from the box from the box and simply found the tissue paper that had once covered her shoes. Fifteen boxes stacked inside of the three stacked by the front door for Monday morning's recycling pick-up. It wasn't too late. She could take the boxes back upstairs and place the shoes safely back inside, but it's like Austin sang that day in the living room, *"the hard part is over,"* then she heard the thump in the living room. Becca ran out of the kitchen to find the tower of boxes tipped over and Stevie sniffing the scene. There, behind the boxes, was Oliver, sitting behind the pile, trying to crawl inside the largest empty box. She looked over at his spot by the TV, his blanket still lying on the floor where he had just been.

A promise kept...

Well, it would have been easier to plant the tube in the lawn if the ground had been softer, but after a few minutes, Becca had the pole securely in the grass, the hose coming out the side as Donald Duck's head stood tall on top. "Are you ready?" she yelled to the boys who stood still in the back yard, looking at the sprinkler looming 3 feet or so above their heads.

"Ready," Mason yelled.

"Ready," Oliver repeated.

Becca ran to the spigot and turned on the water, watching the hose grow wider as the water began to flow through it. "Here it comes!" she yelled back.

The boys ran around in circles as the water rained from the blue hat on Donald's head, Mason in his bathing suit and Oliver in his diaper. Becca sat back in her Adirondack chair, a Diet Coke on the grass beside her, her hot fudge sundae container gripped between her knees. The drink dispenser filled with lemonade, waiting beside her on its stand, even looked a little like the picture on page 28.

Becca watched the boys running in circles as Stevie chased them near the sunken patio. She thought about the busy street, the asbestos, the now-gone tarnished ceiling fan and, of course, the closet, the one downstairs, with the vented doors, that was dark, with what she hoped were cob webs but knew differently.

Sometimes people need a bit of help in recognizing a great work of art that might be a bit unfamiliar…

Becca watched as their little feet became muddy, splashing in the puddles forming below them. It was completely unfamiliar, not at all what she thought her life would be. The sun shined warmly on her cheeks as she raised her spoon up towards the sky, finally, finally recognizing her great work of art.

A finished house…

A short while later, the boys were napping on the white sofas, the many throw pillows surrounding them. Becca sat in perfect Lotus position, legs wrapped up like a pretzel with her feet in the creases of her hips, the soles of her feet facing up to the sky. Her wrists rested gently on her knees, the fingers on her left hand forming a circle, the fingers on her right, still holding the paint roller. She was staring at the now off-white wall in front of her. After many choices and many months, there it was, "Cloud Cover," now replacing the mustard walls and ending the search she had been on. The whole house would soon look like this, she thought. It felt clean, fresh and noncommittal, with the possibility for change.

Her phone buzzed next to her, a long text from Elle… *These three new trainees are making me crazy, CRAZY! One wears her clothes too tight, one is chewing gum ALL DAY and I think the boy is colorblind COLORBLIND! How can you put outfits together if you're COLORBLIND?* with an open-mouthed, closed-eyed, defeated eyebrow emoji at the end.

I guess Elle's got three more kids… Becca smiled, staring at the wall in front of her.

Her phone was buzzing again. Elle? No, a text from Jay…

"Gum?" it asked simply.

She placed the roller in the tray and untangled herself. *Be witty. Remember how you used to be so witty? You can do this…*

"OK. I always keep some next to my bed…" She hesitated, just a moment, before tapping SEND, then touched it ever so lightly as it floated up and appeared in its little bubble.

What love looks like…

"Good morning, Sonny," Becca said, walking up to his desk that Sunday morning.

"Good morning, Becca," he said, standing up. "Dana's all moved in."

"What's your roommate up to?" Becca asked, walking through the door he was holding open for her.

"Sleeping."

"Sleeping?" Becca asked, turning around.

"Yeah, she's sleeping. By the way, tell Dana 7D," he said, giving her a wink.

"What about 7D?" Becca said, confused.

"Someone asked me about Dana. Tell her 7D," he said again, with another wink. *Wow. This place really is magic,* she thought as she pressed the button and the elevator door closed.

Walking down the hall, she readied herself for the newly appointed apartment. Allie's shabby-chic would now be replaced by Dana's more sterile style, she realized. She knocked on the door and turned the knob.

"Bex!" Dana yelled in from the bedroom. "I'll be right there!"

Becca sat down on the sofa and looked at the dining table, set with the four place settings, stacked beautifully at each chair. In the cabinet against the wall, behind the glass, were the creamer, sugar bowl and butter dish, gravy boat and now the notorious salt and pepper shakers, but, also, on other shelves, more plates, more chargers and more bowls, some stacked and some leaning on plate stands for display.

"Pretty, huh?" Dana asked from the hallway, her hair up in a high pony, not a drop of makeup on her usually primped face.

"You got the whole set?" Becca asked confused.

"Yeah," Dana said. "Just didn't feel like waiting anymore. You would be proud. I bought a pair of shoes, too," she said, gesturing for her to follow. As they walked through the hall, Becca looked at the framed pictures on the wall, the largest, one of the five of them at the Thai restaurant with the benches.

"That's a great picture of Katie," Becca said, stopping to take it in.

"Do you remember that night?" Dana asked, looking at it, too.

Of course she did. "I do," Becca said, her cheeks twitching the littlest bit. "That night, when Katie dropped me off, we pulled into the driveway and there was a family of deer eating in my yard. We sat and watched for a while."

"You never told me that," Dana said, looking sadly at her.

"I'm telling you now," Becca said, but not the rest. *The rest is special, very, very special.*

"I'll get you a copy," Dana said, again walking towards the bedroom with Becca catching up. "What do you think?" she asked, holding up a pair of moss green pumps.

"They're beautiful," Becca said. "What will you wear them with?"

"Not really sure, yet," Dana said. "Catch!" and the cashmere beanie floated through the sky towards Becca's open hands. "It's really more your style anyway."

Two hours later, 26 girls raced through the streets of Chicago on a mission, well, several, really. First, in pairs, they ran to Crate & Barrel to pick up five boxes that they had to carry through town to Karen's apartment. Upon completing that task, they needed to go to the coffee shop Karen and her fiancé always went to, find their server and order their "usual." After learning to make and then drinking their half-caf skinny lattes, it was on to the stationary store where they needed to copy, by hand, Karen and Myles's invitation before delivering it to the building it was believed where her ex-boyfriend lived. Then, a mad dash to Dana's apartment, where she and Karen stood, waiting for the first to arrive.

Becca, Allie and Elle had set out the refreshments and had stacked the gifts. "You're sleeping?" Becca asked, looking at Allie.

"I am. I sleep," she said.

"What's going on?" Elle asked, approaching with yet another gift, this one wrapped in a cello bag with a silver bow. "Why am I here on a Sunday afternoon lugging all this stuff around anyway? They say it's going to rain soon. I hope we at least get home first."

"I was just telling Becca about how excited I am for my new class starting after the party today," Allie said, patting her stomach, ever so lightly. "Brand new young artists in search of knowledge, from me. You'll drive me, Bex?"

There were no long curls falling, there was no felt hat. It was Allie patting her belly. Becca was watching her because she was patting her belly. Becca's eyes widened as she understood. "Why not?" Becca said, with a wink. *It's just like magic...*

Two by two, girls entered the apartment, took a martini a la Becca and rested from their adventures. When all the 13 pairs arrived, Dana and Karen walked in.

"Because I'm the older sister, people may think I have a lot to teach you, but the truth is, I have a lot to learn," Dana said, looking at the girl with the perfect eyebrows. "I've actually been taking notes." She reached down and took out the little floral notebook, turning it over, flipping it upside down and beginning to read from the back. "What I can tell you is this. Sometimes, love doesn't dance. Sometimes, love doesn't call three times a day. Sometimes, love doesn't make a plan for a night out. But love does come to see you in the cold, in the dark. Love gives you the yummy burnt cinnamon on your scone. Love gives you the things you want, of course, but also the things you didn't even know you needed. Most recently, I have learned, that love takes you by the arm and leads you home. To my sister Karen and her fiancé Myles. Thank you for teaching me what love looks like."

Becca, Allie and Elle stood silently watching Dana raise her glass to the girl with the perfect—seriously perfect—eyebrows. Becca tipped hers, too, as she wiped away the smallest tear. *Her knowledge of love might be upside down and backwards, but maybe the bad stuff about dating, and the good stuff about love, could meet somewhere in the middle.*

"Should we tell Dana that it didn't rhyme?" Elle asked. "Because, ya know, Karen's actually rhymed."

But first a quick visit
with a friend…

"You're just like everyone else here, Becca, I mean it. I am not going to treat you any differently than I would treat anyone else. Got it?" Allie said, standing in front of a large wooden box, then gesturing inside.

"Got it," Becca said, walking up next to her and reaching inside the box, pulling out a folded, portable chair. "Where to?"

"We're meeting by the Blume at 4:00. Be ready."

Becca walked quietly down the hall, the folded, portable chair, swinging into her ankle only once in a while. She made her way up the stairs and turned into the gallery on her left. There, she found her college-aged classmates, sitting in front of the painting of the large sphere, cracked through the middle with its sharp points and edges, the men shoveling, lifting and hammering to fix the devastation, the woman on her knees and reaching for the sky.

"Thank you for getting here on such a stormy day," Allie said, turning around to face the class with her cat-eye glasses on. It was the glasses. People were looking at her because of the glasses. She was so good. "Josh Blume, 'The Rock.' 1944. Destruction and reconstruction, really. Thoughts? Amy?"

The young girl in the striped tights underneath her ripped jeans took her pen out of her mouth. "It's scary. The woman seems scared. Maybe the rock fell on her kids or something?"

Allie turned towards the painting then, placing her hand on her belly again. "Maybe," she said. "How about, you? With the orange bag? Your name?"

"Bex," Becca said, her small lisp still evident even after all of the therapy in Ms. Seager's room.

"OK, Bex," Allie said while trying to keep a straight face. "What do you think? Is she scared?"

Becca looked at the woman in the brown dress, her hair pulled back in a low ponytail, kneeling in front of the cracked rock, while the men worked. "Maybe," Becca said, "but maybe she's angry, too."

Allie turned around again to look at the painting in front of the class. "What's she angry about?"

"Well," Becca said. "Maybe she had a nice life before the rock fell."

"Maybe," Allie said.

"But she's wasting time."

"Wasting time?"

"Yeah," Becca said. "She needs to get to work like the others. She's got a lot of rebuilding to do."

Allie stood with a small smile on her face. The tears in her eyes more visible through the nonprescription lenses. "Thank you, Bex," Allie said. "Anyone else?"

An hour later, class was dismissed with an assignment: two paintings that have something in common, a theme, a color scheme, a feeling. Becca could hear the thunder and looked at her phone. She could wait out the storm right here before getting the boys, she thought, and she planted herself on the wooden slat bench in the center of the contemporary room. The storm reminded her of that day in her dress, on the curb in the rain. Had it been a year already? She had made it. She chuckled as she remembered Hillary's whole Four Seasons speech. She had gotten to know herself pretty well in that time. *I can spend a lot of time with someone like me,* she thought.

"It's about the space landing," she heard from behind her. Becca sat very still and listened as the two people behind her talked about her Twombly.

"I mean, the numbers, that's his thing," the man went on. "He used all kinds of media. He used house paint, glue, charcoals…"

Becca tried not to turn around and hoped they would discuss the painting longer, as she was hanging on each and every word.

"They say it's a study of floating and falling, or falling and floating…" one continued.

Becca let out a little giggle and slapped the bench, just a bit. *That's funny,* she thought, *I've kinda been studying that, too…*

There is 100 percent chance that I am right where I should be, she remembered. *So, that's why I hadn't noticed you before,* Becca thought, smiling at the canvas in front of her. *I simply wasn't ready for you until HERE, NOW.*

Down on Weee Street…

There is always room for some change, she thought, as she drove down the winding street.

Let's try this again. "Do nothing." And she turned all the voices off in her head.

"Ask your body." And she did. After a few moments of listening, she smiled, just like her body had told her to do.

"Reverse." No, she thought, never again. She would only look backward to see how far she had come, or to look in the rearview mirror. There, she could see the very top of five fingers on her left and two on her right. Tiny hands reaching up to the sky in anticipation of Weee Street coming into view.

She could see the framed roof of the new monstrous house peeking out above the new stucco gate. The stone gate with the tile-filled windows was long gone. When Becca had seen the trucks there months ago, she had been so angry that they were tearing down something so old that had survived so much just to be replaced by something bigger and newer. Now, it made more sense to her. Maybe something has to be destroyed so it can be rebuilt stronger. The new house had been built at a slight angle to the street. Maybe going upside down wasn't completely necessary but, by shifting your view, you can change your perspective on things. Sure, the framing was almost complete, but it's the final finishes on the inside that take the longest, Becca knew.

"Are we there yet, Mommy?" the voices sang out from the backseat.

She drove by the old house that was featured in her book, the house that had been returned back to its original floor plan by removing the newer wing. She had admired the owners for losing some square footage in efforts to keep things as they were, but realized something today: The stone wall continued in front of the next house too, as if part of the property had been sold. They had made way for the modern mansion on the lake right next door. She thought about that day she had been driving by with the sleeping boys, the day that the workers had come back, carefully placing the stones into the wall where they had been missing. She had figured that there would always be a seam there, a place that you could tell that there had been damage done but had been repaired. She had noticed that in that spot, there was no delineation between old and new, broken and fixed. The repair had been seamless. She had hoped that maybe her repairs would be seamless, too, that maybe *someone* would look closely and if they did see that something was different, realize it all fit together somehow just fine anyway. She tipped the rearview mirror enough to see her reflection smiling back at her.

Someone just did.

There would always be low-flying hawks. She just had to keep her eyes open and be on alert. She was still the girl who couldn't get lost in the city if she tried. The girl who could sing, but only in her car. The girl who loved to dance alone in her room. The girl in the blue rain sicker. But now, she was also the girl who could play guitar, do yoga, paint a house and pimp out her driveway...

*Hidden wedges and platform shoes, fake cheeks, fake bags, fake walls...
Everyone has something that they hide behind but, if you're lucky, maybe there
will be a crack, an open seam, for one to peek in or maybe, even, if you're really
lucky, for one to peek out...*

"We're here," she answered, tipping the mirror back to catch sight of five
little fingers on her left and just the tiniest top of two on her right. Glancing
into the passenger seat, Becca could see all of her Post-It notes now stuck on
the seat next to her—*the girl with the perfect eyebrows, an unexpected introduc-
tion, a little bit of magic, start with A Princess Story, Seamless...*

You can write your own story.

She pressed her waffle stomper, without the heel cushions hidden inside,
down on the gas, the black and red laces dangling just above the dried pink
paint on the sole. "Put them up high!"

"Weee!"

258